A Book Club's Guide To Murder & Mayhem

A Suzie Tuft Cozy Mystery

Bethany Barker

ISBN: 979-8-9890320-4-4

Cover design: David Ter-Avanesyan https://ter33design.com/

Cover image: AdobeStock

Published in the United States of America by Harbor Lane Books, LLC.

www.harborlanebooks.com

Chapter One

I listened with rapt attention, mouth ajar, as Georgianna Borelli detailed how she killed Kat Slothenburg by burying a knife six inches deep in her chest. Unabashed, Georgianna described the gruesome act in detail, declaring, "That snake, Kat, had it coming." A startling gleam shone in her eyes.

Aghast at my friend's candid confession, I tightened the grip on my glass. The exuberance emanating from her sent chills down my arms.

Her red lips curved in a triumphant smile. Georgianna raised her wine goblet in a manicured hand. "And that, my friends, is how Kat died in my latest manuscript."

Ta-da! I, Suzie Tuft, as well as the other four Bearfoot Book Club ladies, gathered in Georgianna's spacious living room, released our collectively held breaths.

A retired schoolteacher and full-time author, Georgianna fabricated the most devious ways to kill her enemies —on paper. Her imagination seemed to have no limits. She made my college textbook writing look dull and boring by comparison. Of course, given our different subject matters, I couldn't imagine my audience, captive students, reading their texts with jaw-dropping enthusiasm.

Our book club ladies devoured all of Georgianna's award-winning novels and looked forward to her latest foray into the world of murder and mayhem. We considered ourselves fortunate to have a hometown celebrity within our group.

"Another successful murder in the books," I laughed. "Pun intended."

I settled back against the white Aria sofa I shared with Bre Christofanos, our resident bakery owner. "What an imagination. Your vivid descriptions hook me every time."

"That's the plan," Georgianna said, looking mighty pleased with herself. Her spiky silver hair provided the perfect crown for her round face.

"Another bestseller," Bre commented. She wore her long, dark hair swept up into a ponytail today. Dressed in a pastel peach tunic with tiny blossoms and beige leggings, she looked as sweet as the treats she made for her shop, Bre's Bakery.

"You mentioned Kat deserved the stabbing, but the real tragedy for me was destroying her CeCe blouse," said MaryLou Mondra, a clothes snob and the most outspoken one in the group. Her attire, a mint green silk designer blouse over black dress pants, was more suited to a board meeting than our casual group of book lovers. A local councilwoman, she was privy to the town's secrets and spread them around faster than the common cold.

"How do you come up with your brilliant ideas?" Bre spread cheese on a cracker and took a dainty bite.

"Turn on the news," MaryLou replied.

Bre squirmed. Conflict of any kind made her nervous. "I can't listen to all the tragedy without feeling depressed."

We were fortunate our little Pennsylvania community of Bearfoot didn't suffer the maladies reported in the national news. Even though my dog and I lived on several isolated acres on the outskirts of town, I never worried for my safety. In fact, the town was borderline sleepy except for the occasional parade or festival.

Georgianna raised her well-sculpted eyebrows. "You read my murder mysteries."

All of us, as well as half the town, had attended Georgianna's book launches and signings held at Bre's Bakery.

"The difference is your stories are made up, and you don't write gory details or show explicit photos." Bre turned to me. "Suzie, why don't you give up stuffy academic writing and create a novel?"

Why hadn't I chosen to write something fun? Heaven knows my life provided enough material for a soap opera. Instead, I played it safe by accepting academic work, although I had an ex-boyfriend I wouldn't mind knocking off in a mystery novel.

"For the time being, my college texts and business books pay my mortgage."

"Right. You have a trip this week," Georgianna said. "Convention?"

I shook my head. "An appointment in New York with an editor to discuss writing a series of business books. The convention is in the fall in San Diego." I set my glass on a coaster.

"Isn't San Diego where you met your ex?" MaryLou asked.

She would remind me of that disastrous error in judgment. I cringed inside. "Yes, but he won't attend this year."

"Wish I could land a free trip to San Diego. I've never been to California," said Jess Waters, my best friend since grade school. Her short, dark hair and brown eyes contrasted with my blue-eyed, blonde features. At a slender five foot two, Jess's waiflike appearance was deceiving. She had the stamina of a pit bull and the tenacity of an obstinate cat. She also wore the brightest neon colors she found.

"I put in a lot of hours writing and researching for that trip," I countered. "None of it was thrilling, either."

I thought of the upcoming trip to San Diego, the third to my favorite city. I fell in love with the area, visiting years ago when my first textbook was a featured item at a college book fair. I enjoyed the diversity, the history, and the weather. The only blight on my memories was that I'd met my ex at that college fair.

"What time is your flight to New York tomorrow?" MaryLou asked.

"Two-twenty. I'll spend the night and fly home Tuesday evening." MaryLou would, no doubt, file the details in her brain for future gossip distribution.

Jess sighed. "Wish I could go to New York with you. The spring blossoms will be on display. Remember the time we flew to the city for a concert when we were in college?"

How could I forget? I didn't want MaryLou in on the story. To stop Jess from revealing the details, I added, "I'm staying for one night, and I'll be in meetings all day."

"I love New York City," Bre said.

"Yeah." Georgianna fluttered her fingers in the air. "The excitement, the energy, the shopping."

Jess brightened. "Why don't we arrange a book club trip to New York?" she suggested. "We'd have loads of fun."

"And lots of laughs," I said.

"We'll see a show and dine at a fine restaurant," Bre added.

"And drink wine." Georgianna tilted her glass toward Jess. "I'm in. My publicist can arrange a book signing there."

MaryLou, who was afraid of missing something if she left town, huffed. "Are we going to discuss the book we read? I can't stay here all day."

Did she worry the rumor mill spun without her?

"I enjoyed this one," Bre began. "The main character was a smart, gracious woman. I give it a nine."

From there, the discussion continued for half an hour. Afterward, we chose a novel to read for the next meeting. We rotated meetings once a month at our various houses. Bre's turn to host next time meant I would gain a pound or two from her yummy baked goods. We bid Georgianna goodbye and filed out to our cars. As usual, Jess and I stood in the driveway talking for several minutes before leaving.

* * *

Monday morning, I pulled to the curb of The Bearfoot Pet Lodge and coaxed my dog, Hunter, out of the backseat. "Come on, boy. I don't want to miss my flight." It's not that I wanted to board him, but he couldn't go with me on a business trip. Reluctant, he trotted to the door, but his tail wagged in earnest when he spied his favorite doggie sitter, Elly. She greeted us both and assured me she would take good care of Hunter.

The rest of the day went as planned. My flight landed on time. The meeting with the editor resulted in a three-book deal, and he entertained me at dinner with his dry sense of humor. He was particularly witty after he consumed a couple of drinks. Or maybe I just thought so after I drank a glass of wine.

My return flight on Tuesday, scheduled for late afternoon, allowed time for a leisurely breakfast in the hotel restaurant and two hours to stroll through Central Park, one of my favorite New York City sites. A Vinyasa yoga class was doing downward dogs near The Yoga Trail. Blankets dotted the grass where sunbathers awaited the sunshine.

I ambled around the beautiful gardens, stopping to admire a horse-drawn carriage pulled up in front of waiting passengers. Too soon, I returned to the hotel and rode the shuttle to the airport.

At two, I arrived, anxious to fly home to Hunter. Disappointment overtook me when the airline announced a delay.

The plane landed at Pittsburgh International Airport at five forty-five. With a forty-minute drive home, I missed the deadline to pick up Hunter before the lodge closed for the night. I counted on Elly to care for him until morning.

Arriving at my house, I was greeted by perfect weather for a May evening and pulled into the garage. I was happy to be home. Although I enjoyed the hustle of New York City, I loved the peace and quiet of my secluded house in the woods. I carried my overnight bag to my bedroom, changed from dress shoes into my old, comfortable walking shoes, and headed out for some much-needed exercise.

I took my daily dance—er, I mean walk—on the rarely traveled, mile-long road spanning the one hundred eighty-five acres of undeveloped woods surrounding my house. My nose twitched when the smell of a decaying animal drifted on the breeze. Having discovered the occasional carcass of a deer or wild turkey who'd met its match with a two-ton vehicle along this stretch, I recognized the odor immediately.

As far as I could see, the road ahead remained free of rotting debris. I turned the volume up on the music blasting from my cellphone as if that would somehow turn down my olfactory senses. It didn't.

The stink hung on the breeze, permeating the area and increasing in intensity as I neared a gully alongside the road. Like a driver slowing down to gawk at an accident, I crept to the berm, craned my neck, and squinted into the chasm.

The crowded trees stood at majestic attention, a haphazard army. Full-dressed pines grew among trees whose limbs bore only spring buds, offering me an unobstructed view.

Something was down there all right, but it wasn't an animal's red tie flapping in the wind near a thicket of ferns and brush twenty feet below. The tie was anchored to a huge hump, half covered by the undergrowth. I moved in for a closer look and spied a boot sticking straight up in the air in another spot.

My screams shook the tree branches, sending squawking birds to flight. I stumbled backward. My heart pounded louder than the drums beating in my earbuds, one of which fell out during my whirl of distress.

From the sickening stench and the boot reaching toward the sky as motionless as a tree trunk, I was certain the person needed a coroner's vehicle instead of medical help. Dry fall leaves and plant litter covered most of the body. Men and women both wore the type of boot on the person's foot. As curious as I was to learn their gender, I couldn't bring myself to go all the way down the hillside.

My legs refused to work at top speed as I scrambled away, until a gray squirrel ran in front of me. Startled by the bushy-tailed creature, I jumped straight up in the air and landed on both feet with a thud before breaking into a sprint.

After putting distance between the poor dearly departed and myself, I slowed my pace, trying to regulate my breathing to something close to normal. I bent over, my stomach roiling. When the nausea passed, it occurred to me this would be a good time to call the police. Straightening, I took out my phone and dialed nine-one-one.

A monotone voice answered. "Nine-one-one. What is your emergency?"

"A dead body."

"Excuse me? Are you calling to report a death?"

"Yes, a death."

"What is your name and location?"

"Suzie Tuft. I'm on Woody Lane."

"You're on a woody lane?"

"No. I mean, yes. It is woody here. That's how the road got its name, I suppose."

The operator's monotone ticked up a notch. "Do you know the victim?"

"No. I mean, I don't think I do."

"What's your address, ma'am?"

"One Woody Lane."

"I'll send the police. Wait there for them."

"You mean here? In the middle of the road?"

She paused so long I thought I lost cell service. "At the address you gave me where the person died. Stay on the phone with me until the police arrive."

"The person didn't die at my house. I was out for my walk, minding my own business, dancing to my music, when I caught the whiff of a dead animal."

"You were dancing in the middle of the road and came upon a dead animal?"

"That's what I thought at first, but the deceased is a human."

"You found a dead person in the middle of the road? Was he hit by a car?"

"He's not on the road, but over the hillside. Of course, I don't know if he is a he or a she. I didn't go close enough to find out." Blue and red lights flashed in the distance. "Here come the police."

"You can hang up now," the operator said.

A navy and white police cruiser slowed, then stopped beside me, lights still flashing. The window lowered slowly, and a chubby, clean-shaven face appeared. "We're investigating an accident on this road, ma'am," the detective said. "I'm going to ask you to go home unless you witnessed the incident."

"No, not an accident. I mean, the death might have been an accident. I didn't see how it happened."

"You aren't a witness, then?"

"No, but I called you."

The officer on the passenger side checked his computer. "According to this, the call came from One Woody Lane."

"That's my address, but I called nine-one-one from here. I spotted a body in the gully, and the operator told me to wait at this place for the police."

"The report said the victim was at One Woody Lane," he repeated.

"No. There's no dead body at my house." I raised my arm and pointed. "He's up there." I dropped my arm. "I mean, it's technically down there. Over the hill."

The men exchanged a look that seemed to indicate they thought I was either a nutcase or hallucinating.

"Stay put," the driver commanded. The vehicle rolled to the side of the road, half in the weeds, and stopped. Two men emerged—one tall, handsome, and built like the guys on a gym poster ad, and the other, a head shorter and thick around the middle.

I wondered how the handsome detective managed to look crisp and neat in his impeccable suit, while his partner resembled a wilted bag of lettuce.

The stout officer was a little gruff for my liking. Hands on his hefty hips, he instructed in a no-nonsense, demanding tone, "Start from the beginning, and state what happened here."

"Not right here, but up the road." I nodded with my chin.

He heaved a sigh and sternly repeated, "From the beginning."

I was nervous enough without him barking orders at me. I'd never encountered a dead person before today. That kind of discovery affected your brain. "I was out for my daily walk, listening to my music, doing a little road dancing." I gave him a brief sample of my moves that would put Trudy Vardine, the local dance teacher, to shame. He wasn't impressed.

"When did you discover this body, ma'am?"

His constant use of ma'am grated on my nerves. I wasn't *that* old. "A few minutes ago, when I called nine-one-one."

His gaze settled on Officer Handsome for a moment. I imagined his eyes rolling as he said, "Let's take a look at this alleged body."

Officer Gruff's sarcastic tone suggested he didn't believe me. I couldn't wait to deflate his smugness. Of course, I hoped no one sneaked in from the other side of the woods and stole the body.

The three of us strode to where the ground dropped away from the road on the right side of the guardrail. I stopped a few feet from the place and gestured. "On the right side. Down several feet."

Officer Gruff told Officer Handsome to stay with me while he trudged on alone.

"Do you smell that?" I asked him.

"Yeah. Can't miss it."

"I thought an animal had died. Then, I spied a red tie and a boot."

Up ahead, Officer Gruff pulled a gadget from his belt. I figured he notified someone to pick up the body. "Bring her over here," he called out toward us.

I backed away. "I don't need to see that again."

A granite-hard expression on his face, Officer Gruff waved us forward.

Officer Handsome said, "I'm sure this is uncomfortable for you, but since you found the body, we need to gather pertinent information." He extended his right arm in an *after you* gesture. He stayed close, which helped to put me at ease.

Officer Gruff paced back and forth in front of the guardrail, his thumbs tucked into his belt. "Tell me again how you happened to spot the slight protrusion of a boot down a twenty-foot drop."

His accusing tone irked me. "I smelled him. Can't you?" Wrapping my forefinger and thumb around the right lens of my sunglasses, I adjusted them. "And I have very good vision with my contacts."

I received a hard look, then he glanced down the hill as if measuring my words against the distance. He waved me away with a flip of his hand. "Take her back to the car and wait for me. The coroner is on his way." His curt dismissal both pleased and irritated me.

Officer Handsome and I sauntered back to the police

cruiser. "You did fine," he said. "Notifying us was the right call."

His compassion calmed me, but I wondered if I was smack dab in the middle of a good-cop, bad-cop routine.

"Are you okay?" He pointed toward the car. "Do you want to sit?"

Claustrophobic, the steel mesh cage visible through the window didn't appeal to me. "Uh, no thank you, sir." I presumed standing on the road was more comfortable. Probably the less intimidating choice, too.

"I'm Detective Pagarelli. Sorry for the inconvenience, but you'll need to wait here. My partner may have more questions for you."

He reached in through the open car window, retrieved a small notebook from the visor, and flipped the page. "In the meantime, why don't I take down some information?"

The smoothness of his voice had a mesmerizing effect on me. I didn't mind giving him my name, address, and phone number. I would've liked his personal information, too, but figured it was inappropriate to ask. I did notice the bare ring finger on his left hand, though.

"Where is your house located from here?"

"About half a mile that way." I indicated the direction.

He did a three-hundred-sixty-degree turn, his gaze flitting over the woods on both sides of the road. "Not much around here but trees."

"The closest house to mine is a mile in any direction."

He seemed to consider the fact. "You don't live out here alone, do you?"

"Me and my one-hundred-fifty-pound Siberian tiger."

His eyes widened. "You do realize it's illegal to keep wild animals as pets?"

His naivety was cute. "I'm kidding. He's a Siberian husky."

"Where is he? He'd be good protection on this isolated road."

"I can't say how much protection he'd be, but his size and bark are enough to scare people. Hunter is a cuddly baby at heart. He's apt to lick you rather than fight you. He's at a boarding kennel because I arrived home too late to pick him up today. I'll get him in the morning."

He leaned a hip against the side of the car, notebook poised in one hand. "Were you on a trip?"

"Yes, New York."

"Visiting relatives?" he asked.

"No. Work."

"What kind of work do you do?"

"I write textbooks and give talks at seminars. My publisher has an agency in New York City and invited me to come and discuss a new project."

"A writer, huh?"

I waited for him to make the usual comment about always wanting to write a book but never having the time. Instead, he made a few notes and asked, "Will you be staying alone tonight?"

"Yes." It had been quite some time since a man called on me.

He crossed his arms over his muscled torso, the notepad dangling in his hand. "You're not frightened? I mean, with the victim found close to your home and your dog at the kennel for the night."

Was he hinting he could keep me company? "I'm by myself lots of times when I travel to unfamiliar places and stay in strange hotels. I've become used to it."

"Does your home have a security system?"

"Why? Are you thinking of breaking in?"

My teasing fell flat as Detective Pagarelli's face reddened. "I, um...until we figure out what happened here, you can't be too careful."

"I do have an alarm system, and I'm capable of taking care of myself."

"Oh?"

"I have a handgun and a concealed carry permit."

He snapped to attention. "Do you have a gun on you?"

"No, sir." I was going to ask if he wanted to search me, but I didn't want to embarrass him again.

He pursed his lips, his expression slightly suspicious. "I'm surprised you aren't carrying. I would think a weapon would give you peace of mind out here all alone with no one around for miles."

"You gave the reason why I don't feel the need for a gun." I spread my arms wide. "No one around for miles."

"Except we have a dead body over the hill," he reminded me.

I scrunched my forehead. "Point taken."

"You take safety precautions with the weapon, I hope."

"Locked up, as we speak. A few friends and I took gun safety courses, and we practice at a local club."

An engine rumbled in the distance, signaling the approach of a vehicle. A black van, followed by an ambulance with lights flashing but no siren blaring, came into view.

"The coroner," Detective Pagarelli announced.

Detective Gruff flapped his arms with the velocity of an alarmed bird's wings while conversing with the coroner and two paramedics. My sympathy went out to them as they made their way over the embankment. I doubted it ever became easier to examine the dead.

Sometime later, the paramedics reemerged. They returned to the ambulance and dragged out a stretcher, black bag, rope, and something resembling a large tool chest. Quickly, they disappeared over the edge of the road again.

Detective Gruff's head rose from the void, followed by his stocky frame. He strolled toward us with his *I'm in charge* demeanor. With a flick of his head, he asked Detective Pagarelli, "Did you get her information?"

"I did."

"And her statement?"

Pagarelli tapped the notebook. "All here."

"Why don't you see if Ms..." Gruff stared at me with a questioning gaze.

I let the anticipation of an answer hang in the air for a few moments. "Tuft. Suzie Tuft."

With another *I want to roll my eyes* expression, he said, "Take Ms. Tuft home, will you? Take the car. I'll be here for a while. I can catch a ride with the coroner."

"Copy that."

Gruff spun around, stomping away without another word. Detective Pagarelli opened the back door of the car.

"I can walk," I explained. "My house isn't far."

Even from a distance, Gruff overheard me. "Detective Pagarelli will drive you home," he called out, his tone more of a command than a courtesy.

"I live around the bend. It's not worth starting the car." I stopped short of explaining which bend.

Gruff had halted, but he blew out a breath and waved an arm overhead. "Whatever." His mannerisms indicated he wasn't okay with the decision, but he wanted rid of me.

I was thankful. I didn't exactly want to be there, either.

Detective Pagarelli gestured. "After you."

I thought it would be rude to put in my earbuds and

listen to music, so I decided to take the conversation route. "Your partner acts like I did something wrong."

"You didn't. He does everything by the book. Wants to obtain everything we need to find out who our victim is and how he died."

Pagarelli had a long stride. I was glad my daily walks gave me the stamina to keep up with him. We entered the curve in the road, and he glanced around. "I don't see your house."

"You won't until we're close. It sits down over the hill on the left, about a quarter mile further."

He slid me a sidelong look. "Around the bend, huh?"

"If you want to get technical, it's not this bend." I put on my best apologetic face. "I couldn't see myself caged in the back of a police car. I have a thing with claustrophobic situations, especially when I can't escape when I want."

He said, "You're lucky I'm the detective walking you home today."

"I know." I paused, then asked, "Do you live in the area?" I hadn't seen him before around town.

"We're required to reside in the township. How long have you lived here?"

"Going on ten years. I walk every day, if possible. Until now, this road's been quiet and uneventful. Never any dead people, only animals."

He nodded. "Do you have many visitors?"

"A few friends and family members."

"Have you seen any suspicious people or cars in the area?"

"Either of those could be considered suspect with the lack of houses nearby. I've run into a few walkers over the years who ventured out this way from housing plans."

We rounded another bend, and the roof of my house came into view. "This is my place."

"Speaking of cars, is that yours in the driveway?"

He was a head taller, and I had to peek between the tree branches for a view of the white Honda. "It's Jess. My best friend." Her presence lessened my nervousness.

His voice lost its conversational tone. "Did you call her?"

"No, but her husband is a paramedic. He listens to a scanner."

He nodded. "It's better that you don't discuss the details of the discovery until we've worked the case. If this is a murder, we don't want anything to tip off the killer."

My feet halted with his last word. "Do you think he was murdered? Couldn't he have simply lost his way and fallen over the hill? Hit his head, passed out, and died from exposure?"

A hint of a smile tugged at the corners of his mouth. "I believe you've been reading too many mysteries. But, yes, he could've fallen. The coroner will determine the cause of death after an autopsy. While we wait for those results, please don't discuss what you've seen."

"I won't." *Except with Jess.*

As we neared the driveway, Jess jumped out of the car, clad in a lime green jumpsuit, and rushed to meet us. She knocked into me, throwing her arms around my shoulders.

"I was worried. Are you alright? Jake heard they found a dead body by your house." She studied my face, then brought her fingers up to cover her mouth. "Wait, did you find it? Oh, you poor thing."

"Who's Jake, and how did he hear about the victim?" Pagarelli asked.

"My husband," Jess said. "He's a paramedic."

"Where is he?"

Jess averted her eyes. "Working."

I pried myself loose from her grip. "He doesn't know you're here, does he?"

"He may have said to stay away from the area." She flapped her arms. "How could I, though, when you're my best friend?"

I introduced Jess to the detective.

She blanched and held me at a distance. "You aren't a suspect, are you?"

"Not unless you just put the idea in Detective Pagarelli's mind." We both turned his way.

He shook his head. "You're not a suspect." He addressed Jess. "Ms. Tuft is a witness, that's all."

Jess slapped both hands to her cheeks. "You witnessed the murder?"

"No," I answered.

Pagarelli interrupted. "We can't confirm murder. It could be a tragic accident. The autopsy results will help us make a clear determination."

"This is creepy," Jess whispered. "You must be terrified out of your mind. Come stay with us tonight."

"I can't deny it was a shocker, but I'll be okay at home."

"At least you have that beast of a dog." She looked around as though expecting to see him amble around the corner of the house. "Where is Hunter?"

"He's still at the doggie hotel. They were closed by the time my flight landed."

Jess placed a hand on my forearm. "Then, I insist you come to our house."

Pagarelli spoke. "A sensible idea under the circumstances. Do you want me to escort you inside before I leave?"

Yes. "That won't be necessary."

Jess edged closer to me, patting my back. "I'll stay with her while she packs a few things."

With a tip of his hat, the detective said, "I'll be going, then." He turned to leave. "I'll be in touch if we have more questions for you at a later date, Ms. Tuft."

"You have my cell number." *Call me anytime.*

He walked up my driveway with an easy stride, slowly disappearing from sight behind the trees and branches. I couldn't help admiring his tall, muscular figure the entire way. Although I'd sworn off men since my former boyfriend, Mike, cheated on me, I had to admit, Pagarelli tempted me.

Chapter Two

As soon as he disappeared behind the trees, Jess latched onto my arm. "Tell me everything." Her eyes glittered, and I imagined her rubbing her hands together in anticipation of a juicy story. "Were you creeped out finding a dead body? Was it all rotten and stuff?" She clutched her throat. "You're braver than I am." Raising the back of her hand to her forehead, she sighed in a dramatic fashion. "Such a ghastly sight! I would have fainted on the spot."

Not likely. Jess coaxed the gory details out of her paramedic husband every time he assisted at a horrible accident. How did I know? She repeated the particulars to me with shocking clarity, much to my revulsion.

Three years ago, Jess married her college sweetheart, Jake. At five ten and of sturdy build, Jake was as protective of Jess as a lion guarding his territory. He was a handsome man, and they presented as a striking couple who turned heads.

"I wanted to pass out," I confessed, "but feared

tumbling down the hill, where they'd find me tangled up with the rotting body."

"Eek. Now I'll have that horrid image in my head."

Until Jake comes home with a more horrible story. "I didn't see enough of the body to diagnose the condition. The boot pointing in the air did me in." I imitated the ramrod straight appearance. "I didn't go down the hill to examine him up close and personal."

"I would've."

Oh yeah, you would. "When you fainted and rolled down beside him."

Jess clicked her tongue. "I didn't mean literally. I'm a naturally curious person." She made no apology for her gruesome interests.

"That, you are."

"Did you scream your head off?"

I felt around the top of my head. "No. It's still attached."

"Be serious."

"Yes. I screamed loud enough to shake the birds from the trees. Then, I ran toward home. When my common sense and breath returned, I called nine-one-one. The operator stayed on the line until the police arrived."

"Then, Mr. Hottie showed up." Jess fanned herself with one hand.

"Unfortunately, he was with a humorless, gruff detective who made me show him where I found the victim."

"Murder victim?"

"They haven't determined if it's a murder, Jess. The poor man could have fainted and rolled down the hill."

"Ha, ha."

"Truthfully, he could have fallen while hunting. Broken

his neck. They won't determine a cause until after the autopsy."

"If they're doing an autopsy, they're suspicious."

"Not necessarily. Authorities request one when a death happens under unusual circumstances."

"This is unusual, all right. The most excitement ever on your road." She put a finger to her bottom lip. "Ooh, there may be more bodies in your woods."

My stomach did a disturbing flip. "Stop. Just stop."

"What?" She opened her arms and twirled. "It's a huge area. Hardly anyone ever wanders off in there."

"Except hunters who ignore the *No Hunting* signs."

"Too bad your Hunter wasn't with you. He would've investigated."

"I'm glad he wasn't. He could have destroyed crime scene evidence."

Jess's face brightened. "Ah ha, it *was* a murder."

"I didn't say it was a murder. I meant, if it turned out to be a crime scene, I wouldn't want Hunter to ruin the chance of finding a killer."

"Still. Sounds mysterious."

"Here's the real mystery..." I replied, my eyes glinting.

Mouth hanging open, Jess leaned in close.

I whispered, "We have to wait for the autopsy results."

Her mouth pursed. She frowned, shooing me away with her hands. "Go pack."

"Really, Jess. I'll be fine here. I'm not afraid."

"I'm afraid for you. Now, pack your things. I want to leave here before dark."

The truth was I didn't want to be alone with time to think about my gruesome discovery. Lucky for me, I hadn't unpacked the suitcase from my business trip. I tossed the dirty clothes from my luggage, replaced them with clean ones, and turned off the bedroom light. Staying with Jess seemed extreme, but a bit of caution wouldn't hurt. I had no idea how the body ended up over the side of the road or how long it had lain in the woods. If someone did harm him, he or she was running free.

Keeping details to myself about the corpse proved difficult with Jess quizzing me during the ride to her house. Since we shared everything, I caved and provided her with the few details I'd been warned to keep quiet about.

"You can't tell anyone about our discussion. Pagarelli advised me against talking about the ongoing investigation."

Jess blew out a puff of air. "You're my one and only best friend. Who would I yak to?"

Uh, let's see. MaryLou, Georgianna, and Bre.

She turned her face toward me, raising her eyebrows. "Speaking of Detective Pagarelli, he's a hot one."

"I hadn't noticed." *Liar.*

Jess cracked up. "Of course, you didn't." She refocused her attention on the road.

I would have had to be blind not to notice Detective Pagarelli's appeal. The man could pose as a centerfold for one of those calendars the police and firemen modeled for sans shirts. I hoped, these days, I was too smart to fall for a handsome face. I mustered my most indignant voice. "For your information, I was too shaken to think straight. He had all these questions about me finding the dead person. I concentrated on my answers."

"If you say so." She fixed me with a smug grin.

I crossed my arms, mirroring the stance of a defiant child. "I do."

"I think he likes you."

Twisting in my seat, I stared at her. "How did you come

to that ridiculous conclusion in the few seconds you met him?"

Jess kept her face forward, but I gathered from the way she bit her lip that she sensed my scrutiny. "He looked at you as if he had you under a microscope."

"He's a police detective. I imagine he studies everyone."

"He said he'd be in touch." She did another eyebrow lift. "You gave him your cell number."

"In case he has more questions for me about the discovery. Sheesh, Jess."

"Don't sheesh me. You're the one who hasn't been on a date in ages. I'm saying this could be an opportunity for you."

An opportunity to have my heart shattered again. My ex, Mike, was sweet and thoughtful when we met. A gorgeous man, yes, but his ability to make me feel loved was what endeared him to me. And he was funny, always making me laugh. We were happy. Until we weren't. "I'm not ready."

"Don't let Mike Hansen take any more of your life."

We were together for two years and were broken up longer. The first few months after I left him were a rough, emotional rollercoaster. Crying. Denying. Blaming. Depression. I congratulated myself for putting him further out of my mind every day. Eventually, I found contentment and a new happiness in my life. Did I want to risk disrupting my tranquility for another man?

We arrived at Jess's house, and she thankfully moved on to a different subject. "I have leftover meatloaf and can throw together a salad."

"Fine with me."

During dinner, I retold the story of finding the body to Jake for what seemed like the tenth time, but in actuality was only the third. The weight of the evening's discovery settled on my shoulders, exhausting me.

In Jess's guest room later that night, I had time to digest what occurred. I relived the moment Detective Pagarelli stepped out of the patrol car in all his six-foot-plus masculinity, and the kindness I'd seen in his unusual colored eyes when he spoke to me in a soothing voice.

I admonished myself for fantasizing. His interest in me was nothing more than interviewing a witness.

* * *

My first time in a police station the next day for questioning rattled me. My foot tapped out an unrecognizable, nervous beat. The bleak setting was every bit as intimidating as television dramas portrayed. Putrid green, peeling paint tainted the bare walls. A darkened observation window covered one wall, and a surveillance camera spied on the room's occupants from the water-stained ceiling.

I sat stiff as a mannequin on one side of a cheap, scarred wooden table that had seen its best days years ago. The gruff detective from last night sat bulldozer-rigid across from me, his stern expression shredding my nerves further. Why couldn't nice, comforting Detective Pagarelli be the one to interrogate me? Wanting to focus on anything but this detective's face, I stared at the cup of weak tea cooling in front of me.

"I'm Detective Whiteford."

My head jerked up at the sound of his gravelly voice disturbing the silence. I couldn't decide if I should shake hands with him. I opted to clench my trembling fingers in my lap. "Hello."

Keeping his eyes lowered to the folder before him, he

fingered the edge. "You're probably wondering why I called you down here."

"I assume it's about the body I found." It didn't take a rocket scientist to figure that one out.

"It is." He adjusted his plump frame in the chair, sat back, and stared at me. "Explain to me how you happened upon the victim, beginning with when you left your house for a walk."

Can't you remember from yesterday? "I told you and the other detective everything last night."

He tightened his lips, regarding me as if I couldn't understand his simple request. I related the story again, trying not to leave out pertinent details.

"Do you usually stop and check out the hillside?"

"Sometimes."

"Why yesterday?"

"I told you, I smelled something dead. The odor came from that area, so I looked. Call it curiosity. Those woods are posted against hunting. I wanted to see if someone shot an animal."

He rested his elbows on the table, his clenched hands under his chin. "Except it wasn't an animal." He smiled, but it was far from genuine. "Debris covered the body except for the boot. I'm surprised you spied him at all."

Was he dense or on an ego trip? "The piece of red material tossing on the breeze caught my eye. When I realized it was a tie, I moved closer and spotted the boot."

Whiteford picked up his pen. "Have you seen any strange cars or people on your walks during the last week or two?"

"No. Cars rarely travel my road. I mean, the township's road."

He noted my answer on a piece of paper but remained silent.

Not one to appreciate a lull in the conversation, I plowed on. "I call the road mine because my house borders the woods running its length. It's sort of a super long, private roadway for me."

He cleared his throat.

My brain urged me to quit talking, but my mouth wouldn't cooperate, even to stop myself from asking, "Do you live in a rural area?"

His steely eyes bore into me. I nearly gulped aloud.

"I've got a question about the timing of finding the victim," he said. "You stated you walk every day. Did that include the days before your discovery?"

Did he even read the statement I gave to his fellow detective? "As I told Detective Pagarelli, I was out of town for two days on a business trip. My flight arrived at the airport at five forty-five, and I drove three-quarters of an hour home. My legs needed a stretch after the cramped plane ride. A walk seemed perfect since there's daylight until almost eight these days."

"Ever heard of Christopher Ryder?"

"No." I blinked several times as understanding kicked in. "Is that the poor dead man's name?"

"Yes." He leaned back, resting his forearms on the chair. "He was on his way to speak with you."

Taken aback, I grabbed the edges of my seat, worried I'd fall over. "What? Why?"

Whiteford studied me. "He was an estate lawyer. He was in the area to deliver a letter about an inheritance."

"To me?" I shook my head. "There's a mistake. None of my friends or family members died, especially not someone who would include me in their will." I leaned forward, my forehead creased. "Are you positive?"

"Very. We contacted his next of kin, who put us in touch with the law firm where Mr. Ryder worked. The senior attorney claims Ryder was in the area to speak with you. You never met with him?"

I'd never heard of him. "No. As I said, I was on a business trip in New York."

"Did he call you?"

"No."

Whiteford scratched his chin in slow motion. "He checked into a hotel room three nights ago. Perhaps, he attempted to reach you when you were away."

"I didn't have any messages or missed calls."

"Maybe he found out you were out of town and decided to scout the area to see where you lived." He tapped his fingertips on the arm of his chair. "Unless he was planning a surprise visit."

"None of this makes sense." My palms were sweaty. It felt as though the room was closing in on me. "Who did the attorney represent?"

He lifted a paper from the folder in front of him. "Mr. Mike Hansen."

The room spun. My muscles had turned rubbery, and I sagged against the back of the chair. Eyes closed, I clutched my tightening chest, my breathing restricted.

"Are you okay? Ms. Tuft?"

I forced open my eyes, nodded, and tried to focus through the black dots distorting my vision. My thoughts were jumbled as I tried to process how my ex-boyfriend from years ago had not only died, but also included me in the disposition of his possessions. We had the kind of breakup that made a person wish to never hear from or see the other party for the rest of their life.

The detective pushed the Styrofoam cup toward me. I sipped the lukewarm tea for several seconds to compose myself.

"Thought you were going to faint on me. I take it you're familiar with Mr. Hansen."

If Whiteford was a decent detective, and I suspected he was, he'd discovered that Mike and I had dated. "Yes. But we haven't seen each other or spoken in years. Last I heard, he lived with another woman. Why would Mike leave anything to me?"

"I imagine Mr. Ryder was here to tell you. Did you notice his car when you found him?"

"No."

He scratched his head. "Got to wonder how he ended up in the woods along that deserted road. His office said he drove here alone, but his car is missing. Someone left his body over the hillside. Any idea who would commit the crime?"

I looked up and shook my head in answer, but also to clear it. "I don't know him or anything about him, nor am I familiar with any murderers."

My eye twitched, and my forehead perspired. I gulped down the rest of the tea. Talk about looking guilty.

Whiteford must have recognized my obvious discomfort. "We don't suspect you had anything to do with Mr. Ryder's death. We're trying to patch together missing details."

A chill ran through me. They didn't suspect me? Why even bring that up? Of course, I wouldn't be a suspect. The perspiration on my forehead dampened my bangs.

The paper in his hand crinkled as he scanned it. "They are sending another representative to inform you of the inheritance. We'd appreciate your cooperation in updating us on what you inherited, in case it has a bearing on this incident."

"Was the man I discovered murdered because he planned to contact me?" My eye twitch worsened.

"We're still investigating."

Guilt over the man's death overcame me. "What if someone tries to kill the next attorney?"

He held up a hand. "Let's not assume anything. We'll be on the alert. Extra police will patrol your area."

His no-nonsense tone did little to quell my rising panic, which must have shown on my face.

"Do you feel safe in your home?" he asked. "You should consider staying with a friend until this is resolved."

"I have a first-rate alarm system and Hunter, my husky. He tends to be intimidating when he feels I'm being threatened. I feel safer at home than anywhere else. And I'll be extra cautious." I'd also keep pepper spray in my pocket until the murderer was found.

"Okay." He shuffled his papers into a pile and tapped them on the desk. "We're done for now." He stood and slid a business card across the table. "Call us with questions or if you remember any additional information. We're here if you need us."

"What I need is this mystery solved."

"We're on it." He slapped the folder closed. "Thanks for coming down. I'll walk you out."

Shuffling down the hall behind him, I tried to inconspicuously divert my gaze toward the other offices in search of Detective Pagarelli. No sign of him, to my disappointment.

* * *

Roaming from room to room at home failed to work off my nervous energy. I decided fresh air was in order and dangled Hunter's leash from my fingertips. "Who wants to go for a walk?"

Hunter's nails clicked on the wood floor as he scampered toward the door, tail wagging. As usual, he beat me to it.

"Hold on a sec, boy." I ran back to the study and slipped a can of pepper spray into my pocket, thinking it was a shame that murder had come to my peaceful world.

Hunter led me down the driveway, stopping to sniff one of my azaleas. He poked his head under the bush and withdrew a Mont Blanc pen between his teeth, my favorite writing tool.

"Thanks, Hunter. I hate it when my pen disappears. Must have fallen out of my purse." I slipped the Mont Blanc into my jacket pocket and urged him up the driveway.

Foregoing my walking music, I used the time to contemplate what I'd learned about the body I found. According to Detective Whiteford, the man was on his way to deliver an inheritance letter to me. What on earth could Mike have bequeathed me that was worth a man's life? Why stop Ryder from informing me of the will contents? Who killed him?

I could think of no reasonable answers to those questions, or for the killing, but I was determined to find an explanation. His death was tied to me, and I wanted to help bring his killer to justice.

My livelihood depended on researching facts for my textbooks and articles. How different could investigating a murder be?

I spent the remainder of my walk mentally plotting my goal of solving the case and a few details about how to accomplish my mission. I would talk to the new messenger from the law office to learn what I inherited. I'd compile a list of people who would resent the fact Mike gave me even a dime from his estate. So far, my list included Mike's brother, Tom, and his recent live-in girlfriend, Samantha Banks.

Tom, ever the mooch, would think he was entitled to his brother's estate. Samantha, who had lived with Mike since she broke up our relationship, would never want me to get a cent from him out of pure jealousy.

I drew a blank as to who would kill to keep me from finding out Mike named me in his will. And why would he? Furthermore, what did Mike own worth more than a few bucks? I'd paid when we went on dates. I lent him money and cooked meals for him. I'd even made his car and cell-phone payments during our last months as a couple when he couldn't scrape together the cash. Had I suspected he was spending his paychecks on drugs then, I would have stopped.

Now that another attorney would be contacting me, the wait for a phone call drove me crazy. I had a mind full of questions, and they required immediate answers.

Hunter growled, and I became aware of my surroundings. Although intending to avoid the place where I'd found the victim, I stood within a few feet of yellow police tape flapping in the wind. I shuddered at the sight. "Let's turn back, Hunter."

The dog's head bobbed about as he sniffed. A low growl rumbled in his throat once more. "What is it? Do you smell the body?" I inhaled a whiff of air. "I don't smell anything now."

He tugged at the leash and barked as if he intended to tear someone or something apart. My arm sockets protested, but I hung on as he leaped forward.

Rustling sounded from the gully. Had the killer returned to the scene of the crime? I stood there, incapacitated by fear, a scream stuck in my throat.

A head materialized from the abyss, and my scream found its way out. Hunter went nuts. My hands burned where I held his leash with all my strength. I couldn't reach for the pepper spray.

A man emerged and waited on the side of the road, shouting, "Sorry! Sorry." He raised his hands in the air. "I mean you no harm."

He didn't strike me as a hunter with his styled hair and designer jeans. I backed up, yanking on my dog's restraint. Overexcited, Hunter danced around my legs.

The stranger lowered his arms, patting the air in a *calm down* motion. Eyes wide, he asked, "Does your dog bite?"

"Easy, Hunter," I urged. The dog switched from barking to growling.

"I'm Corey James. I work at Blockhart, James & Ryder, LLC. I'm an estate lawyer. Please accept my apology for scaring you." Fear tightened his face. His eyes never wavered from my snarling dog.

"Hunter, heel." The well-trained animal he was, Hunter parked his rump beside my feet and sat at attention.

Briars and slivers of rotted bark decorated the man's jeans and sweatshirt in a haphazard pattern. Twigs tangled in his bootlaces. I didn't mention the pieces of fern in his hair.

"I'm sorry to frighten you." He plucked at the debris covering his clothing. "I wanted to see where Christopher died." His voice caught on the last two words. "He was a colleague. A good guy. I can't believe someone would hurt him on purpose."

Hunter and I stared at him with wary eyes.

"Are you, by chance, Ms. Tuft?"

Who was this stranger who knew my name? "Why do you ask?"

"I know Ms. Tuft lives on this road but have only seen woods so far. I figured someone walking out here in the middle of nowhere must live close by. I'm here in lieu of Attorney Ryder."

"I'm Suzie Tuft."

"I wanted to make an appointment to see you during the next couple of days, and, well..." He swept his arms toward the crime scene. "I don't know. Morbid curiosity drew me here." His face reddened as he explained.

"Where's your car?" I asked.

He glanced over his shoulder, lifting his chin. "Up around the bend a piece. I wasn't positive where Christopher was discovered, but the police said he was over a hillside on this road. Thought I'd have a better chance of finding the place on foot." He pointed. "I came across the police tape." He ran a hand through his hair, dislodging the fern. "I understand you found him."

I nodded.

"Sorry you had to endure the shock. How are you doing?"

This guy was sorry a lot. Reminded me of myself for trusting Mike. "I'm glad I found your friend before...any animals did."

His horrified expression made me wish I'd left off the last part of my comment. He stroked his hair again, rotated his head in different directions. "This is a deserted road."

His eyes settled on Hunter. "Guess you don't have to be afraid."

"Hunter won't hesitate to protect me." I patted his head.

The man visibly gulped.

"I need to finish walking him."

He reached into his pocket. The action was enough to make me loosen my grip slightly on Hunter's restraint and become painfully aware of the pepper spray's location. But Mr. James only produced a business card and held it out to me. "Would it be alright if I called you? Mike Hansen employed us to deliver an inheritance to you upon his death."

I didn't move. "Why would he do that? We've had no contact with each other for years." I realized too late I had spoken sharply.

The attorney dropped his hand to his side, still clutching the card. "Mr. Hansen was a recovering drug addict. I believe he wanted to make amends for something in his past regarding you. Do you live near here?"

"Down the road." That should give him a clear picture. Not.

He advanced closer, the business card stretched out in front of him. A menacing growl rumbled in Hunter's throat. Mr. James halted.

Touching the pepper spray in my pocket, I gave Hunter's leash a tug. Mr. James stepped backward, hand still extended.

I stretched out and accepted the card. He pulled another one and a pen from his pocket. Flipping the card over, he asked, "May I verify your phone number?"

I rattled off the digits.

"If convenient, I'll call you in the morning and set up a time to meet and go over the paperwork."

Curiosity gnawed at me. "Fine."

"My car is in the direction you're headed. Do you mind if I walk with you?"

"Suit yourself." I nudged Hunter in between us. Mr. James clung to the berm of the road as he followed a step behind us. Guess he wasn't a dog lover.

Chapter Three

"Well?" Jess stood, hands on hips, tapping her foot. Her long, flowy fuchsia and egg yolk yellow top matched her flamboyant personality. As usual, her nail color coordinated with the day's outfit. I couldn't figure out how she managed the feat when I barely found time for a manicure.

"Picture those cop interrogations on TV."

She scrunched her lips. "That bad?"

"Harrowing. Detective Gruff's name is Detective Whiteford. Good thing he's not a doctor. His bedside manner would intimidate the hardiest of patients. He said I wasn't a suspect, which made me think they considered me at some point. Thank goodness I was in New York." I swiped my bangs from my eyes. "And police station tea tastes as if it's brewed from moldy weeds."

She shooed me into the living room. "Sit down. I made a fresh pitcher of iced tea and baked a batch of brownies—from a box, not from scratch like Bre's."

Jess returned a couple of minutes later with the baked goods and tea. "What'd he say about the body?"

"He confirmed a murder was committed. Whiteford didn't add anything new about the victim or his condition."

Jess opened her hands in a begging motion. "Give me something." Her mouth hung open.

Witnessing her salivating for the gruesome details, I gave her a few crumbs. "Promise me you won't tell anyone about this."

"I promise. Don't I always have your back?"

Always. "The victim was an estate attorney on his way to see me about an inheritance."

"An inheritance? Who died?"

I took a breath. "Mike."

"What?" She recovered, slapping her thigh. "The rat finally got what's coming to him."

I thought about the early days of our romance. Mike hadn't always been a rat. "Shh. Don't speak ill of the dead."

"Consider the remark as payback for making me *ill* for the way he treated you."

"Don't joke. This is serious."

"How'd he die?"

Jess's question stumped me. "I was too shocked and nervous to ask Whiteford."

Her face deflated like a balloon losing air. "Don't bother applying for a news anchor job any time soon."

"Not a chance."

She broke off a piece of brownie. "So, Mike died and left you an inheritance." Jess popped the morsel in her mouth. She brushed crumbs from the front of her shirt. "Why would he give you anything? The man had nothing worthwhile to his name." She flapped a hand in the air. "Besides, Mike lived with that witch he had the affair with, remember?"

Remember? My heart seized as the old pain I'd fought hard to overcome flared. "How could I forget?"

Jess didn't notice my distress. "How will you find out what you inherited now that the attorney is dead?"

"The estate firm has sent another lawyer."

"Who?"

"Corey James. Hunter and I met him today on our walk."

"On your road?" Her eyes widened. "Looking for you?"

I pictured the man's unkempt appearance and somber mood. "He wanted to see the place where his attorney friend died."

"Gruesome. Did he say what Mike left you?"

I don't really care or want anything from Mike. "No details yet. Mr. James is going to call in the morning and make an appointment to discuss it with me."

"Did he give you his number? Can you call him?"

Why would I want to? "He did, and no."

She collapsed against the sofa cushions. "I hate waiting."

* * *

Prompt for the appointment he'd made with me, Corey James flashed a smile and waved a finger when I opened my front door. Dressed in an expensive navy suit, white shirt, and multi-striped tie, he bore little resemblance to the disheveled man I'd encountered on the road with twigs stuck to his boots and fern leaves in his hair. "Hello, Ms. Tuft."

Hunter growled at my side. I patted his head to reassure him it was okay. Opening the door wider, I stepped back. "Come in."

His expression wary, Mr. James glanced at the dog. "I don't think he likes me."

I stroked Hunter's head. "He's a guest, boy." I pointed toward the kitchen. "Go lie down."

Hunter retreated to his bed, but he twisted his head to keep an eye on the attorney. I led Corey James to the dining room table, where I had set out freshly baked chocolate chip cookies. The smell of coffee brewing permeated the air as it percolated in the kitchen.

"Coffee or tea?" I asked.

He deposited his leather briefcase on the floor, unbuttoned his suit jacket, and tugged on the back of a chair. "Coffee would be great. Black."

Minutes later, a steaming cup of coffee in front of him and iced tea at my place, we settled in for the meeting.

"As I informed you," he began, tugging his shirt cuff over his gold Rolex, "I'm here to officially deliver your inheritance from Mike Hansen."

"Why would he name me in his will? We've had no contact for years."

Mr. James lifted his briefcase to the table and released the locks with a ping. "Mr. Hansen made it clear to Christopher—Mr. Ryder—that he owed you for taking advantage of you years ago. A recovering drug addict, he wished to make amends for the inconvenience he caused when you were a couple by providing you with a monetary gift."

"You mean when he cheated on me?" I mumbled.

If he heard, James ignored the remark. Delving into the briefcase, he lifted a single sheet of paper. "According to Mr. Ryder," he said, "Mr. Hansen deeply regretted his actions toward you."

The Mike I'd dated would never have admitted he

wronged me unless he had a complete overhaul of his personality, conscience, and compassion.

The attorney slid the paper toward me with the tip of his manicured index finger. "Here is the letter explaining your inheritance."

Curiosity was the sole reason I refrained from crumpling it and sending Mr. James on his way. As I picked up the proffered document, the words *the deceased, Mike Hansen* shook my bravado. I imagined the shock was to be expected since we'd been close at one time. Maybe it was conceivable that Mike had left me a trinket or two.

This wasn't the case. Reading further, my confusion quickly turned to astonishment. There, outlined in black and white, was a list of what I'd actually inherited. Mike had bequeathed me ten acres of land and a cabin with its furnishings, along with all possessions and any money on the property therein.

"Land? A cabin?" I gaped momentarily at Corey James. "This is ludicrous. We weren't even engaged. Why would he bequeath valuable assets to me?"

I held the letter out to Mr. James, between two fingers, as though it would burst into flames. "There must be strings attached. Why didn't he give his possessions to the woman he lived with?"

Mr. James lifted his coffee cup, ignoring the letter in my outstretched hand. "Mr. Hansen left her the home they sometimes shared and its contents. He intended this property to be awarded to you." He put the cup to his lips and sipped.

I wondered about his choice of words, *sometimes shared*, but stopped short of asking. "What does this mean?" I pointed to the specific phrase regarding any money therein.

He leaned in to read the document. "I imagine if there

is money at the cabin or anywhere on the land, it's yours. Perhaps, he has a safe on the premises."

From his case, he lifted a legal-sized folder jammed with papers and explained he'd compiled the documents to transfer the property to me. "You're required to sign in several places to settle the matter."

I waved them away with a flick of my wrist. "Forget it. I won't incur his mortgage."

"Insurance paid off the mortgage upon his death." He handed me a tri-folded document with the word *deed* inscribed across the top in prominent, bold letters.

Knowing how angry Mike was about our breakup, he'd probably left me a dilapidated building with years of back taxes. I tapped the unopened document against the table. "Let me guess, I now own a hut on some strip of worthless land?"

"Hardly." He slipped an appraisal form in front of me and pointed out a figure. "The house alone is worth four hundred fifty thousand dollars."

The value threw me off balance. Flabbergasted didn't begin to describe the extent of my shock. I felt the color drain from my face.

James reached over and raised my glass in front of me. "Are you okay?"

My whirling brain was about to explode. "No." I downed the tea, though a glass of wine would have done more to steady my nerves. "This has to be a joke."

"It isn't. Everything is legal. There are no hidden costs."

"What about back taxes? Liens?"

"No liens. Taxes are paid in full." He laid a bound stack of photos on the table, withdrew several from the top, and spread them out. "The realtor took these when Mr. Hansen bought the cabin."

I left the photos lying there, but stretched over for a closer view. The one-story log structure was half hidden by trees, but I could make out huge windows and stone pillars. The pictures of the interior showed an open-concept great room, dining room, and kitchen area. All rooms were devoid of furniture. A wall of windows, rustic ceiling beams, and a floor-to-ceiling fireplace were focal points. Another stone fireplace lent ambiance to the master bedroom. I scanned pictures of two other bedrooms, a mud room, and laundry. The opulence was far different from anything Mike ever had either before or while we dated. The very notion was illogical.

I noted the dates; an appraisal from four months ago and a deed recorded two years ago.

"How did Mike go from jobless to owning a half-million-dollar home? Rob a bank?"

James dismissed my comment with a chuckle and laid down another paper. "This is a detailed list of your inherited possessions. Of course, there may be discrepancies from what you find at the property due to Mr. Hansen adding or subtracting items prior to our drawing up and filing this revision for him."

I planted my elbows on the table, positioned my fingers on my temples, and closed my eyes. "Wait a minute. Let me process this before you go on." Picking up my glass, I pushed back my chair. "I need another cup of tea. More coffee?"

He handed me his cup. "Please."

I rested against the kitchen counter for a moment, my head in my hands. It was all too unbelievable to comprehend. Hunter nudged my leg, and I stroked his fur. "Want to go outside?" He ran toward the door. I let him out into the fenced-in yard. With a sigh, I refilled the coffee cup and tea glass.

Although my hand trembled, I managed to place the hot liquid on the table without spilling it and scalding my guest.

James gripped the cup handle. He, too, looked in need of caffeine. "I understand this large of an inheritance is a lot to take in."

"You think? Believe me, if you knew Mike and the circumstances surrounding the stormy end of our relationship, you'd be as shocked and perplexed as I am."

"When their circumstances change, often people do, too," he said.

I snatched the deed from the table and waved it in front of his face. "This much in three years?"

"In my business, I see fortunes come and go in a blink." He tapped the inventory. "Why don't we see what's here?"

He went over the two-page, legal-sized papers with me. "Besides the normal home furnishings, the cabin contains valuable artifacts and antiques. Many are listed here, and I have pictures of them, unless he removed something within the last two weeks or neglected to designate them. Before you dispose of anything, consider calling in an estate auctioneer."

It seemed absurd Mike would go antique shopping. "Are you certain they aren't garage sale items?"

He ran a finger down the value column. "I guarantee you, these assessments are correct."

The figures included a lot of zeroes.

"A four-car garage contains an SUV, a boat, and a riding mower." James aligned more photos on the table. "A tool shed and a garden shed are located next to the cabin."

I had trouble keeping my jaw from dropping. Staring at the condensation forming on my glass, I concluded there had to be a catch. I dropped back in my chair, pushed the list away from me, and crossed my arms. "I don't want any of this. I won't be responsible for any credit cards or other debts of his."

The attorney shook his head. "Everything in your inheritance is debt-free. Mr. Hansen even provided a separate account to pay for inheritance taxes."

"How? Did he win the lottery?"

James smiled as if I'd made a ridiculous remark. "Christopher Ryder claims your boyfriend inherited several thousand dollars when his parents died. He made lucrative investments with it over the years. You aren't going to be stuck paying a dime."

"Ex-boyfriend," I corrected him. "No way could a few investments pay for all of this and his girlfriend's place. Mike must have obtained the bulk of his money illegally."

"According to the records Christopher kept, Mr. Hansen was a stock day trader. He made a small fortune and parlayed it into a huge payoff. He was even teaching Christopher the art of day trading."

I fingered a corner of the deed. "Have you been to see this place? According to these photos, the *cabin*, as it's referred to in these documents, is not an everyday hunting camp."

"I've only seen the photos here. I doubt Mr. Hansen hunted there, though I could be wrong."

"What if I don't want the property?"

"You may dispose of it however you wish. Sell it, or give it to charity."

"Don't you find it odd that someone I've had no contact with, who had a life with another woman, is giving me a small fortune with no strings attached?"

"I've bequeathed stranger things under stranger circumstances."

I didn't see how. "What about his brother? What did Mike leave Tom?"

"Mr. Hansen bequeathed only you and Ms. Banks gifts." Not so subtly, he glanced at his watch. "Let's begin," he suggested, handing me a Mont Blanc pen. It seemed we had the same taste in writing tools.

He withdrew a bloated batch of papers from the legal-sized folder. Flipping through each page, he explained why I needed to sign the documents and then directed me to the appropriate signature lines.

A strange shiver wound through me, causing my name to distort as I penned it on each indicated page. I had an eerie thought Mike was about to jump out of hiding and yell, "Gotcha."

James dated and countersigned as a witness below my name. When I finished signing the last document, he detached a copy of each and handed them to me for my own records. He gathered the originals, securing them with a huge binder clip. "My assistant will file these when I return to the office."

Having felt as if I'd been writing for an hour, I massaged my fingers as I questioned my sanity. What if, down the road, these possessions became a nightmarish weight on my shoulders? I couldn't help thinking Mike had a delusional hidden motive for revenge because I'd left him and refused to take him back.

"Your hand is probably cramped from signing," James said, breaking into my thoughts. "But the law requires us to be thorough."

From the few papers left in his briefcase, James withdrew a nine-by-twelve manilla envelope. "This contains keys to the cabin, garage, sheds, as well as the SUV and boat. All the proper ownership documentation, insurance, and property tax information are included.

"Mr. Hansen retained us to handle all title transfers and name changes. Your signature on all necessary documents allows us to begin the filing process. We'll mail the updated materials to you."

Too many unanswered questions swirled in my mind. "Did you know Mike?"

"I wouldn't say I knew him. I met him once when he came in to see Christopher, who handled his business the past three years."

"Three years? He had this fortune three years ago?"

"Not all of it. He bought the house two years ago. The antiques and the boat were more recent acquisitions." Resting his forearms on the table, James crossed his right hand over the left. "I understand he attained sobriety, then sought legal representation to draw up a will after receiving his inheritance. He returned several times to make additions as his estate grew. He had one brother, and no legal marriage or children of his own. I assumed you were his main benefactor because he still loved you."

The last comment baffled me. We'd made a clean break. The first few months Mike had pleaded with me, but I stood strong in my refusal. He'd cheated on me. How could anyone call that love? He gave up and hadn't contacted me in nearly three years. "Did you learn how he died?"

"Heart attack. He lingered for a few days. Christopher visited him in the hospital. Mr. Hansen stressed his final wishes should be carried out as directed in his will as soon as possible after his death."

I extended the deed toward him. "Maybe Mike wasn't in his right mind when he left this to me."

"He was as sane as we are."

Did sane even define me these days?

"You were the only person included in the will when he first came to our firm. He amended it later to include a house and possessions for Ms. Banks."

Everything about this situation raised additional issues in my mind.

As if sensing he might be trapped with a barrage of my questions, Corey James closed his briefcase with a brusque snap of the locks. "My number is on my card if you have further questions. Please don't hesitate to reach out to me."

"Thank you. I'm sorry about your friend."

Pain flickered in his eyes. "Christopher was a terrific guy. It must have been quite a shock when you found him."

"It definitely was. Did he have a family?"

He nodded. "A wife and five-month-old daughter."

My heart constricted. "How awful for them. Please extend my sympathies if you speak with his widow."

"I will." He donned his suit jacket, smoothed his tie, and lifted the briefcase from the table. "Thank you for the coffee."

A few minutes later, he pulled out of the driveway, leaving me to figure out why Mike's final wishes included me and why Mr. Ryder died attempting to contact me. Learning he had a wife and baby only made me more determined to help find his killer.

In the dining room, I picked up the deed and the listing of possessions. Mike bought the cabin not long after we broke up. The question of why he would leave anything to me when I'd completely cut him out of my life kept swirling in my mind. Not to mention, how could he have made that kind of money in day trading? The man had harbored little ambition and no knowledge of the stock market when he was with me. He barely kept a decent job about a year into our relationship, claiming his various bosses hated him. It was more that Mike hated work.

I dumped the keys out of the envelope and scattered them with my fingers. So many. Tags on rings identified which were for the house, SUV, boat, and sheds. An index card taped to the garage door opener had a number written on it. Another indicated the code for the cabin security system. I lifted a large, heavy key marked *gate*, which aroused my curiosity. Had Mike built himself a fortress?

I brought Hunter in from the backyard and refreshed his water dish before stashing the deed and list of possessions in my purse. I needed to discuss this outlandish inheritance with Jess in person.

Driving, I mulled over Mike's irrational last will and testament. An old friend of Mike's told me his parents had died, but he still had his worthless brother. Why didn't he leave the cabin to him? Mike had been generous enough in giving him money borrowed from me.

Jess poured me a glass of unsweetened iced tea while I filled her in on the strange afternoon.

"A deed?" She plopped down in a chair, looking as baffled as I was. "As in, he gave you property?"

"Yes."

She waved a dismissive hand through the air. "Yeah, a falling-down shack built over an abandoned strip mine."

I spread the deed out on the table. "According to this, the total value of the place is four hundred fifty thousand dollars." I let that sink in before adding, "The cabin sits on ten wooded acres and is fully furnished."

Jess gaped, astonished at the photos I placed before her. She picked one up in each hand, practically drooling. "No way. Get a load of the size of this place. My gosh, the main room is magnificent. Did he rob a bank?"

"No."

She guessed again. "Hit the lottery?"

I chuckled. "My thoughts exactly, but no." Preparing to drop another bombshell on her, I handed over the two pages detailing the possessions. "Here's a list of furnishings and other assets I now own, too."

Her wide brown eyes skimmed the list. At one point, she drew back from the paper and then brought it closer again. "Artifacts, antiques, an SUV." She looked up and squawked, "He left you a vehicle?" Jess slapped the document with her right hand. "He couldn't even afford a bicycle when he was with you."

"Keep reading."

"A boat? He left you a boat?" She huffed. "You've got to be kidding. He's been living the good life all these years?"

"Mr. James claims Mike inherited several thousand dollars when his parents died and increased it through investments."

"Right. He wouldn't recognize an investment if someone shoved it down his throat. Decline all this stuff before you're the one stuck paying off his debt."

"Nope. I own everything, free and clear." I held up a finger. "No mortgage." I raised a second finger. "No credit card or other debt, either."

Jess slouched against the back of her chair, arms limp at her sides. "I'm stunned." Her facial expression confirmed her words.

"No more than I am. That's why I'm here." I scooped

up the papers and raised them with one hand. "Isn't this ridiculously excessive?"

"Yes. Why would creepy Hansen leave you property? There must be a hitch."

"I asked myself that question, and I intend to find answers."

"How?" she demanded. "He and his lawyer are dead. You said this new one didn't know Mike."

"I'll contact Samantha."

"Ha," Jess scoffed. "The witch won't tell you anything."

"I'm kidding." I would never contact Samantha, nor would I expect her cooperation. "I research educational materials, Jess. Investigating an inheritance can't be much different. I could be the one to solve the murder for the police."

"Setting your sights a little high, aren't you?"

"Assembling a four-hundred-page college textbook with an instructor guide and online materials isn't a piece of cake, you know," I replied, my tone a little too abrupt.

Undaunted, Jess brushed me off. "Yeah, yeah."

I pulled a small spiral notebook and a pen from my purse. I turned back the cover and jotted down the questions I had. Why did Mike give me the property? Why was Ryder murdered on his way to tell me?

On the next sheet, I listed my research goals. Step One —Check out the property. Step Two—Have it reassessed. Step Three—Note anything unusual. Step Four—Interview Mike's other friends to determine if any of them heard about the property.

Peering over my shoulder, Jess asked, "Come on. Do you think he had friends with that freeloader personality of his?"

"Everyone has a friend or two."

"What if you don't find one of his?" She challenged me with raised eyebrows. "Or what if his only friends are thugs, same as his brother?"

"There's always Samantha."

She rolled her eyes. "There's no way she'll give up info. Remember how snobby she was when you found her with the jerk? I wanted to slap her cussing lips for spewing all those mean things."

"She'd have sued you."

Jess crossed her arms over her chest, reminding me of a stubborn teenager. "You should've let me anyway. Taking her down a peg or two would've made my day."

I flipped the notebook cover closed and dropped it into my purse. "It wasn't your fight."

Jess placed her hands on her hips. "Are you kidding me? I would do anything for you. You're my best friend."

"And you're mine." I gathered up the papers. "I have to go before this conversation turns all sappy sweet."

"What about his brother?" she asked. "What did Mike leave the scoundrel?"

"According to the attorney, Mike only named me and Samantha in his will."

Jess blew out a breath, fluttering her blunt-cut bangs. "Bet he didn't take that well."

Mike's brother, Tom, was a sly character, and he hunted for ways to make a fast buck without straining himself. I never trusted him. "I can't imagine he did."

She picked up the deed, examining it. "Where is this place?"

"Punxsutawney."

She burst out in hysterics. "Hansen the punk left you property in Punxsutawney? Punk, Punx, get it?"

"Unfortunately."

She scrunched her face. "How far is Punxsutawney?"

"About two hours from my house. I mapped out a route."

"When are we going to check it out?"

"This weekend." I stood, slipping my purse strap over my shoulder. "If you can ride along Saturday morning, I'm leaving at seven."

"Do you want Jake to come?"

"That would be wonderful. We have no clue what we'll run into."

"Another dead body?"

"Jess, please. Don't tempt fate."

Chapter Four

Saturday, Jake loaded a small cooler of drinks into the backseat of his truck for the trip to the cabin. I added a tote of fruit and snacks.

"Sit behind Jake," Jess instructed, getting into the front seat. "We can communicate better." Both of us needed a clear view of each other's hands to interpret the gestures that accompanied our oral comments.

Jake set the GPS for Punxsutawney, and we were off, greeted by a gorgeous sunrise. The forecast for lots of sunshine throughout the day signified a pleasant trip.

"I can't wait to see this place after a glimpse of those photos," Jess said. She glanced over her shoulder into the backseat. "Bet you can't, either."

My anxiousness stemmed from not being able to shake the feeling that accepting Mike's generous gifts was a terrible idea that would boomerang and somehow ruin me. Leaving him on such unpleasant terms only aroused my suspicion of his generosity. "I want to prepare the place for the market as soon as possible."

"You could change your mind after a tour," Jake said.

"Might turn out to be the perfect getaway. Nestled in the mountains far from interruptions, it may even spark your creativity. Lots of authors have writing retreats."

Reluctant to change my mind about the sale, I said, "No cabin of Mike's could ever be a writing haven for me."

"Why'd the guy leave you property worth a fortune in the middle of nowhere in the first place?" Jake asked.

"I have no idea. We hadn't spoken since I broke off the relationship."

"Creep," Jess corrected. "Not a guy, a creep for cheating on her."

Mike didn't start out as a creep. He was a respectable book salesman when we met. In fact, we were nearly perfect for each other. Or else, I fell so hard I overlooked his faults. Two years into our relationship, I found him in a drugged state. He claimed that was the first time he'd used drugs and that it would be the last. Our story unraveled completely when I caught him using again while cheating on me, and I left him. Why, then, would Mike include me in his will?

"That's what makes me curious about his motives," Jake said. "I mean, we're not talking about property worth a few measly thousand."

Jake's words sent a ripple of dread through me. As detached as he was from the situation, Jake had also concluded Mike's actions were crazy.

"Guilt," Jess said. "For being a horrible person and treating Suzie badly."

"Four hundred fifty thousand dollars buys a lot of penance," Jake said.

My thoughts, exactly.

"No, it doesn't," Jess argued. "You can't put a price on Suzie's pain and suffering."

The relationship wasn't all painful. I thought about our hikes in the woods, eating pizza while enjoying our favorite football games, intimate dinners in our favorite restaurants. Then, how the pain of my broken heart had devastated me. My chest tightened.

Jake eyed me in the rearview mirror. "What's your take on all this, Suzie?"

I swallowed. "I can't begin to guess Mike's motives. After seeing the property, I plan to talk with people he hung out with and find some answers."

"Does anyone rent the cabin seasonally?" Jake asked. "The place would bring in a nice extra income."

"Good question. The attorney didn't mention it, and I didn't think to ask."

The conversation shifted from Mike to pleasant topics, and I relaxed for the next hour.

Consulting the GPS, Jake announced, "This is where we turn."

"We do?" A narrow road led into the dense woods, reminding me of the land around my home, only darker and more crowded with evergreen trees. The area was devoid of any immediate signs of life, human or otherwise. Desolate came to mind.

Jake left the highway and entered a narrow, tree-lined dirt road. He dodged one enormous pothole, only to clunk into another. He struggled with ruts that made steering difficult.

The thick forest boxed us in on both sides. Through tree trunks, I discovered a small stream on the left, glistening where the rising sun struck it. In another month, the leaves on the cluster of oaks and maples, along with the briars and weeds, would create a barrier to conceal it. Fir trees already hid it in patches.

To the right, trees clumped collectively to form a wall of bark and pine. Not one house was in sight. Jake braked as a large antlered deer darted in front of the car. The woods were no doubt teeming with other hidden wildlife.

The road began to unfold into a smoother section of tar and chip, almost as if two different road crews had maintained it. "At last, a decent road," Jake said.

A little further along, an iron gate rose in front of us, blocking the entrance from the road. The closely aligned iron bars formed spikes at the top, a deterrent to someone wanting to climb over them. Signs stating no trespassing scattered on the gate and the adjacent trees sent clear warnings. With fat pines hogging the space on either side of the gate, it would be impossible for a vehicle to circumvent the fortress.

Jake stopped the car. I fished the largest key out of the envelope and handed it to him. He unlocked the gate, drove the car to the other side, then relocked it.

We passed rows of trees with fresh budding leaves and dense brush for what seemed a half mile before the cabin came into view.

Calling it a cabin was an understatement. The photos from the attorney didn't do justice to the log and stone dwelling that stood before us. The place resembled a picturesque lake house with a front wall of A-framed windows and a wrap-around, screened-in deck. A stone chimney crawled up the left side of the structure and rose three feet above the dark blue tin roof. Two dark, walnut-stained Adirondack chairs sat on either side of the front door. A stack of logs rested against the porch. Two smaller block-style buildings sat on the opposite side.

"Oh, wow." I wondered if I'd entered a painting, or

maybe the Twilight Zone. The place was palatial. My house would fit in the oversized garage.

We sat in stunned silence for several moments until Jake gave a low whistle.

"Ditto," Jess added. She swung around in the front seat and tapped my knee, breaking my stare.

The only words I managed were, "I'm speechless."

Jake pulled onto the gravel driveway, where a forest of towering pines encroached. A few yards of grass surrounded the buildings. Through the trees, a fleeting shape flitted, too small for a deer or a bear.

We crawled out of the car and stretched our legs. Rotating our heads every which way, we resembled a bunch of lost tourists.

"Peaceful," Jake said. "And beautiful."

"Isolated," Jess added.

Imagining Mike's ghostly spirit on the scene, I wrapped my arms around myself to still the shiver running through me.

We mounted the rough-hewn porch steps. Leftover dried leaves from the winter had gathered in the corners. I unlocked the door, and we entered single file. I led.

Crossing the threshold behind me, Jess gasped. "Ugh." She held her nose. "What reeks in here?"

I held my breath against the stench.

Jake stepped inside, chuckling. "Musty with a side of dead mouse, I'd guess."

"Stinky," Jess corrected him. "Where's the air freshener?"

"How could such a beautiful place smell this awful?" I asked.

"You ladies haven't been to many hunting camps. This is how camps smell when opening them after being closed for a while. If anyone's been here recently, they've kept the place shut up tight." He gestured. "Don't close the door. I'll see if I can open the windows and air the place out a little."

He found a light switch and gave us a view of the once darkened room. Collectively, we drew in a breath. The interior stunned us, and not in a good way.

Jake let out another low whistle. "I didn't expect this." He walked to one of the great room windows and fought with a heavy flower-print swag that swathed a pole and cascaded down on either side. He raised the decorative window shade and, with a grunt, heaved up the window-pane. The distinctive scent of pine drifted in on a breeze.

Jess and I stood rooted in place, gawking at the room's furnishings.

A royal blue sofa adorned with gold tassels running along the bottom stood proudly before a carved mahogany table. Bold striped pillows and a knitted afghan rested on it. Straight-backed parlor chairs with gold upholstery sat royally on the opposite side of the table. A colorful print area rug covered the wooden floor. The furniture was better suited to a nineteen-twenties parlor decorated by someone with dreadful taste.

The sofa table and two side tables were covered in lacy doilies, presumably from a bygone era, judging from the discoloration. Candelabras, glass animal statues, vases, an ornate gold clock, and a marble bust of a lady all vied for space on available surfaces. A mahogany and glass cabinet mounted on one wall held a china tea set trimmed in gold and a white vase with gilded handles.

The fireplace itself was a magnificent stone structure, diminished only by the tawdry statuettes adorning the oak mantle.

"Is that wallpaper on the walls?" Jess asked, squinting.

I stepped back, running a hand over the covering. "Yep. Flocked blue roses."

"Yikes." She placed her palms against the sides of her face. "I'm in a time warp."

"I pictured a hunting cabin having deer heads and taxidermied fish bodies on the wall," I admitted. "Lamps made of antlers. Buffalo hide rugs. Faux leather furniture."

"From staying in my share of camps," Jake said, "I can say this is no hunting cabin. No hunter would be caught dead decorating the place in this manner. No offense to departed Mike."

Instead of animal heads, gaudy sconces dripping with crystals glinted at me. I shook my head, trying to clear my disbelief. "What was he thinking?"

"What *is* this place?" Jess asked in an incredulous voice.

"A nightmare," Jake replied. "Why would someone ruin such a great house?"

"I wonder if he thought a hideous decorating scheme would deter would-be pillagers when the cabin was vacant." It was the first, and only, idea that I could come up with. I was too baffled to think.

Jake guffawed. "More than likely, someone who broke in would think this place belonged to some old couple lost in time who didn't own modern electronics—computers, widescreen televisions, and cellphones—all burglars' favorites to steal. If robbers didn't realize the value of the antiques, they'd think this was a bunch of worthless junk. They wouldn't waste time looking for valuables."

He disappeared into the kitchen area. We marched after him, his little soldiers. The kitchen presented a stark contrast to the living room. It was modern with white cabinets, gray granite countertops, an island in the middle of the floor, and a log table with bench seating. The sleek appliances were current models and stainless steel, including a microwave and lantern-style lighting.

I stopped short. "What in the world?"

"Exactly." Jake opened the refrigerator and poked in his head. "Hey, look at this."

We crowded in for a closer look at the shelves, filled with bottled water, soda, beer, wine, and two bottles of coffee creamer.

"Huh," Jess and I said in unison.

Jake juggled three waters in his arms. "Here."

Jess pushed away the one he offered her. "Maybe it's poisoned."

Jake laughed, twisting off one of the tops. "If I fall over dead, enjoy the insurance, baby."

He only had time to gulp a mouthful before Jess whacked his stomach. "Jake."

His mouth flew open, spewing water like a spouting whale. He coughed violently.

Jess jumped back with a screech. "You're drenching me."

Catching his breath, Jake croaked, "Well, who hit me while I was drinking?" He guzzled down half the bottle.

To take the focus off their argument, I opened the freezer. Plastic containers and bulging freezer bags filled the space. "That's a lot of food."

"Wild animals he killed," Jess surmised, mopping her face with a paper towel.

"Yum." Jake wore an amused look on his face. It gained him another arm swat from Jess.

I opened a cabinet beside the refrigerator. The shelves there were stocked with canned goods and canisters. "This place has more food than my house."

"What do you need food staples for? You never cook," Jess said.

I couldn't argue with her on that one.

"Old Mike wasn't going to starve," Jake said. "He could've hidden out here for months with this stash."

"Why so many supplies for a camp when he shared his main residence with Samantha?" I wondered.

Jake put an arm around Jess's waist. "Unlike me, some men meet with their buddies for weeks of hunting and fishing. He could've been planning for a hunting party."

"Mike enjoyed camping and hiking. Except, he used a two-man tent." I glanced around. "Why wouldn't he furnish this place like a rugged country cabin rather than a boudoir?"

"Because he was a nutcase," Jess reasoned.

"Do you think the toilet works?" I asked, hopeful.

Jake turned on the kitchen faucet, and water flowed freely. "I'd imagine."

Spotting a hallway, I followed it to the bathroom. There, I found a testament to a nineteen-fifties throwback as far as furnishings. Pink and lavender wall tiles greeted me. A thin horizontal black tile band of color ran around the room halfway between the floor and ceiling. The bold geometric white and black tiles on the floor looked out of place. I crossed the room to the lavender toilet and pushed on the handle to flush it. To my relief, it functioned. I washed my hands in the matching pedestal sink with a heart-shaped cake of rose soap from a cupid soap dish, then dried them on a linen hand towel trimmed in pink tatting. I peeked behind the shower curtain, which was cloaked in pastel swirls, to see the color of the tub. More lavender. The design and furnishings had a woman's touch.

I returned to the living area, calling out, "Toilet works."

"Next," Jess shouted, then scrambled down the hall. I laughed when I heard her shriek. Jake's head jerked toward the sound.

"Garish," I explained.

"You could've warned me," Jess groused upon her return. "The wall tile almost blinded me."

I feigned innocence. "And spoil the surprise?"

Jake crossed the room to the stone hearth. "I'll start a fire to take off the chill."

He opened the fireplace screen. "Found the source of our smell." He held the red tail of a dead squirrel.

Jess and I scrunched our faces. "Eww."

Jake held the critter's tail between his finger and thumb all the way to the front door. When he returned, he went about plucking kindling from the log basket and piling it in the grate. He lifted his chin toward the dining room. "Why don't you open those doors, Suzie, to circulate the air and clear out the stuffiness?"

I ran my hand over the cherry wood table as I passed by, admiring the design on the four upholstered chairs nestled around it. Dust clung to my fingertips. I swiped it on my jeans before sliding open the patio doors. The screened redwood deck provided an impressive view of the woods. A wrought iron pub-style table with two stools sat to the right of the door, an old-fashioned wooden rocker to the left.

Besides the natural beauty of the trees, a small pond and white gazebo a short distance from the deck created a tranquil scene. The remnants of dead flowers and ornamental grasses surrounding the gazebo suggested spring and summer would bring a colorful display to life. Drawing several cleansing breaths, I filled my lungs with the fresh air. A squirrel shot across the yard, startling me. My hand struck my chest, and I gasped. The vermin raced up a nearby tree and across an outstretched limb. He sat staring at me with beady eyes, chittering at my intrusion. I wondered if he'd found the dead squirrel Jake disposed of somewhere outside.

Stepping back through the doorway, I noticed Jess holding an odd vase in one hand with careless abandon. She brandished it toward me. "Have you ever seen anything this ugly?"

The spherical moss-green vase was about ten inches high and covered in brownish-black fireflies with fluorescent yellow spots that poorly imitated their light. It didn't impress me, but I appreciated history more than Jess. "Careful. You could be juggling an antique."

She wrinkled her nose. "True. It does remind me of somebody's old junk."

I pulled my cellphone from my back pocket and snapped pictures from several angles. "Turn it over to see if there is an inscription on the bottom." I photographed the signature and date stamped in gold.

From my purse, I retrieved the list of valuables the attorney had given me. "We'll check this and other items around here to determine if they're worth anything." Running a finger down the column of numbers, I found relevant values. "Uh, Jess? You're holding a porcelain vase worth eight hundred and fifty-five dollars."

She nearly dropped the vintage china. We gasped in unison as she regained control. Using two hands and a delicate touch, Jess set the vase on the table beside the couch. She backed away, her eyes still wide. "How could this eyesore be priced that high?"

"As they say, beauty is in the eye of the beholder."

She huffed and took the paper from me. Perusing it, she shook her head. "These values are outrageous." She gestured around the room. "What if some of these whatchamacallits aren't on the list?"

"According to the attorney, this inventory might be outdated. He suggested keeping everything and contacting an appraiser for verification and value. Let's catalog whatever we think would sell at an estate auction or to an antique collector."

Jess made a face. "I hear there's a buyers' market for gaudy fringed sofas."

I'd be lucky to give that piece of insanity away. "Anything not sold goes to charity. Leaving these ornate furnishings will turn off potential buyers interested in a mountain cabin."

"Oh, they definitely will."

Jake rose from his crouched position in front of the now blazing fire, came up behind Jess, and peered over her shoulder at the list. "Anything you touch is a potential small fortune." He squeezed her shoulders. "Handle with care, my uncultured little darling."

"Ha, ha." She stuck her tongue out at him.

I gestured around the room. "You and Jess take whatever you want. I'm not keeping anything."

"What would we do with all your junk?" Jess asked.

"Handle it with care?" I joked.

We burst out laughing. Jake remained unimpressed with our wit.

I handed each of them small spiral notebooks and pens I'd brought from home. "Jot down furnishings and descriptions not covered on the list. While you're at it, please keep an eye out for anything that will give us a clue as to why Mike deeded me this property, especially something illegal he did that could entail entrapment."

Jake slid the pen behind his ear. "Let's split up to cover

more ground. Otherwise, it will take us hours longer to go through everything. I'll start in one of the sheds."

"Of course, you will. Don't bring any tools home." Jess picked up her notebook and pen. "I'll take this room. Why don't you explore the bedroom, Suzie? Mike and Samantha may have left some intimate items in there."

I groaned. "Why do you have to be gross?"

She laughed. I frowned. Turning to leave, I stopped when Jess called, "Hey, look at this." She lifted a silver photo frame to eye level, turning it toward Jake and me.

"That's not Samantha," I blurted, taking in the flaming red hair and green eyes ringed in hunter-green shadow and a heavy half-inch of black liner.

"No, it's not." Jess rotated the five-by-seven photo toward herself. "Mike Ole Boy was still engaging in hanky panky. Wonder who she is?"

Jake snickered. "Some made-up bar bimbo, by the looks of it."

I agreed. Her makeup was overdone, hardening her features. The big hair wasn't flattering to her delicate cheekbones, either. She appeared to be in her twenties.

"Do you suppose this was their love nest?" Jess asked.

Jake cut a wide swath through the air with his arm. "A possible explanation for the bizarre decorating scheme. Also, the cabin is far enough from Samantha's prying eyes and isolated enough to hide a mistress."

I didn't believe an adequate explanation existed for the décor and color schemes of the great room and the bathroom, both of which clashed with the modern kitchen.

Jess studied the photo, twisting her hair. "Her teased mop with the little flip on the end is something they wore in the sixties. Maybe her tastes are stuck in that decade. She could pass for an antique herself if she weren't so young."

Jess laid the frame facedown on the end table. "Tell me if you find her clothes and personal items in the bedroom drawers."

"How will I decide if clothing is hers or Samantha's?" I snapped my fingers. "Come to think of it, she might be Samantha's relative or friend."

Jake poked a finger at his chest. "My opinion? The two-timer struck again, and we found his clandestine lair and girlfriend."

"What if she is, and Mike purchased this place for the two of them to rendezvous?" I asked. "What if she thinks Mike is still alive because no one informed her of his death? She could have a house key or the combination to the garage door if she's been living here. What if she comes to claim some of this stuff? Not that I want to be selfish, but Mike didn't give her the cabin for a reason."

"It's possible someone else has access." Jake stroked his chin. "We'd better buy new locks for the doors when we go into town for lunch. I'll change the garage door and security codes, too."

We split up to begin our tasks. I wandered into the master bedroom, off in a wing of its own. More of a suite than a room, the enormous space was tastefully furnished with modern furniture and accessories. A king-size sleigh bed covered in a white quilted bedspread with tiny embroidered trees sprawled near the window. An upholstered storage bench shaped like a half-moon resided at the foot of the bed. A stone fireplace matching the one in the great room, but smaller, took up one wall, its mantel covered in porcelain figurines of various sizes.

I shook off my astonishment. The cabin decorating scheme was such a contrast from room to room. I wandered over to the reading nook, furnished with two cushioned rockers and a bookcase. The setup had to be the girlfriend's idea. Mike didn't read for pleasure. A patio door led onto the deck and evergreen-covered view. I opened the door a few inches to let in crisp pine-scented air, and a serene view appeared before me.

On the dresser, an eight-by-ten silver frame displayed a photo of Mike and the woman whose picture Jess had found. I picked it up. Mike and the mystery woman were on his boat, taken on a sunny day. Their passionate kiss and arms wrapped around each other confirmed they were intimate, punching a hole in the theory she was a relative or Samantha's friend.

Who was she, and why didn't Mike bequeath her the cabin since it was apparent the place held memories for them?

I was wickedly gratified to think boyfriend-stealing Samantha was secretly betrayed by someone who'd employed the same tactics she did. It reinforced the wisdom of my decision to leave Mike before our relationship progressed toward marriage. I snapped a picture with my cellphone, intending to learn the identity of the unknown woman.

I began searching the room. The first dresser drawer yielded an explosion of men's underwear, socks, and T-shirts. I tossed them on the bed. More T-shirts and two pairs of jeans were in the second. I removed the drawer and turned it upside down on the bed to empty the remaining contents.

A woman's neatly folded undergarments and tank tops occupied the third drawer. I assumed the lacy bras and matching panties belonged to the woman in the photo, although they could be Samantha's.

With apprehension, I opened the nightstand drawer,

hoping I wouldn't find more evidence of an affair. It held a handgun comparable to the one I owned, a few insignificant personal items, and a dog-eared paperback romance. I removed the gun, checking to see if it was loaded. No ammunition. I placed it atop the stand. Everything else, I dumped on the bed.

His and hers walk-in closets organized a handful of flannel shirts and feminine tops. A pair of worn men's work boots sagged on the floor beside a pair of hiking boots. Opposite them, I found a woman's tennis shoes and boots. The tag on the ladies' wear said size large. I smiled in satisfaction because I wore a medium. It was petty, yes, but it's the little things.

Two clear plastic boxes sitting on a shelf in Mike's closet drew my attention. I pulled them down and placed them on the dresser. One box held a lot of papers and photos. The other contained envelopes, cash, and coins that jingled when I set it down. I would examine the contents more closely later.

I stripped everything from the drawers and closets, heaping the items on the bed to pack in some of the many boxes Jake brought. If the girlfriend and Mike's brother didn't claim the things during the next two weeks, I'd donate them all to a charity.

Using one of several keys the lawyer had given me, I opened the gun safe in the corner. Two rifles, another handgun, and a compound bow were stored inside. Arrows and boxes of various ammunition rested on the bottom shelf of the cabinet. Mike was more particular about the care of his firearms than his underwear. I added the handgun from the nightstand and relocked the case.

The spa-style bathroom was another surprise with its soft lighting and row of half-burned candles on the vanity.

River rock flooring, double shower, whirlpool tub, and bucket-style towel warmer created a relaxing spa atmosphere that taunted my aching back. Where did this creature-comfort version of Mike come from?

The vanity held a plethora of personal items for both a man and a woman that required boxing for disposal. I switched off the light and went back to the bedroom.

Jess walked in, carrying empty cartons. Her eyes perused the room. "Is that another photograph?" she asked, pointing to the heap on the bed. She didn't miss a thing.

"Of the happy couple? Yes."

She extricated the picture. "Ha. He was sneaking around on Samantha. Serves her right. The man-stealing witch got what she deserved."

"*If* she discovered he was having an affair. This place is far from where Samantha lived with Mike and well concealed in the woods. She may have been oblivious to his cheating." I gestured toward the doorway. "Find anything interesting out there?"

"Lots. I checked quite a few things off your list." Jess clutched a statue lying in the middle of the bed. "This is an antique. I remember seeing the illustration and description."

"We'll put it with the others."

Peeking in the bathroom, Jess let out an expletive. "This is living right. Jake needs to build me a haven. Is that a vial of lavender oil?" She removed the cap and inhaled deeply. "Heavenly. I would love this kind of pampering." She set the bottle down. "Who would have thought Mike would be the type to indulge in such pleasures?" Returning to the bedroom, Jess flung open the closet doors. "This is unfair. Jake and I share a space a fourth this size." She turned back to the mess on the bed. "What are you going to do with all this garbage?" She pawed through the heap.

"Pack it for a few days. If no one claims it, donate."

She picked up a bra with two fingers. "I say, burn the lot."

"I might do that, too. For now, I'll discard the health and beauty items but pack the clothing."

"Why not just toss everything now?"

"What if his girlfriend wants her belongings? Maybe his brother will want some of Mike's things."

"Too bad. They're yours now to do with whatever you want." Her voice held no empathy.

"I'd rather store them for a few weeks than face either's wrath for disposing of their personal things without notice."

Jess threw her hands up in the air. "As usual, you're too nice." She grabbed an empty carton and placed it on the bed. "Go deal with the bathroom vanity. I'll pack this stuff up."

I guessed there would be overly dramatic balling and stuffing of clothing, but at this point I didn't care about wrinkles. Ten minutes later, I reappeared, carrying a box filled with the trash from the bathroom vanity. Jess had placed two boxes of clothing on the closet floor.

"Do you need help with that?" Jess nodded toward the box in my arms.

"It's not heavy. I'll put it in my trash at home."

She followed me out of the room. "Are you packing the antiques?"

"I'm undecided about taking the valuables, or leaving them and contacting an auctioneer to conduct an estate sale here."

Jake appeared at the front doorway at that moment, having overheard our conversation. "You should take the smaller antiques home, the vases and statues. You'll make out better using an antique dealer in town. I don't suspect you'll draw the antiquing type of crowd up here. Guys look for cheap hunting camp furniture and guns."

"Speaking of guns, a cabinet in the bedroom has several," I said. "Check out the rifles and handguns. If you want any of them, we can do the transfer paperwork. I don't hunt, and I have no need for the rifles or the bow."

"I'll look. We should remove items of value that are easy to steal today, though. We can come clean out the rest another day."

Jess said, "I've had enough for now. I think we found most of the valuables on your list from the attorney. Let's head into town for lunch." She glanced around at all the work still left to be done. "We can come back afterward and load the truck."

Jake put out the fire, and we drove into town. We ate lunch at a worn-out diner with a faded, blue-striped awning. The outside wasn't much to look at, but the inside was clean and the food was tasty. We added a take-out order of fresh baked pie slices and drinks before we left.

At the local hardware store, I bought a can of air freshener and a scented candle to mask the musty smell while we worked. Jake selected a sturdy lock set and a box of contractor-sized trash bags. Unfortunately, it would take more than synthetic scents and garbage removal to make sense of Mike's hidden cabin with its hidden secrets.

Chapter Five

Back at the cabin, Jess wrapped the antiques in old newspapers and carefully placed them in boxes while Jake switched out the door locks. I returned to the bedroom to rummage through the contents of the plastic boxes I'd found on the closet shelf.

After emptying the first container on the bed, I piled the coins and bills, then stacked the papers. I rifled through smaller items—an odd key, a wooden turkey call, club patches. The documents were land surveys, purchase receipts, letters, and random stuff. I returned the money and important paperwork to the container and threw the rest in a trash bag.

When I dumped the second box, several photos turned face up amid the paperwork. Horrified, I couldn't take my eyes off the pictures—of me. Dozens of them. Some recent, all of them random candid shots. I felt a pang in my chest as a shudder wracked my body.

My breath returned in rapid gasps. Mike had spied on me. For how long? How was I too oblivious to notice?

I fanned through the pile, my hands quivering. Several

photos captured me walking with Hunter on my road, taken on different days, evidenced by the variety of clothing I wore. They spanned seasons and years. Hunter as a puppy, later a full-grown dog.

My hands continued to tremble as I shuffled through snapshots of me coming out of the supermarket. Crawling in and out of my car at various places. At church. On Jess's porch. Calling Hunter from my back door.

The hairs on my neck rose, and my heart hammered wildly. How often had he stalked me without my knowledge? Why would he? Was he planning his revenge? Could the deal with the cabin be part of a twisted plan? Mike pleaded with me to take him back for months before turning bitter and hateful toward me. Maybe he'd finally found a way to wreak revenge by saddling me with a huge debt or purchasing the cabin with stolen money.

I sifted through a few pictures of the woman Mike had dated. Most were of her alone. Was his girlfriend aware Mike photographed me? Would she have been curious and snooped through his things when she stayed at the cabin? If so, she'd have found the clear plastic bin, which didn't have a lock. Did Mike tell his mistress he was leaving his property to me even though they dated? Did she try to stop the attorney from notifying me of the property?

I called Jess into the bedroom, panic riddling my voice.

She rushed to my side. "You're pale as a ghost and shaking. What's wrong?" Glancing at the photos, she instantly drew the correct conclusion. "He's been tailing you?" She stared at the images of me and Hunter on my deserted road, then picked up a photograph of me talking with Jess on her porch. "This is my house," she shouted, her face reddening. "That louse!" She texted Jake.

In minutes, he appeared in the doorway. "What's wrong? You two spot a bear?"

Jess shoved the photograph in his face.

His mouth dropped open. "This is the two of you at our place."

"Exactly," Jess replied. "Hansen's handiwork."

He whirled around to me. "Where did you find this?"

I pointed to the closet. "Top shelf."

He picked up and inspected the box lid. "Mike didn't try to hide them. The box is transparent. Lid doesn't lock." He threw it on the pile, then bent over and swiped through the collection of photos.

"What the..." The one he pulled from the pile caused his jaw to harden. "This is our backyard. The picnic we had you over for last fall."

Jess rose on her toes for a look. "He spied on us, too?"

Jake released a heavy breath. "I doubt it. Suzie is the one he wanted. He followed her to our place." Jake tossed the print in the box and browsed through the others. "Guess we now understand why Mike gave you this place."

"What do you mean?" I asked.

"A man doesn't go around taking random pictures of ex-girlfriends for no reason. He was obsessed with you."

I blanched. I didn't want to believe it. The idea sickened me.

Jake scooped up everything and chucked the whole lot into the box. "We'll take these to the police."

"What good will it do now?" I asked. "He's gone. He didn't blackmail me and can no longer be prosecuted for stalking."

"True, but hang on to these in case someone else uses copies for blackmail or something. I'll keep them in my garage for a few weeks. After that, we'll torch them in a backyard barbeque."

Barbequed photos sounded pretty good to me.

Jake stacked the boxes on top of each other. "I'm going back to the shed. I'll put these in my truck on the way. Anything else you need me to take?"

"I'm not finished packing up the antiques," Jess said.

"Text me when you are."

Jess and I returned to the great room to finish wrapping valuables. I snapped a newspaper open and picked up a statue to wrap. "Mike violated my privacy, Jess. If he weren't dead, I'd wring his neck."

"Count on me to stand beside you cheering. What an insane creep. Did you see Jake's face when he realized Mike's photo collection included the intrusion into our backyard?" She shook her head. "I thought he would explode."

"Knowing Mike was stalking me is unnerving, to say the least." I crossed to the dining room to check for any small items of value. Moments later, I heard Jess's voice from the other room.

"Who are you?" she asked.

At first, I thought she was talking to one of the strange antique statues. Then, a rough voice answered, "None of your business."

My heart sputtered. Feet fixed in place, I couldn't see around the half-wall between the rooms.

"You have no right to come in here." Jess's sharp tone hung in the air.

I raced from the dining room to the living area in time to hear the man say, "I'm the owner's friend. Who are you?"

Jess stood her ground like a pit bull. "None of *your* business."

Moving beside her, I appraised the man's Paul Bunyan features and stance. He filled the doorway with his over-sized, nearly seven-foot bulk. Grungy hair stuck out from beneath his filthy cap. The unruly beard trailing down his thick neck was long overdue for a trim.

"I'm Suzie, the owner of this cabin."

The man sneered. "I don't think so. This place belongs to Mike Hansen, and you ain't his girlfriend."

"She's not, and the house isn't his anymore, either." Jess splayed her hands on her hips. "Mike is dead."

The finality of her words startled me as they sank in. *Mike is dead.* Up until now, the craziness of inheriting the cabin had consumed my thoughts, delaying the reality of his death in my mind. It wasn't that I had residual feelings for him, but we'd been close at one time.

The stranger didn't even blink at the news. He knew.

Jess yanked her cellphone from her back pocket and punched in numbers.

The man stepped toward her. "Who're you calling?" he shouted in a gruff voice.

Jess took two steps backward. With the phone to her ear and a hand remaining on her jutted hip, Jess snapped, "My husband. He's out in the shed."

I had to admire petite Jess's bravado while facing the Yeti of a man.

He looked visibly relieved. "Hansen stored some of my things here. I came for them."

"He didn't mention anything to me." Of course, I was bluffing since we hadn't spoken in years.

The man smirked. "Look, lady. I don't care which of Mike's women you are, but I intend to claim what's right-fully mine."

Which of his women? Interesting. "What did you leave here?" I asked.

His jaw hardened. He rested a beefy fist on his hip. "Personal things."

He wasn't backing down and neither was I. "Such as?"

Tucking his thumbs into his belt, he threw back his shoulders and expanded his already massive chest. "I ain't here for no interrogation. Let me find my stuff, and I'll be outta here."

I stood straighter and met his glare. "What are you looking for? I'll tell you if we've found it."

He lunged forward, shoving Jess aside with his thick forearm. "Outta my way."

I fumbled my phone from my pocket but dropped it on the floor. It landed with a clunk, and the stranger kicked it across the room.

Why didn't I pocket the handgun from the bedroom? How could I chase the man out of the cabin? I looked around for something to use as a weapon. I wanted him gone.

My wish was granted. Sort of.

The click of Jake's gun signaled he'd loaded a bullet in the chamber. "Stop right there," he commanded.

Having recognized the sound of an armed weapon, the intruder stopped in his tracks. He whirled to face Jake, a snarl on his lips.

Jake held his ground. "This is private property. The lady asked what were you doing here."

"Claiming what's owed to me." The man's voice was a low growl.

"Which is?"

"None of your business."

"Then, your time is up." Jake stepped aside, wagging

the gun toward the door. "Everything on this property belongs to Ms. Tuft."

The stranger turned sideways, and Jake pushed by him to stand with the women. "To claim anything, you'll have to wait until she has a chance to go through this place." He shrugged. "Unless you got some kind of claim ticket for those goods."

"Listen, buddy..." The man shook his index finger in Jake's face.

Jake leveled the gun at the guy's midsection. "No, you listen, *buddy*. You're trespassing on private property and threatening the rightful owner. Leave, or we'll call the police."

The man sidled past Jake, a scowl on his face. If looks killed, the man wouldn't need a weapon. "This ain't finished," he snarled, then disappeared out the door.

Jake followed him, and Jess and I stayed behind Jake. The stranger climbed into his truck and drove away, gravel flying as the vehicle fishtailed.

Jake disarmed his gun. "Who was that?"

"No idea." My voice trembled. The man was one scary bully.

"He barged in, demanding to recover belongings Mike stored here for him," Jess explained. She sounded frightened now that the adrenaline was starting to wear off.

Jake wrapped an arm around her. "You're shaking worse than oak leaves in a windstorm."

"He claimed Mike had something of his but wouldn't say what," I told him.

Jake stared down the deserted road. "We haven't seen the last of that guy."

I silently agreed and hoped to never face him alone. Without Jake's gun, Paul Bunyan could have taken out all three of us. "Why was he secretive about what he wanted? Do you suppose Mike owed the guy money? Maybe from some illegal dealings?"

"No sense in speculating about what he was after." Jake tucked the gun into his belt and withdrew his cellphone. "I'll notify the local police."

"We didn't catch his name," I reminded him.

"I wrote down his license number in the dirt with a stick before coming into the house to confront him." He shrugged. "Left the pen and paper you gave me in the shed. I had to improvise when the truck pulled up the drive."

Jess patted his cheek. "Aren't you the smart one?"

Jake retrieved the notebook I'd given him earlier and copied the license plate number onto a page. "The sheds are loaded with new tools of all kinds. I'll lock them for now and come inside to help you two. Good thing we're taking the antiques with us."

Jess choked out a laugh. "Yeah. If he wants the sofa, he can have it."

Jess and I headed inside the house to continue wrapping antiques. Jake reappeared a few minutes later and made a beeline for the kitchen. I heard cabinet doors creaking open and banging closed.

"Hey, ladies. Come here and look at this."

Jess and I stopped what we were doing and strode to the kitchen.

"I found this taped to the back of the refrigerator." He held what appeared to be a roughly drawn map.

"Why did you look behind the refrigerator?" I asked.

He grinned. "My detective skills come from binge-watching crime shows. I searched in the usual places for valuables—the freezer, the junk drawer. I checked for fake cans in the pantry." He tapped his forehead. "Then, I remembered a police show where they pulled out the fridge and found drugs. I guess some criminals tape things to the back of the stove, refrigerator, and cabinets."

He walked over to the table and smoothed out the paper. "I think this is a map of the cabin and surrounding property, but I can't figure out why Mike hid it."

Jess and I leaned over the table. Jake traced a line running through the middle of the page. "See? Here's the road we drove in on, off the main highway." He repositioned his finger to the left. "This large square represents the house, and the smaller one is the garage. Here's what appears to be the pond, beyond the deck." He shifted his hand a couple of inches. "Here's a clearing where someone drew a row of eight pine trees. They're significant if someone sketched the exact number of pines. This large blob could be another body of water because of the odd borders, maybe a lake. Then, we have a row of six pine trees in this area."

"What's the dot?" I asked, touching my index finger to the map.

He drew the paper closer to his eyes. "I can't tell, but it can't be a smudge. See these other ones? They're tiny, but noticeable." He traced a path to five additional dots.

"Yes."

Jake tapped his chin. "Maybe we'll find a marker by the trees."

"A marker for what?" Jess asked. "Buried treasure?" She chortled.

He folded the diagram and shoved the paper in his back pocket. "That's what we need to find out. The map could lead to something of value." He walked to the patio doors. Jess and I fell in line behind him.

I brought my hand to my forehead, shielding my eyes

from the sun. Scanning the area, I spotted the row of eight pines in the distance and pointed. "There."

Both heads turned in the direction I indicated. "The trees from the map," Jake said, squinting. "Wish I had binoculars. Let's go have a closer look."

"Are you kidding? Suzie and I are not dressed for hiking." Jess lifted a foot. "We aren't wearing boots."

Jake glanced down at our canvas shoes. "This is early in the season. The weeds haven't had time to grow high. You should be okay."

Jess stuck out her bottom lip. "Fine for you to say. You're wearing work boots."

"You don't have to come."

Curiosity nagged at me. I stepped forward. "I'm coming."

Jess let out a sound between a groan and a huff. "You're not leaving me behind with Mike's maniac friend in the area."

The three of us set out toward the row of pines. Making our way to our intended destination was difficult with the underbrush and piles of dead leaves. Wearing sneakers instead of hiking boots hindered our progress, but it didn't deter us.

A gnarled tree root tripped me, yanking off my tennis shoe. "Argh." I caught myself on a limb to keep from falling, but my sock-covered foot landed in damp leaves. *Yuck.*

Jake retrieved the shoe, slapping it against his leg to shake off the dirt.

I hated to slip my wet sock into it, but I had no choice. After the fiasco, I took more care where I stepped. So focused on the ground before me, I would have knocked myself senseless with a low-lying branch if not for Jake's astuteness.

"Watch out." He grabbed my arm, stopping me. My head was mere inches from the tree.

"Eww!" Jess yelped from behind us.

While Jake saved me, Jess stepped into a soft, smelly pile of animal excrement. She flung off her shoe and wailed, "Scrub that off!"

Jake sighed audibly, pulling up a clump of moss to use as a makeshift cleaning rag. "Will you two pay attention to where you're walking?" He made a face. "This is disgusting." After wiping the sneaker as best he could, Jake led us onward.

We reached the line of trees without further mishap and hiked to the place marked on the map. Jake walked all around, examining the ground. He checked the area surrounding the other trees. "Nothing is on the tree trunks or ground."

"Maybe something is buried here," I suggested, stomping on the weeds.

"Possible." He studied the land. "It doesn't seem disturbed, but we've got nothing else to go on. We'll come back with shovels." He raised an arm. "Let's go on to the lake."

The lake turned out to be a pond the size of a football field. A row of six pines at one end resembled a goalpost.

Jake unfolded the map and spread it out to display the section where we stood. "There's a dot by the row of pines." He tipped his head, indicating the direction. "Onward."

We trampled the weeds at the edge of the water near the trees. "Look at the fish." Jess pointed at two glistening fish swimming inches below the surface.

Jake whistled. "They'd make a tasty dinner."

Jess frowned.

We searched around the pines for anything that might

account for the dot on the map, coming up empty-handed once more.

Jake scratched his head. "Unless something is buried in the marked spots, the six map dots are useless to us."

"The marks are there for a reason," I said. "Did you see a shovel in the shed?"

He held up a couple of fingers. "Two shovels, as a matter of fact."

We retraced our steps. Jess and I were careful to avoid a repeat of our earlier mishaps. When we arrived at the cabin, Jess kicked her shoes off on the porch. "These revolting things need to be scrubbed. I'd throw them away, but I didn't bring another pair with me."

"How about the ones we found in the closet?" I asked.

"No thanks."

Jake pulled the shed key out of his jeans pocket. "I'll get the shovels."

Jess's shoulders slumped. "Can't we leave and have a nice dinner on the way home? Forget about the dots?"

Jake jiggled the keys. "I'm too curious to leave now, but I promise we'll stop at a nice restaurant later."

I, too, was curious.

Jess blew out a breath. "Let me scrub my shoes with soap and water first."

Jake held up a hand. "I don't want to hear whining the entire time. Bring a bottle of water and a book to read while we're digging."

"Maybe I'll take a snack, too," she added, stomping toward the porch.

"Don't eat my pie," Jake called over his shoulder before we turned to make our way to the shed.

Hooks on the wall held shovels, axes, rakes, and other tools. A tool chest about four feet in height sat against another wall beside a bag of grass seed. A shelf held smaller hand tools, flowerpots, and other gardening items.

We gathered what we needed for digging, and the three of us trekked back to the line of trees. We stopped at the first dot on the map. After careful study, Jake laid it aside and picked up a shovel. "Try this area." He motioned his hand in a wide circle. "Let's see what we can dig up." He chuckled at his own joke. "No pun intended."

Yes, it was. Jess and I groaned.

Jake and I started working at opposite ends of the spot. I brushed aside the leaves with the tip of my shovel. Breaking ground was difficult, the earth still hard from the winter. Although Jake made progress, I barely scraped the surface.

Jess spread out a beach towel she'd found at the cabin and sat. "I'll switch with you when you get tired, Suzie."

No way could my diminutive friend excavate the concrete dirt when I had to jump on the shovel to make a dent. "Okay."

Although the weather was cool near the trees, sweat soon moistened my forehead and bangs. Still, I shoveled. Digging down about two feet, my shovel hit something, making a tinny sound. "Here," I called, dropping the shovel. My nerves snapped with excitement at the thought of a treasure.

Jake crouched down on his knees, scooping dirt with a smaller shovel. "It's about a foot across."

Jess squeezed in between us. "Let me see."

Standing, Jake grabbed his shovel and poked around the edges. "I'll dig a wider hole."

What resembled the lid of a large popcorn canister appeared. Jake worked the item loose, unearthing a tin with faded pictures of puppies.

"A rusty old can." Disappointment grabbed me as my hopes of finding buried treasure waned.

Jake wrenched off the rusted, dented lid. He whistled, pulling out a banded clump of hundred dollar bills. Then, another. "There're thousands here."

The more green he pulled from the can, the higher my enthusiasm skyrocketed.

Jess did a happy dance, clapping. "The lout came through for you."

In all, Jake stacked twenty bundles of banded hundreds in my arms. Twenty thousand dollars. My smile faded. What if Mike stole the money? My arms became rubbery. "What am I supposed to do with this?"

"The cash is on your land. So, it's yours, according to the will."

Jess stopped dancing and pointed. "I'm going over there behind that tree to—you know."

I dumped the cash into the can and pushed down the lid. "What if the money came from a bank robbery?"

"Didn't the attorney notify you that any money on the property is yours?" Jake asked.

"I doubt he knew Mike hid thousands in stolen cash."

"You have no proof it's stolen."

"A suspicious buried fortune? I understand Mike well enough to believe he could pull off a heist." I swatted at a flying insect.

"Yeah. It doesn't take much to add two and two and come up with four with that character," Jake agreed.

He glanced at the tin of cash, then at me. Something flashed in his eyes. "You realize what this means, don't you? Those other dots may represent cans of hidden money, too."

My hand went to my throat. "Oh."

Jess returned and grabbed my free hand. "Treasure hunting is so exciting."

"Depends on the origin of the money," I said.

"Let's go find out if I'm right about the other locations before we start celebrating." Jake picked up the tin and pounded the lid on tight. "Can you carry this, Suzie?"

I stood rooted to the ground, dumbfounded. Could I somehow get into trouble with the law if Mike stole the money? Would they consider me a suspect?

"Suzie."

I recovered my senses and accepted the tin.

Jake grabbed the shovels and swung them up onto his shoulder. "Are we ready, ladies?"

"Wouldn't miss this kind of excitement for the world," Jess answered. Finding money had energized her.

We hiked to the pond, where we dug up a smaller can. I gasped at the twenty thousand dollars inside. "This is insane."

"Yeah. At this rate, you'll be insanely rich," Jess exclaimed, beaming.

I stared at the money, clutched in my fists. "I have to turn this money over to the police."

Jake leaned on his shovel handle. "No, you don't."

"Finders keepers, as they say," Jess chimed in.

"If I discover the money is stolen, I'll have to give it back."

Jake lifted his hands. "Give it back? To who?"

"Whom."

"What?"

"Give it back to whom, not who," I explained to him.

Jake huffed, apparently not pleased with the impromptu grammar lesson. Jess thought the exchange was hilarious.

"Okay, you can't spend the money in case the bills are from a bank holdup and are marked. You do research for a living," Jake reasoned. "Find out if there are any unsolved bank robberies your ex could've pulled off. In the meantime, put the money in a safety deposit box at your own bank."

"Maybe." I spread my arms wide, the same questions gnawing at me. "Why leave this place to me? Why not Samantha, or the woman in the photo?"

"For all you know, he planned to leave Samantha and hid the money so she didn't have access to it. Or, maybe he wanted to make up for his past treatment of you, as the lawyer said."

My brain wrestled with the idea of Mike leaving me thousands of dollars as reparation for being a lousy ex. It was out of character for him. "How could he be certain I would find the map?"

Jake lifted a shoulder. "He couldn't. He chanced it for some reason."

I stared at the hole, thinking about the possibility of no one ever finding the hidden cash. "The money could have stayed buried forever."

"Unless someone knew the cans were hidden." From his back pocket, Jake withdrew and opened the map again.

I clicked my fingers. "The guy who threatened us." A chill raced down my back.

"Could be him," Jake agreed, turning toward the way we came. He shaded his eyes. "We need to be careful of someone following us."

Goosebumps rose along my arms as I scanned the area, convinced Mike had outwitted a partner by burying the money they stole.

Jess whispered, "We should go home."

Dread seeped into my bones. "Maybe that's why

someone murdered Ryder. To keep me from finding this place until whoever hid the money could recover it."

Jake tapped the lid of the can in my arms. "Don't let your imagination run wild."

"But it does make sense," Jess said, eyes wide.

Jake spun her around. "This way. Follow me."

We found the rest of Mike's stash in four more smaller cans. One hundred and twenty thousand dollars in total. How did Mike legally obtain that much cash? If he did, why bury the money on his property? I didn't see how he could have counted on someone finding the fortune at all.

When we dug at the last dot marked on the map and unearthed another can, Jake forced the lid off and fanned himself with a bundle of bills. "This back-breaking work was worth the trouble."

He handed me the can and reached for my shovel. "I'll carry that. You and Jess carry the money."

"I'll take the three small ones." Jess juggled the cans in her arms. She left me with the popcorn tin and two others.

My nerves were on edge as we hiked back to the cabin. "What am I going to do with all this?"

"As I said, open a safety deposit box and store the money until you figure out a plan."

Gratitude for my friends spilled over. "You and Jess are so helpful. If I had a free hand, I'd hug you both."

He thumped a shovel against the cans I held. "You're welcome."

Jess clinked her cans against mine. "We love you."

We arrived at the cabin, dirty and sweaty. Jess swiped her brow. "Guess this means a nice restaurant is out. I'm filthy."

"You can shower here," Jake suggested.

She frowned. "And put on these grimy clothes?"

With a glint in his eye, Jake said, "Maybe the mystery lady has something sexy you can wear."

I laughed at Jess's curled lip. Jake earned himself an arm punch.

Jess and I set our loot on the deck steps. Breaking into a grin, she popped the lid on one of the containers and grabbed a fistful of cash. She waved it at me. "This isn't enough for the heartache Mike caused you, but it's a start. Once you sell this property, you should have a nice travel fund."

Would I? Or would I be on my way to a jail cell? "Unless Mike was a thief and left me the house and money hoping I would be held criminally responsible if I kept everything."

"Doubtful."

"Why? He was furious when I wouldn't forgive him for the affair. He begged me not to leave him, Jess. Remember how he stalked me?"

"And he never quit from the looks of the photos you found," Jake said. "Those photos taken at our house were recent."

"You may be right about Mike doing this to incriminate you," Jess said. Holding the wad of bills between two fingers, she dropped them back into the can. "Sorry, Suzie. With your luck, he stole the loot. What are you going to do now?"

"Put the money in a safety deposit box, as your husband suggested. As for the property, it remains to be seen whether I sell it."

Jess drew back, her face scrunched in confusion. "Keep the cabin? With the attachment to Mike and his girlfriend?"

"What I mean is, if Mike bought the property with

illegal funds, I can't sell it. I'll need to do some investigating before making any decisions."

Jake sidled up to Jess. "Why don't you girls freshen up a bit? I'll condense the money into the popcorn tin and stow it in the trunk. We shouldn't let the can out of our sight. After we close up the place, maybe we can find a not-so-fancy restaurant that'll serve us."

"Yes," Jess said. "Let's go home and forget we ever stepped foot in this garishly decorated cabin."

Jake glanced at me. "Until next Saturday, when we come back to go through the other bedrooms."

His willingness to help touched me. "You two don't need to waste another day here. I appreciate what you've done today."

"If we don't drive you, you'll run up here on your own."

He was right, of course. I needed to finish searching and cleaning the place to see what I was dealing with before selling.

Jake seemed to read my thoughts. "I'm not comfortable with you being here alone. We'll drive you next week. Same time. Besides, I have the other shed and the garage to go through." He grinned like a kid at Christmas.

Chapter Six

The Bearfoot Book Club ladies called an emergency meeting Sunday afternoon to talk about the victim I'd found. We settled ourselves in Bre's spacious living room with glasses of wine. The coffee table held dessert plates of baked goodies so fresh the smells of cinnamon and vanilla still hung in the air. Bre owned the town's bakery, and she tried her new recipes on us in hopes of including them in the cookbook she was writing. We loved being her taste testers.

Her long, dark hair was drawn up in a bun, the way she wore it at the bake shop. Over a white cotton blouse, she wore a frilly pink apron with Bre's Bakery embroidered in white. I noticed a dab of chocolate on her right sleeve, possibly from the eclairs she'd baked us.

MaryLou wasted no time bringing up the body I discovered. "We hear you've had some excitement near your house." She fingered the gold chain dangling from her neck.

Before biting into a cherry tart, I corrected her. "Horror, not excitement."

Bre swallowed a bite of iced lemon cookie and licked her fingers. "We want to hear the specifics."

Georgianna raised her wine glass, tilting it toward me. "Yes. Tell us about the body you found."

It didn't surprise me that MaryLou got right to the point. She was used to running town council meetings with a no-nonsense attitude. I was taken aback by Bre's interest, though. She usually avoided unpleasant news. I imagined Georgianna's mind churned with possibilities of a new novel plot. And Jess, who I'd already told the gruesome details, eyed the goodies.

"I was on my usual walk when the rancid odor of something dead gagged me."

Bre wrinkled her nose. "Gross. We had a dead mouse in the garage once. It stunk up the entire house. We had to tear the place apart and clear out tons of stuff to find it."

MaryLou pinched her nostrils with thumb and forefinger, the nails of which were polished with red acrylic. "Nothing rivals the odor of a rotting rodent corpse." The other ladies agreed.

Bre set another plate of delicacies in front of us. "Wouldn't you think someone would miss the guy? He'd have lain there a long time if he was rotting."

Another mention of the word *rotting* triggered a sudden whiff of decayed flesh. I gagged. Would I ever be free of that awful stench?

Bre whirled around. "Are you alright?" She picked up a bottle and rushed toward my chair. "Need more wine?"

I held out my glass, watching as the pink liquid splashed into a rising pool of bubbles.

"Eat a cracker." Jess held out the cheese and cracker board. "Maybe you ate too many sweets."

Bre looked stricken.

"No, everything is delicious. Discussing the smell triggered the horrible memory of the odor rising from a gully along the road. When I peered down, a red tie and a boot sticking out of the moss and dry leaves caught my attention."

MaryLou, ever the drama queen, laid a hand on her cheek. "Did you scream? You'd hear me yelling a mile away."

A chorus of, "Me too!" arose around me.

"I yelled so loud the birds fled the trees." Sharing my reactions with these ladies didn't embarrass me. Half of them would have passed out upon finding a body.

"Who could blame you?" Georgianna spoke in a motherly way. "I nearly fainted when my grandson broke his arm. I constantly worry for the children."

MaryLou reached for a mini raspberry muffin, sprinkled with a generous coating of sugar. "Is this a new recipe, Bre? You know that raspberry is my favorite flavor." Without waiting for an answer, she turned to me. "How did you know the man was murdered?"

"I didn't. In fact, I thought he fell while hunting or hiking. I called nine-one-one. The police came shortly afterward. They called the coroner."

"Did you see the body?" MaryLou asked. "Was it gruesome?"

I waved the tart in my hand. "I didn't go down the hill to see the victim, and I wasn't near enough when they brought up his body." I finished relating the basic information, only to be hit with a barrage of questions, fired from all of my friends at once.

"Who was he?"

"How long had he been dead?"

"Where is he now?"

"How did you flush the horrid smell out of your nose?"

"Do you have nightmares?"

I raised my hand. "Ladies, please." They quieted, settling down, but with the eagerness of a group of preschoolers anticipating the narration of a scary story. "The police are waiting for autopsy results."

"My gosh." Bre paled. "If he was murdered, we have a killer running loose." She drew in a deep breath. "What if he attacks children next? Are the police searching for him?"

As usual with our group, things were getting out of hand. No doubt, the wine contributed to the growing paranoia. "The news outlets haven't confirmed the victim was murdered. The police are still investigating."

Bre leaned forward, elbow propped on her knee, full wine glass in her hand. "Did the police interrogate you?"

"They did."

"I read somewhere that the police often suspect the one who finds the body," MaryLou said. She popped a strawberry in her mouth.

Her nonchalant attitude had me working to keep my tone neutral. "Fortunately for me, I was in New York meeting with my editor at the time."

Jess asked, "Who would suspect Suzie, even if she was home?"

I appreciated Jess's confidence, but the police had a murder to solve. "They did their jobs, looking at all possibilities. The detective who first questioned me was abrupt and grumpy. His partner, though, was friendly."

Ever the ray of sunshine, MaryLou didn't let me off easy. "The one who was tough on you obviously suspected you had something to do with the killing."

Her insinuation grated on my nerves. "Imagine my pleasure to prove him wrong."

Georgianna set down her plate, topped with a crumpled napkin, on the end table beside her. "I understand one of the police at the scene was Detective Pagarelli. He's my neighbor's nephew. Such a gentleman. Handsome, too. I assume he's the *friendly* one you spoke of." She wiggled her eyebrows.

Jess was all too keen to chime in. "You should have seen the way he looked at Suzie." She placed her hands under her chin, batting her eyelashes.

The other ladies couldn't contain themselves. My face heated, and not from the wine. They were always trying to find me a suitable boyfriend. Sometimes, being the only single one in the group was a pain, but I wasn't willing to settle for just anyone. I wanted to be truly loved and to feel secure in that love. Occasional flings were not for me. I wanted the real thing.

"He called her," Jess added, beaming.

I clarified. "To come to the station to answer questions."

Bre brushed cookie crumbs from her apron onto her napkin. "Do they have a suspect?"

I shook my head. "They're telling me as little as possible."

MaryLou said, "Georgianna, you write murder mysteries. Who do you think killed the man?"

"There's not much to go on." She turned to me. "What's the vic's name, and where is he from?"

I suppressed a smile at her use of the shortened term for victim. "Christopher Ryder, an attorney from Punxsutawney. Other than that, I only heard what's reported on the news." I shot Jess a look. Earlier, I'd warned her not to reveal all the details I'd given her.

"An attorney." Bre mulled the information over while twirling the stem of her glass.

"In that case," MaryLou announced with confidence, "The murder has something to do with the property Hansen gave you."

I glanced at Jess.

She threw up her hands. "I didn't say anything!"

MaryLou scoffed. "I learned of the property from a source."

Why wasn't I surprised? MaryLou heard everything that went on in the town through her grapevine of gossipers.

"Tell us about the property," MaryLou said.

Jess happily accommodated the request. "It's a gorgeous house in the middle of the woods in Punxsutawney."

"Again with a house in the woods?" MaryLou made a *tsk, tsk* sound with her tongue. "Don't you get tired of not having neighbors, Suzie?"

"I don't, but I'm selling the place."

"You should see it," Jess gushed, her eyes big as saucers. Between the two of us, we went on to describe the living and dining areas, bathrooms, and the master bedroom.

"Sounds perfectly lovely," Georgianna said.

Too bad the cabin was a gift from Mike. I would feel uncomfortable staying there, even as a vacation home. "I'm auctioning off the antiques here in town and having an estate sale up there," I explained.

Jess raised her index finger. "We also found a picture of Mike and a mysterious woman."

MaryLou perked up. "What about Samantha? He lived with her." Tapping her wine glass, she said, "This is getting more interesting by the minute."

I could visualize her brain swelling with the possibility of new gossip. I gave Jess a look, telling her not to answer or comment. She shook her head, focusing on her wine.

"Maybe she's the killer," Georgianna suggested, her expression pensive.

"It's possible," MaryLou answered. "Someone didn't want Suzie to inherit the property. Any ideas, Suzie?"

Oh, I had my suspicions, but too many people were on my list to make an assumption. "I have a couple of people in mind."

"Who?" MaryLou asked.

I knew better. She would spread my suspicions around town in a minute. I didn't need the aggravation that kind of fallout would bring. "Not enough details to point to anyone in particular."

"What about Samantha?" she pressed. "She can't be happy that Mike gave you a gorgeous home."

No, she won't be.

Georgianna raised her right index finger. "If you never found out about the cabin, Samantha might have squatted there indefinitely. I've read of people squatting for years in abandoned houses. You wouldn't expect Mike to give you the place. All she had to do was keep the attorney from notifying you."

"Interesting, but would she kill to stop him?" I asked.

Georgianna lifted a brow.

"They could have struggled, and she accidentally killed him," Bre suggested.

Jess huffed. "Samantha is mean enough to take down an elephant in a fight."

A huge smile spread across Georgianna's face. "Look at us. Sitting around talking about a victim and suspects. Our little book club is in the middle of a hometown murder mystery."

MaryLou pursed her lips. "Except we don't have a great detective to solve the crime."

Georgianna leaned forward, commanding our attention. "Not all mystery novels feature seasoned detectives. Sometimes, an ordinary housewife solves the crime. My own manuscript has a tea shop owner as the amateur sleuth."

Jess nodded. "It's true. An average person could solve a crime. We ought to be able to put our heads together and do it."

"This is the most exciting meeting we've ever had," Georgianna decided. "And these scones are delicious, Bre."

"Thank you." Bre smiled, delighted. "But remember, ladies, this is a real-life murder, not a novel plot."

"With an actual murderer," I added. Even though these women were my closest friends, Bre's reminder drove the point home; I needed to heed Detective Pagarelli's warning not to divulge too much information ahead of the police records and press releases.

* * *

First thing Monday morning, Jake met me at the credit union with the buried treasure he'd stored in his garage for safekeeping. He handed me a navy canvas bag before pointing to a group of chairs off to the side in the lobby. "I'll wait over there." Then, as if to reassure me, he added, "This is the best solution until we figure out the source of the money."

I stepped up to a plexiglass window, where a perky young teller with a smile that nearly swallowed her face greeted me. We exchanged pleasantries, and she asked how she could help.

"I want to rent a safety deposit box, please."

"Certainly. Are you a member of our bank?" Her singsong voice was an octave too high for my liking.

I provided my identification and the additional required information for the rental agreement.

Miss Cheery folded her hands on the counter. "What size of box would you like?"

"How large of a box do you have?" I hefted the tote bag onto the ledge.

The size of it threw her into a bit of a tizzy. Her eyes widened a half inch. She was so stunned that bystanders could have thought I handed her a note saying, "Give me all your money." Her smiling ruby lips now formed a perfect O, and her eyes blinked in rapid response. In hindsight, her shocked reaction indicated I probably should have kept the bag on the floor.

Suspicion clung to her face. "Is this a bag of money? You won't accrue extra income in a safety deposit box."

"No, important documents." No sense in increasing her alarm by revealing the truth.

Her lips tightened in a thin line while she proceeded to finalize my paperwork. She didn't seem to believe me, but I didn't care. I had never experienced such a change in behavior toward me.

Miss Not-So-Cheery-Now led me to a room where rows and rows of gray metal boxes filled the wall. She explained the procedure I would use when accessing my valuables. Then, she retreated toward the outer door to provide me privacy. I stashed the cash, wondering if I'd committed a crime. For all I knew, I had.

When I finished, the teller returned to secure my box and led me out to the lobby. We wished each other a pleasant day, fake as the gesture was.

Jake crossed the room to meet me. "How'd it go?"

"Okay until I set the bag of money on the counter."

He stopped. I did, too. "You didn't tell her it held a hundred and twenty thousand, did you?"

I was glad I hadn't.

* * *

An hour later Jake, Jess, and I sat in front of Detective Pagarelli, describing the encounter with the stranger at the cabin.

"What's the man's name?" Pagarelli asked, pen poised above his notebook.

Jake and I glanced at each other. He cleared his throat. "He didn't say. We didn't ask."

The slight stiffening of Pagarelli's shoulders indicated his displeasure with the answer. "Can you describe him?"

I raised my hand like a student called upon by a school-teacher. "Paul Bunyan."

Detective Pagarelli stared at me, his expression a cross between wondering if I was joking or if I was insane.

Inwardly, I cringed. *I wish I'd kept my mouth shut and let Jake do the talking. I don't want Pagarelli to think I'm a ditzy blonde.*

Jess's head bobbed up and down. "Exactly."

Her agreement didn't change the detective's expression.

"Sort of." Jake came to our aid. "Gigantic, burly guy." He imitated a bodybuilder pose. "Easily six foot six. Caucasian."

I made a circle above my head. "Filthy brown tassel cap. Tufts of greasy black hair stuck out all around the edges." I tugged on my hair to show him what I meant.

"A black, bushy beard with gray streaks covered his ugly face." Jess rubbed her hand over her mouth and chin.

Again, Jake clarified our convoluted descriptions. "His

full beard extended to his chest." He laid his upturned palm on his midsection to demonstrate the length. "Was dressed in hunting clothes. Camo jacket over a red plaid flannel shirt. Camo pants and hiking boots."

"All he needed was an ax slung over his shoulder." I imitated the pose, which gained me another mixed expression from Detective Pagarelli. He pointed the back end of his pen toward me.

"He threatened you?"

Jess struck her chest with a thumb. "Me first. I was in the room he barged into without even knocking."

"Was the door open?"

I nodded. "To clear out the dank odor."

The detective's gaze settled on me. "Where were you when the man arrived?"

"In the adjoining dining room. I heard Jess ask his name. He snarled that it was none of her business. I entered the room as Jess told the man that Mike had died and the house belonged to me. He didn't care. Insisted he left his personal property at the cabin and wanted to collect it."

I gestured toward Jake. "When Jake said he had to wait until I went through everything, the man went crazy."

"He pushed me out of the way," Jess said with a scowl.

Pagarelli focused on Jess. "Did he hurt you, Mrs. Waters?"

She shook her head. "Scared me, though. The two of us couldn't stop a man of his size."

The detective glanced from Jess to me. "Did he mention a gun or threaten violence of any kind against either of you?"

Jess answered, "No, but my husband came to our rescue."

Jake changed positions in his seat, leaning his right

elbow on the chair arm. "He backed off when warned that we'd call the police." He paused. "I revealed I had a gun."

Pagarelli maintained eye contact with Jake. He waited.

"I notified the local police," Jake continued. "Got his license number." He pulled a piece of folded paper from his jeans pocket and handed it to the detective.

"I'll run this plate and contact the Punxsutawney police myself. This may have a bearing on our victim's case."

Oh, great. Another suspect to add to my list.

Pagarelli leaned against the table. "Do you think you can describe him to a sketch artist? All of you?"

Something clicked in my memory. "Jake, what about the security system? The outside cameras might have filmed him coming up to the door."

Jake snapped his fingers. "You're right. Detective Pagarelli, the cabin has a high-tech security system. Plenty of cameras around the building and grounds."

The detective noted the new information. "We should be able to pull something from them with your permission." He nodded at me. "Good catch, Ms. Tuft."

I basked in his smidge of approval.

The plastic box of pictures from the cabin sat on the floor beside Jake's chair. He lifted the container and balanced it on his lap. "We have another issue to discuss with you, Detective Pagarelli." He unlatched the lid and removed a stack of photos.

"We found these in a closet at the cabin. It's proof that Hansen stalked Suzie the last couple of years."

Pagarelli shuffled through a handful of images, lingering on a photo of me. His face darkened.

Jake held up two of the photographs side by side. "You can see these were taken in different years because of the change in Hunter's appearance. All in all, the photos range from years ago to recent weeks."

Pagarelli picked up the picture taken at Jess and Jake's place. "Whose house is this?"

"Ours," Jess said. "The creep followed Suzie to a cookout in our backyard."

He looked at me. "You didn't know Hansen took these?"

"No." I wished I would have been smart enough to catch Mike in the act.

"It's difficult to spot a stalker who doesn't want to be seen," Pagarelli explained. "Hansen hid well out of sight."

He handed the photographs back to Jake. "Since the perpetrator is deceased, there is no legal course of action we can pursue."

Even though I came to the same conclusion earlier, Detective Pagarelli's confirmation disappointed me. The invasion of my personal space would haunt me for a long time.

"We know." Jake returned everything to the box. "I mentioned the photos in case they were relevant to your investigation."

"Thanks. You don't need to leave them here for evidence, but please hang on to the container for a few weeks."

Jake secured the lid. "It'll be in my garage."

Pagarelli rose. "I'll see you to the main entrance."

We thanked him and left the station.

Halfway to the car, I clicked my tongue. "We should have told him about the money we found."

"Do we have to go back in there?" Jess asked with a slight whine. "This place is unnerving."

Jake shrugged. "We can tell him later. Wait a few days

until we get everything figured out with the cabin. The money will be safe at the bank."

The situation was all too much. The property. The money. Discussing the stranger and the stalking photos. My emotions were in turmoil. "I could use a chocolate-covered pecan ball."

Jess hooked her arm through mine. "I'm in."

Jake opened the car doors for us. "My treat, ladies."

We stopped at the ice cream shop, where I ordered a pecan ball with hot fudge and Jess ordered a chocolate sundae. Jake got a milkshake, and he seemed to appreciate watching Jess and me devour our treats.

The ice cream managed to restore my mood, and once Jess and Jake dropped me off at home, I called Corey James. I wanted information about the photo of Mike's girlfriend, but I wavered about asking him. When he answered the phone, I used the direct approach. "Do you know the name of the woman Mike dated while living with Samantha?"

Silence stretched for several moments. "I'm afraid I don't. What makes you think he was seeing someone?"

"A photograph of the two enjoying themselves on Mike's boat. Also, a woman's clothing and personal items are at the cabin."

"This is news to me. We notified you and Ms. Banks of Mr. Hansen's wishes. No one else came forward to claim a share of his estate except his brother, who has no legal claim. Perhaps, if I saw a photo of this woman, I'd recognize her. Do you have one?"

"Stored in my phone."

"Can you text it to me?"

I opened my photo gallery, copied the image of the two of them on the boat into a text, then hit send. James didn't speak for a few moments, but I waited to hear his response.

"I've never seen her," he said, "But this shows they were intimate."

Another roadblock. "As they say, a picture is worth a thousand words. Thanks, anyway. I had hoped to return a box of her things. Maybe she'll contact me at some point."

"Sorry I couldn't be of more help. You are under no legal obligation to locate her, but you might think about placing an ad in the local paper."

"I'll consider it." I paused. "Do you suppose she received word that Mike is deceased?"

"We would have no reason to apprise her. She could have learned of his passing from a friend or the Punxsutawney papers if they printed his obituary because of his residence there."

My mind sorted through the information. "I wish there was a way I could contact her."

"I don't know the woman."

"Thanks. I was thinking out loud." I hung up, wondering how to learn the woman's identity. Perhaps, she could tell me where Mike obtained the money to build the house. Did she pay? Why didn't he name her as his heir?

Detective Pagarelli came to mind as a source for finding the woman, but I rejected the thought. Why would he bother locating her for me to return a couple of boxes? He was busy investigating a murder.

If someone notified the woman of Mike's death, she might leave a note on the cabin door with her contact information. If Mike didn't contact her from his hospital bed, and no one in his circle of friends knew she existed, she may think Mike is still alive.

My mind, exhausted from the ordeals at the bank and with Detective Pagarelli, needed to escape to another world. I curled up in my favorite chair with a popular novel from my stack of to-be-read books, a cup of chamomile tea beside me.

A half-hour into my book, the doorbell rang, jolting me out of an intense scene. I unfolded myself from the chair and stumbled, attacked by the feeling of pins and needles stabbing my feet. I didn't move quickly enough because my visitor resorted to louder knocking.

I limped to the door, yanked it open, and froze. Samantha Banks, my ex's former live-in girlfriend, stood steady as a statue, her expression stony and hostile. Black, frizzy hair exploded around her gargoyle face. Her eyes reminded me of the shooting daggers that sprang from cartoon characters' orbs. Rattled, I realized Hunter was in the backyard instead of with me. Thank goodness the glass storm door was locked between us. Hopefully, she wouldn't cause trouble. *Ha.*

"We need to talk." Not even a hello was tacked onto her command.

"About?" I folded my arms over my chest.

The grooves in Samantha's forehead deepened. "Mike's attorney told me I inherited the hovel we lived in, but none of his money. I made it my business to find every dime of his." She flashed a folded piece of paper. "I have a copy of the will stating he left you a house filled with antiques. I viewed it online." She slapped the paper against her thigh. "I live in squalor compared to the log home you inherited. His will also mentions an SUV, a boat, and money." She twisted her lips in a smug sneer. "I can't guess where he found the cash to buy a second home but, believe me, I'll end up with everything he owned." She shook the paper at me. "He won't get away with hiding assets from me. I hired a lawyer to take back the property you stole from me."

I settled a hand on my hip. "Excuse me?"

"Don't act all innocent. I suspected for a long time he was seeing someone else." She poked the glass with a wicked fingernail. "You snuck around with Mike behind my back."

My mind shifted to the unidentified woman's photo at the cabin. "I wouldn't stoop low enough to cheat with a cheater."

She crooked her neck. "Why else would he give you part of his estate?"

"I asked myself the same thing, with no logical answer. You lived with him. Why didn't he leave his entire estate to you?" I rushed on before she had time to respond. "As for your accusations, I haven't seen or talked to Mike since I left him. I'm as puzzled as you are about why he gave me the cabin and property. Maybe he had a guilty conscience for the way he treated me when we were dating."

She grunted, sticking her pug nose up in the air. "From what I heard, he bent over backward to make the relationship work."

I blew out a puff of air. "Clearly we experienced different versions of Mike."

She thumped her chest. "I'm the one who lived with him. I should be his sole beneficiary."

Her smug, selfish attitude was one of the reasons I disliked her so much. "Well, you aren't."

Fury contorted her features, which threatened to tear her face apart. "If the stupid law firm hadn't informed you of the will, you wouldn't have any idea the house existed."

"Are you blaming the attorney for fulfilling his professional obligation?"

Her hands balled. "You weren't a part of our lives. It should have stayed that way. Ryder had no right to interfere."

Samantha's words sent a ripple of fear coursing through me. Had she tried to stop him from contacting me?

Her rigid demeanor reminded me of a drill sergeant in a movie. "Turn over the keys and the deed."

I mimicked her stance. "No. I'm putting the place on the market once I've cleared the clutter."

She was taken aback by the notion. "You can't do that."

Not only could I, but I could take her down a peg, too. "By the way, I found a drawer filled with female clothing at the cabin if you want them back, although I'm surprised you're into silky thongs. I took you to be a panty kind of girl. And those sexy black lace negligees. Wow."

The crease between her brows turned into a crevice. "You're lying. I was never there."

"Oh." I brought my hand to my mouth, feigning innocence. "The frilly intimate apparel isn't yours? Sorry, I assumed *you* were the owner. Hmm, once a cheater, always a cheater, as they say."

Samantha became enraged. I thought her eyes would burst out of her head. It was evident from her scarlet face that her blood pressure had soared from normal to dangerous in an instant.

"You...you..." she sputtered.

I held up my hands. "No, not me. He kept a secret lover at the cabin."

"Shut up." She plastered her nose to the door, once again reminding me of a pug. "Mike loved me. He would never cheat on me. You're lying to make me as miserable as you are." She huffed and slapped her hands on her hips. "It won't work."

I had a deep desire to show her the photo of Mike and his mistress but didn't want her to explode, causing a mess on my door.

"We're finished here, Samantha."

She shook her fist. "Not until I have the deed to the property in Punxsutawney."

"No." I closed the door.

She repeatedly kicked the bottom of the glass door while stringing together a plethora of swear words that would make a sailor blush.

Hunter's bark echoed from the backyard. I went to the kitchen and opened the backdoor. He bolted through, dashed past me, and stopped where Samantha was carrying on in earnest. He joined in the ruckus, snarling and yapping.

Samantha's yelling grew louder. I threw open the main door. Hunter jumped up on the glass, nails clicking, jaws snapping. Taken by surprise, the woman shrank back in wide-eyed terror.

"Get off my porch or I'll open the storm door."

She paled, backing away. Near the bottom step, Samantha turned and ran down to the driveway. She jumped in her car and took off.

Closing the door, I stroked Hunter's head. "You scared her away, big fella. Let's get you a treat. And one for me, too."

Not wanting Hunter to eat his bone alone, I dug into a package of chocolate chip cookies. I contemplated informing Detective Pagarelli of the confrontation, but Samantha left without incident. I phoned Jess instead.

"You won't believe who showed up at my door." I filled Jess in on what had transpired.

"Wish I could've seen her face when you told her about cheating Mike. How satisfying was that?"

"Very. She accused me of being his mistress until I mentioned the intimate apparel at the cabin. Then, she claimed Mike would never cheat on her. Samantha left in a snit."

"Why didn't you let Hunter have a go at her? He'd teach her a lesson."

I picked up a piece of a broken chocolate chip that had fallen on the placemat. "And saddle me with a lawsuit?"

"Think of the enjoyment, though."

"Think of the expense." I popped the morsel in my mouth.

"How did she find out about the cabin?" Jess asked. "Mike went to a lot of trouble to keep the place hidden, especially since he had a girlfriend there."

I considered it for a moment. "The attorney informed her. She flaunted a copy of the will." I laid the cookie aside. "Get this. Samantha said Ryder shouldn't have interfered."

"That's a threat," Jess said. "Tell Pagarelli."

"This inheritance is nothing but trouble," I muttered.

"Whatever. The place is legally yours. Go through with your plan to sell. You can't allow Samantha to undermine you."

"I feel guilty accepting something so valuable under the circumstances."

"Don't. Mike left Samantha an ample chunk of his estate. If he wanted her to own everything, he would have written his will differently." Jess paused. "Are you going to report Samantha to your special police detective?"

I released a sarcastic, "Ha, ha," and said with serious-ness, "I have no *special* detective, but I'm debating whether to call the police."

"The police have a duty to take care of pesky nutcases, Suzie. Turn Samantha in tomorrow. I'm certain Detective Pagarelli would be happy to assist you." The humor in her voice was unmistakable.

"Enough with the innuendos about him, Jess. Goodbye."

She was right about informing Pagarelli that Samantha visited, but I'd already met with him today. I decided to wait until morning to call. I returned to the sofa, picked up my novel, found my place, and zoned out. Instead of focusing on the plotline, however, my thoughts veered to the one thing I shouldn't have been thinking about at all: Detective Pagarelli.

Chapter Seven

Tuesday morning, Pagarelli called and asked me to return to the police station with Jess and Jake. He wanted to brief us on the man who'd barged into the cabin.

"We've identified the man who threatened you as Tyler Ribar." He extracted a picture from a folder and placed it in the middle of the table.

"That's him," we replied in unison.

"Have any of you heard of the guy before?"

We all shook our heads. I leaned over for a better view. "Were he and Mike friends?"

"According to the Punxsutawney police detective who interviewed Mr. Ribar, he and Mr. Hansen were, yes. They hunted and fished in the area. The police there warned Ribar not to trespass again on your property. Ribar claimed he left things with Mr. Hansen for safekeeping. He wants them returned as soon as possible."

"How do I determine what belongs to him when Mike isn't here to verify anything?" I asked. "We haven't gone through all Mike's possessions. The attorney gave me a copy of what's recorded with the law firm, but he cautioned the list may not have been updated with the latest purchases."

"The detective questioning Mr. Ribar told him to write down what he is owed." Detective Pagarelli handed me the note.

"Money and personal items? Could he be any vaguer?" I asked, reading the message.

"That's exactly what the detective asked him. Ribar claims the items are personal." Pagarelli shifted in his seat. "I wouldn't doubt he was trying to lay claim to stolen merchandise. Ribar has a record of being in and out of trouble over the years, including theft. He was convicted of shoplifting several electronics from a big box store. He also pulled off a fundraising scheme that bilked people out of hundreds of dollars."

The paper crumpled in my fisted hand. A thief? What did Mike get himself, and me, into this time? "Do you think stolen goods are stored at the cabin?"

"Hard to tell. If you find anything suspicious, call me."

My mind raced ahead to the money we'd found buried there.

"Here's the thing." Detective Pagarelli twirled a pen between his index finger and thumb. "Even if you give Ribar money, there's no guarantee he'll leave you alone. If the guy's a criminal, he could see this as an opportunity for a quick score."

Pagarelli switched from twirling the pen to tapping it against his left palm. "My concern is he may see you as an easy mark and threaten or coerce you in the future."

"He's right," Jake said. "Hansen could have bragged that the antiques at the cabin were worth a small fortune."

I turned to the detective. "Ribar was a thief. What if he and Mike joined forces to steal money?"

"There is no reason to suspect a collaboration at this time."

Because you don't have all the facts. I said, "Let's say you find out he robbed a bank. What would happen with my inheritance?"

"We would do a thorough search of the grounds, the house, and the other buildings, then confiscate anything illegal. Your inheritance would be tied up for a long time."

"I plan to sell everything. How long should I wait?"

"That depends." He eyed me suspiciously. "Do you have reason to believe Mr. Hansen gained his possessions illegally?"

My insides contracted. I had alerted his perceptive police senses. The guilt of my omission about the buried cash weighed on my conscience. I blurted out, "We found a hundred twenty thousand dollars at the cabin."

Jake coughed. Jess squirmed. Detective Pagarelli stared at me.

I hurried to explain. "Not *in* the cabin. In a field, a long way from the house."

Pagarelli positioned his elbow on the desk, rested his chin in his palm, and continued to stare.

I blathered on. "In tin cans we dug up. Six of them." I gulped. "One hundred twenty thousand dollars in total."

Pagarelli lifted his head. "You found a hundred twenty thousand dollars buried on the property?" He worked his jaw.

My babbling ceased. I shrank back in my seat, wishing for an invisibility cloak.

He turned to a clean sheet of paper in his notebook. "Were you aware Mr. Hansen had buried the cash?"

I shook my head. "No, Jake found a map."

Jake's gaze was lowered as he played with his watch-band. This time, he did not come to my rescue.

Detective Pagarelli waited for me to continue.

"The map was taped behind the refrigerator. We noticed these dots scattered in several places. We thought they meant something."

Much to my relief, Jake broke his silence. "Six tiny dots placed on the paper at random places led me to believe they were clues. We hiked to one of the areas indicated by a dot, but we didn't see anything unusual. Nothing out of the ordinary was at the second marking, either. We went back for shovels and excavated each of the areas. It goes without saying, we were shocked to find different sizes of cans filled with hundred-dollar bills."

Detective Pagarelli drew in a deep breath and released it slowly. "Let me get this straight. You three…"

Jess interrupted, fingers held in the air. "Two. I didn't do any digging with them."

Traitor.

The detective expelled another sigh. "The *two* of you found a small fortune buried in six places on the property in question, and you are only now bringing it to my attention?" His expression changed from rebuke to disappointment, from a frown to a scowl.

"I'm sorry." I was reminded of being scolded as a child. It felt silly to say aloud, but I added, "We forgot to tell you yesterday."

"Forgot?" He scratched the figure on his notepad. "Where is the money now?"

"Stored in a safety deposit box at my credit union." The hole I'd dug for myself grew bottomless. I wondered how to climb out with my dignity intact. "I'll bring you the money."

"That won't be necessary at this point." He ripped a

sheet off the notepad and passed it to me. "I'd like the name and phone number of the credit union, if you don't mind."

I wrote the name and scrolled through my phone for the number, which I added to the note. Although I should have remained quiet, my mouth rambled on with the speed of an auctioneer. "James said money found on the property was mine. We didn't know if the money was legally obtained. We decided the best course of action would be to save it somewhere safe until the police investigated Mike. If he robbed a bank or store, you'd inform us, and I'd relinquish the money."

He nodded but kept his eyes diverted to the notebook. "Maybe the killer was after that money and killed Ryder for not telling them where it was hidden."

My explanation hadn't made him any happier. My shoulders slumped.

"Unless we discover the money was gained illegally, it remains yours." He made a few more notations, then glanced up. "Anything else you want to add?"

I squirmed under his intense scrutiny. "No. Nothing. I'm sorry I didn't tell you sooner."

He set the notepad aside. "We've been investigating Ryder's murder from the angle that someone didn't want you to have the cabin out of jealousy. With a significant amount of money at stake, the motive expands to other possibilities. It's conceivable someone saw Hansen bury the cans. Or the money could have belonged to the killer, who needed time to search for the cash before you retained ownership of the property. Those would be reasons for wanting to stop the attorney from notifying you of your inheritance."

"Oh." The room heated, stifling me. Foolishly, I hadn't connected the money to a motive for killing.

"The perpetrator may not have meant to kill Ryder," Pagarelli said. "He or she may have gotten into a heated argument, which escalated. Can you think of anyone who knew about the cash?"

"No. The attorney didn't mention buried cash, but he said the will stated any money at the property belonged to me. I assumed he meant a few bucks Mike might have had lying around."

"Not a hundred and twenty thousand?" he asked.

"No way. The last contact I had with Mike, he was penniless and on drugs."

Pagarelli pushed back his chair and stood. "Let me work this approach. I'll contact you if I need anything else from you. I appreciate the three of you coming in today."

Once outside the police station, my regret at keeping the money a secret increased. The displeased expression on Detective Pagarelli's face stuck in my mind. I didn't want him to be disappointed in me. Quite the opposite.

Jake plucked his truck keys from his jacket pocket. "He didn't take our omission of the money well."

"No, he didn't," Jess agreed.

I sighed.

* * *

At home, armed with information from Detective Pagarelli about Tyler Ribar, I searched the Internet for more details. Aside from his address and phone number, Ribar's arrests with convictions surfaced. Mike probably met him at a local bar on one of his trips to Punxsutawney.

I had a crazy urge to contact Ribar and ask about his relationship with Mike. Could he identify the woman in the photo with him? I didn't care about Mike's connection with her, but I wanted the facts about how he managed to buy the cabin and antiques. Maybe she was the wealthy one who kept him in luxury. If not, what kind of scheme had netted him nearly a million dollars in assets in the few years since we parted? Why didn't he bequeath the mystery woman his property? Did she know Samantha shared a house with Mike?

I gave up the quest for information and decided to do a load of laundry. Water poured into the washing machine, foaming up the soap I added. Before tossing in clothes, I checked that all pockets were empty. Forgotten tissues that shredded and clung to my clothes irritated me.

I stared at the water as the basin filled. All of a sudden, I remembered something from Samantha's visit. I'd forgotten to tell Pagarelli about her remark concerning Ryder. Guilt nagged at me about disappointing the detective by not informing him of the buried money. My stomach flipped. *Great. He'll think I withheld another detail from him on purpose.*

Finished loading the washer, I texted Jess. My cell-phone rang within seconds of sending the message.

"You know what you have to do," Jess said. "Call Detective Hottie."

"Will you quit calling him that? He has a name. Detective Nathaniel S. Pagarelli."

"When did he give you his first name?"

"I read his badge."

I hung up and dialed Pagarelli. He answered on the second ring. "Ms. Tuft, how have you been since this morning?"

Not so wonderful. "When I came to the meeting at your office this morning, I had intended to tell you about a visit from Samantha Banks."

"Let me guess, you forgot."

His voice held a touch of humor. *Should I be relieved or insulted?*

"Samantha demanded I sign the cabin over to her. She was angry and vowed she would take it from me. She hired a lawyer. I slammed the door in her face."

"And?" His keen observation accurately deduced there was more to the story.

I disliked admitting I'd used Hunter as a deterrent, but I confessed. "She pounded on my glass storm door, yelling profanities. I opened the exterior door, and Hunter jumped up on the glass. Samantha cowered, but she continued ranting." I paused for an awkward moment. "Until I threatened to let him at her."

I thought I heard him snicker. He cleared his throat. "Did she threaten you with physical harm?"

"Sort of, but that's not what bothered me. She said I wouldn't have known about my inheritance if the law firm hadn't informed me, which is true. No one would expect Mike to include me in his will. She said Ryder had no right to interfere."

I heard his pen tapping. "She mentioned Ryder by name?"

"Yes. She seemed to think it was his fault she didn't get the house and property."

The tapping stopped. "Hansen filed a will at the law firm. If Ryder failed to notify you, the firm would send another attorney."

"I don't think Samantha was thinking clearly. She hates me. She accused me of seeing Mike behind her back."

"You weren't, though?"

My face heated with the thought. "Of course not. He cheated on me with her. Why would I ever take him back and put myself through that humiliation and pain again?" I realized my voice was raised, so I brought it down a notch. "I shrewdly informed her Mike had a girlfriend, though."

"Oh?"

"While visiting the cabin, we discovered a photo of Mike and a mystery woman. Then, I found a drawer full of women's clothing."

"Ah, you told her."

"Only about the intimate apparel. I pretended to think they were Samantha's. I refrained from texting her the photo."

Pagarelli laughed, but I was still growing more embarrassed by my pettiness. "You stirred up more trouble for yourself," he said. "Are you worried for your safety with this woman on the loose?"

"No. Hunter scares her."

"Thanks for briefing me on the visit. I'll check Ms. Banks out. Lock your doors and set your alarm, whether you are home or away. If you feel you are in danger, call me. Anytime."

"Okay." I hung up, my mood soaring. Pagarelli said to call him anytime. Too bad he meant for business, not personal calls.

I glanced at the clock. Nearly three. I went to work on the supplemental material for the college text I was working on. An hour later, the doorbell interrupted my thoughts. Hunter sprang from where he lay in his corner bed.

Samantha better not be darkening my doorstep again. The outline visible through the front window sent a jolt of terror through my body.

Tyler Ribar, the mountainous man who'd threatened us at the cabin, stood on my porch.

Hunter, at my side, tilted his head as if questioning why

I hadn't opened the door. I wrung my hands as the bell sounded again. Should I ignore it? Call the police? Hunter barked, pulling me out of my thoughts. Maybe I could learn something about the murder. I ran to the study for my pepper spray. Then, I squared my shoulders and opened the exterior door a few inches.

Ribar's oversized pursed lips poked through the bushy beard surrounding them. Deep furrows marred his forehead below the dirty hat he wore on his unkempt head of hair. All that stood between me and the six-and-a-half-foot giant with biceps the size of my midsection was the locked storm door. And Hunter.

Ribar raised his thumb and a finger to the brim of his hat. "Ms. Tuft."

"How did you find me?" I couldn't keep my voice from quivering.

"Public records transferring the cabin from Hansen to you."

I didn't respond.

"My apologies for barging into the cabin the other day. Can I talk to you about recovering the items I left with Mike?"

Was he sorry, or faking? Could I turn his visit to my advantage? My researcher's brain was fully engaged. "Were you and Mike friends?"

He shuffled his feet. "Yes, for a few years. Fishing and hunting buddies."

Pagarelli had said as much. What I wanted were new details. "Were you friends with Mike's girlfriend?"

A slight widening of his eyes indicated his surprise. "You know about Honey?"

Was that her real name or an endearment? "Only from her photos at the cabin. I boxed her clothing and wanted to deliver it to her, but I didn't have a name or address."

"I can deliver the boxes."

"I didn't bring them home with me. It's up in the air when we'll return to the cabin. It would be simpler if I had her address."

He seemed to be weighing his options. "She works at the diner in town. You can leave the boxes there."

"Does Honey have a last name?"

He chuckled. "There's only one Honey in Punxsutawney."

Not much to go on, but it was more than I'd had.

Ribar rearranged his face into a pleasant smile. "Now, about my stuff. Can I search for it at the cabin?"

Why didn't he come right out and say what Mike owed him? "If you write down what you are missing, I'll check on my next trip."

"How about you give me a key? I'll hide it under a rock when I leave." He smiled, showing off tobacco-stained teeth.

"We set an alarm. I don't want to give out the code."

His pleasant expression disappeared. His voice held a hard edge. "Can I come in and discuss this?" He gripped the locked door handle and tugged.

I leaped back with a gasp, causing a growl to rumble in Hunter's throat. I tilted my head in his direction. "My dog doesn't care for strangers." I sounded brave despite being nervous.

Ribar's face took on a dangerous callousness. "I came here to politely ask for your cooperation. To save you the trouble of a lawsuit. The least you can do is invite me in after my two-hour drive." He rattled the handle.

I froze. Hunter barked, bumping the door with his head.

The man let go of the handle.

Pulse racing, I pushed the main door forward. "You have my address. Send me the list." I sealed the entry with a snap of the lock, my legs jelly as I sagged against the wall in a trembling heap. Hunter's head nudged my leg, his way of assuring me it was okay. I hugged him, listening to tires squeal outside. I peeked out the window in time to see Ribar's tail lights clear my driveway.

I gathered my strength and led Hunter into the kitchen. Still quaking, I made myself a cup of tea to settle my nerves. Minutes later, my head still spun, and I sat staring at the steam swirling from the cup in front of me, the vapor as cloudy as my mind. Was Tyler Ribar after money, or was something else important enough for him to go to the trouble of driving to my home? The possessions we'd discovered at the cabin appeared to belong to Mike and his girlfriend. The only things of true value were the antiques and the guns. If Ribar wanted guns returned, why didn't he say? Did he store something in the garage or one of the sheds?

I checked the time. Jess would be home from work. I texted that I was on my way to her house.

My mind continued to reel. What if Ribar knew Mike buried the money? Maybe he and Mike were in a partnership where they stole cash from a person, company, or bank. My head pounded with the illegal possibilities.

I asked Hunter, "Want to go see Aunt Jess, boy?"

He danced, tail wagging in response. I ran from window to window looking for signs that Ribar had doubled back. Satisfied he was gone, I loaded Hunter into the car, locked the doors, and hit the garage door opener.

I was a bundle of nerves, checking the rearview mirror every few moments during the drive to Jess's.

* * *

"Come in." Jess held open the door. "You look stressed. What's up?"

"I need to talk to you."

After turning Hunter loose in the backyard with her dog, Max, Jess flitted around her kitchen, preparing dinner while I lazed at the table.

"I found out Mike's girlfriend's name."

"What is it?" Jess chopped a red pepper in earnest.

"Honey."

"What?"

"Her name is Honey."

Jess paused, knife in midair, and laughed. "Leave it to Mike to find someone with a name he could use by accident with his live-in girlfriend and not get caught."

"Samantha is no honey. She's more of a bear."

"That, she is. A mean, old grizzly." Jess rinsed a few stalks of celery. "What's Honey's last name? Where's she from?"

"I didn't get her last name, but she works at the Punxsutawney diner where we ate lunch on Saturday."

Jess's head snapped up. She shut off the water. "Really? What a coincidence. Do you think she was there when we were? I wonder if she knows what you look like."

"Had she been working, we would've spotted her red hair. As for knowing me, don't you think she would've snooped in Mike's box of pictures and everything else he owned? After all, how could she trust a cheater? She'd recognize me from his photos."

"True. You can bet I'd find pictures that Jake hid in our closet." She pulled a string on the celery. "How'd you find out her name?"

"Ready for this? Tyler Ribar showed up on my doorstep."

Jess dropped the peeler. She sagged against the counter, covering her mouth. "Oh, Suzie. Why didn't you tell me right away? No wonder you're a wreck. Did he hurt you? Did you call the police?"

I waved away the concern. "Everything is okay. I sent him back to Punxy."

It was Jess's turn to be rattled. "The monster is huge. He could've hurt you."

"We spoke through the locked glass door. Hunter intimidated him. He left."

Jess pushed away from the counter. "That enormous ox could've busted down your door."

"He would have gotten a face full of pepper spray, and Hunter would have taken a chunk out of him."

Jess dried her hands on a kitchen towel, lowering herself in a chair across from me. "Did he cause trouble?"

I relayed the details. "He wanted a key. Can you imagine me giving that thief free rein of the place?"

"At least you turned him down." She hopped out of her seat and began to pace. "You should not be staying alone."

"I have Hunter," I reminded her.

"A dog would be no match for him if he had a gun. Besides, the brute could choke a horse with his bare hands."

Great, now she'd implanted that frightening vision in my mind. "I have a gun."

She crossed her arms, leaning against the oven. "Yeah, like you could actually shoot someone."

"I could fire in the air and scare him."

"Honestly, Suzie. I'm worried about you being by yourself, more so at night. This is frightening."

I picked at the tag on my teabag. "The truth?" I met her stare. "He terrified me by showing up, but he left without incident. I told him to mail me a note with what he claims is his property, and I'll return everything. That should satisfy him. It's strange, though. He never said what he wanted returned."

"Makes me wonder if he's after some sort of contraband. The buried money?"

The exact question had been bouncing around in my mind. "I hope not."

"Did you inform your police detective?"

I pursed my lips. "He's not mine. And, no, I came here first thing."

"Call him." Jess pointed to my cellphone on the table. "He needs to know Ribar went to the trouble of finding you."

"We were at the police station this morning, then I called him about Samantha. Since Ribar left without incident, I'll wait until tomorrow to call."

I wanted to talk to Pagarelli to stay fresh in his thoughts, but I didn't want him to get sick of hearing from me.

"Promise me you'll call him tomorrow, Suzie."

"I will. I promise."

Chapter Eight

Wednesday morning, I dialed Corey James. I got his voicemail and left a message asking him to contact me. Ten minutes later, his name appeared on my screen. We exchanged pleasantries.

"Have you ever heard of Tyler Ribar?" I asked.

"The name doesn't sound familiar. Who is he?"

"Mike's friend. He claims he left personal items with Mike for safekeeping. He refused to give specifics, but he asked for a key to search the cabin."

"Did you give him one?"

"No. I told him to send me a list."

"I strongly advise against giving him a key," he said. "You need to be careful of people who discover you've come into money. They may attempt to take advantage of you."

"Do you think Mike owed him money from a scheme the two devised? Is that where the funds came from to buy the property?"

He spoke in a calm, soothing voice. "I have no reason to believe Mr. Hansen obtained his estate through illegal means. I am, however, suspicious of Mr. Ribar's intentions. He may be trying to swindle you out of valuable assets."

"Could the antiques be his?" I asked.

"Not if they are on the list I provided for you. Mr. Hansen acquired those pieces legally. Our firm can vouch for their procurement. We retained copies of the authenticity papers as well."

"Thank you for returning my call, Mr. James. Sorry to bother you."

"No problem. I'm available to you anytime. I'd be interested in hearing what Mr. Ribar wants. If he gives you an itemized list, please consult me first to verify his claim."

"I will."

"How's the house working out? It's a terrific property."

It is, except for the attachment to Mike. "I'm cleaning and preparing it to sell."

"You should have no trouble selling. Contact me if I can be of further assistance."

I ended the call and proceeded to write a shopping list. The pleasant weather enticed me to drive into town for a few things before settling in to work for the remainder of the day.

The drive presented a vibrant display of blossoms in white and various shades of pink, one of my favorite things about spring. The return of green leaves and colorful flowers delighted me. Even the air smelled fresh.

I finished my errands and decided to stop at Bre's Bakery for a visit and a treat.

"Stopped in for more of your macaroons, Bre."

She packed the cookies in her signature pink box. "I'm tossing in a new scone flavor I'm trying out on customers."

"Yum. What flavor?"

She smiled. "That's a surprise."

Everything Bre baked was scrumptious. I couldn't wait.

On the way home, I noticed a black sedan pull into the street behind me. The car followed me at every turn through town. On the highway, I accelerated. The vehicle sped up, too. My shoulders tensed. Although still daylight, the headlights behind me were two luminous eyes boring into the back of my skull.

Slowing, I signaled left to turn onto the secluded road leading to my house. I figured the other driver would stay on the main highway, as few cars traveled this road. I flicked my eyes to the rearview mirror and caught sight of the sedan behind me. It crept closer until it was inches from my back bumper. My heartbeat picked up speed. I worried the car would end up crumpled in my trunk if I hit my brakes for an animal on the road, or that it would ram my car from behind.

My eyes darted from one side mirror to the other. I struggled to watch for deer and wild turkeys, both of which frequented the area. Had I inadvertently committed an offense to spark a road rage incident? The thought frightened me. Road rage caused a lot of damage and physical harm these days.

Familiar with the road, I pushed my vehicle beyond the speed limit, hoping the other driver couldn't keep up with me. The car stayed on my tail.

I fished one-handed in my purse for my cellphone to call for help. I tugged it out by a corner, but it slipped from my nervous fingers. My heart sank as I heard it thump to the floor. From the corner of my eye, I caught sight of the phone sliding beneath the passenger seat. I dared not divert my attention from the road to reclaim it.

My nerves were frayed, ratcheting my blood pressure a few points. Clutching the steering wheel, I was keenly aware of the isolation that surrounded me. Of course, my mind chose this time to recall a movie in which a truck chased a woman down a deserted dirt road. In the scene, the pursuer sped around her, forcing her vehicle into the ditch. He then blocked her escape with his truck. The narrow road to my house barely accommodated two lanes of traffic, but flustered by my overactive imagination, I edged closer to the middle.

I breezed past my house to avoid alerting my follower where I lived. I feared they would accost me while I waited for my garage door to open.

It seemed to take forever to reach the other end of the road. Hysteria built in my chest with every mile. Finally, the main highway came into view. I didn't bother with the turn signal as I made a left and stomped on the gas pedal. The demon car kept pace. For the first time in my life, I wished for a cop to appear and try to award me a traffic ticket.

Droplets of rain splotched my windshield. *You've got to be kidding me.* Wary of losing control on the slick road, I slowed. A little. Jess's house was close by. If I could get to her neighborhood, surely the car wouldn't follow me there with so many houses around. Coldness swept through me as I navigated the streets, the sedan still shadowing me.

The events of the last few days swamped my mind. Samantha's hatred of me. Her demands and threats. Ribar's requests, then his ultimatum. Ribar drove a red truck. Samantha had visited in a white SUV. Who was tailing me? I didn't want to think that there was someone else who wanted my bothersome inheritance, too.

This was Mike's fault. His stupid bequest to me had fractured my peaceful life. During the past years, I regretted meeting him, but never as much as this week. How could he involve me in his illicit dealings? What other unsavory characters did Mike team up with who wanted what they believed I possessed of theirs?

I neared Jess's house. If the stranger had the audacity to trespass on her driveway, I planned to blow the horn while dialing the police.

Reaching my destination, I parked in front of one of her closed garage doors. The sedan crawled by, but it parked a few houses down the street. I hurried to Jess's front door, hit the doorbell, and prayed she was home.

Jess flung open the door, irritation creasing her brow. A fat tabby cat clung to Jess's popsicle orange shirt by its claws. "Do you have to keep pushing the bell? You have Fluffy in a tizzy." She stroked the cat's fur. "Poor baby."

I scurried inside, flattened myself against the wall. "Lock the door."

Juggling Fluffy, Jess flipped the door lock and threw the deadbolt. "What's going on?"

I peeled myself from the wall. "A black sedan followed me to my house. It was practically in my trunk." My breathing was labored. "I didn't stop, afraid the driver would confront me when no one was around. I came here instead."

The alarm in Jess's eyes caused my fear to turn to remorse. I never thought the sedan would follow me to her neighborhood. In hindsight, I should have driven to the police station instead. "I'm sorry, Jess. In my panicked state, I wasn't thinking straight. Now, I've put you in danger."

"Don't worry. I can only imagine how terrified you were." She secured Fluffy with one arm, wrapping the other around me. "You're trembling. I'll call Jake. He's at a friend's house."

"No. Please. Don't bother him. I need to compose myself." I swiped at my bangs. "I drank two cups of strong tea at Bre's shop. I'm wound up from the caffeine and the sweets I consumed. I can't think logically. Give me a few minutes."

"Where did you lose him?" Jess asked.

"I didn't."

Jess hugged her cat. "He's here?"

I hooked my thumb over my shoulder. "He parked in front of one of your neighbors' homes." I rubbed my arms. "Maybe he lives here, and I imagined he was following me."

Jess shook her head. "Living in this neighborhood, he has no reason to be on your road. He had to be after you. Nothing is on that road but your house and the wild animals." She scratched Fluffy's ears, probably as much to calm herself as the cat. "Did you do something to make the other driver angry?"

"I considered road rage, but I don't remember doing anything wrong."

"When did you notice him?"

"Shortly after I left the bakery."

Jess licked her lips. "Bre does bake delicious desserts. Which reminds me, I need to order cupcakes from her shop."

I cleared my throat. "Jess."

"Sorry. I tend to get off track sometimes when I'm nervous."

No kidding.

"You didn't misinterpret his actions," Jess said. "It's too coincidental for a person to happen down your deserted road, then track you all the way to my place." She brought a hand to her neck. "Do you think the driver is Ribar?"

"He drives a red truck."

Fluffy meowed, causing Jess to resume the ear rub. "He could have rented a car."

"True." Another idea skittered through my mind. "Samantha drove a white SUV. She could have rented another vehicle, too."

"What about Honey?"

I scrunched my lips. "Honey? What would she want with me?"

Jess dropped her arm from my shoulder. "Hello? You stole her cabin."

"I didn't steal it."

"Figure of speech." Jess set Fluffy on the floor, grabbing her phone from an end table. "I'm calling the police." Thinking it an excellent idea, I didn't try to stop her. After a brief explanation, she covered the mouthpiece, turning to me. "What color did you say the car was?"

"Black."

Jess removed her palm and repeated my answer to the person on the other end of the call. She faced me again. "Did you get a license number?"

"No. He was behind me during the drive."

Jess finished the story, gave her address, and ended the call. "They'll send a cruiser to patrol the street. Not much else they can do."

She beckoned with her index finger. "Come on. I'll make you some tea. Caffeine-free herbal."

I followed her fuzzy black cat slippers down the hall. My quaking lessened as I entered her bright yellow kitchen with its sunflower decor. I sank into a chair, releasing a big breath.

"I'm calling Jake." She did so, asking him to come home. Afterward, Jess dropped a teabag in a mug, filled it with water, then placed it in the microwave. When the timer dinged, she set the tea before me.

"Do you suppose this has anything to do with the

money we found?" Jess topped off her coffee before she slid into the chair across from me.

"Yes." I removed the teabag, placing it on the saucer Jess provided. "If Mike stole the money, an angry partner could be looking to collect his share."

"Or the FBI is searching for the money or suspects. You said the car was a black sedan. Isn't that what they drive in the movies?"

She made a valid point. "It could be law enforcement, I guess." My stomach flipped. "I hope they don't suspect me of wrongdoing since I own half of Mike's estate."

"Three quarters." Jess slapped a palm on the table, making me jump. "I can't believe miserable Hansen is causing you this much trouble from the grave."

I rubbed my fingertips across my forehead, mumbling, "Neither can I. My nerves have consumed me since finding Ryder. These last few days have thrown me over the edge." I picked up the mug. "I'm beginning to think Mike intended the inheritance, along with the wackos attached to it, as payback for leaving him."

Jess raised her cup in a cheers gesture. "Sounds like the Mike Hansen we knew and despised."

"Why didn't I refuse to accept the property?"

Jess patted my forearm. "It'll be okay. The police will figure this out." She stood. "Let's take our drinks to the family room and relax."

The doorbell chimed the instant we sat down. Expecting the police, we both went to answer.

I grabbed Jess's arm. "Don't open the door without looking to see who is here."

She lifted a corner of the living room curtain, then unlocked and opened the door.

Pagarelli tipped his hat. "Ladies."

Surprise mixed with relief coursed through me. I was lucky Detective Pagarelli responded each time I called the police. His presence almost made the torment I experienced bearable. Almost. While I was happy to see his handsome face, the circumstances surrounding his visit wore on me.

Jess stepped aside. "Come in, Detective." Behind his back, she wiggled her eyebrows at me, mouthing *he's cute*. I ignored yet another of her matchmaking hints, although I appreciated his rugged persona.

We gathered in the family room. My nerves tingled when he removed his hat and sat beside me on the sofa. His short, dark hair was perfectly groomed. The scent of masculine aftershave wafted toward me.

Jess offered him coffee, which he politely declined. He turned his intense gray eyes toward me. "I understand someone in a black sedan followed you."

I nodded.

"I observed a black vehicle parked down the street," he confirmed. "I glanced at the person behind the steering wheel, but it was too dark to make out the driver's face. I slowed enough to read the plate number as I cruised by to turn around in the cul-de-sac. When I started back this way, the car pulled into the road before I caught up to it. I didn't pursue it, but I'd guess whoever was driving suspected I was here to investigate." He checked his notebook. "The vehicle is registered to Samantha Banks."

My cup clinked against the end table, nearly slipping from my grip. Lukewarm tea sloshed over my fingers. I wiped them on a napkin.

Pagarelli observed my behavior with cool interest. "I gather you didn't tell me the whole story about her."

His voice sounded strange through the buzzing in my head. *She's stalking me?*

Jess spoke. "Samantha is Mike's girlfriend." She waved a hand. "Or rather, she was until he died. On Monday, she dropped in on Suzie. Gave her a hard time."

A stern expression crossed Pagarelli's face. "Didn't I say poking the hornet's nest would cause you trouble?"

"She drove a white SUV, not a black car," I said.

"It's possible the SUV belonged to Hansen. I'll check his registration." He jotted something in his notebook. "Any idea why Ms. Banks followed you?" He cocked his head. "I mean, besides the fact that you taunted her when she visited you."

"Anger over the will? Had I realized she was the one following me, I might have slammed on my brakes."

He didn't need to verbalize that intentionally causing a wreck was illegal. His expression admonished me.

I swallowed hard.

Detective Pagarelli stroked his chin. "Her motive could be to frighten you."

"She's a first-class witch," Jess grumbled. "Samantha resents Suzie. Always has."

I followed up Jess's remarks with a few of my own. "All of that is in the past. Samantha is furious Mike left me part of his estate."

Jess grinned. "She went crazy when you told her about Mike's girlfriend, Honey. On purpose." She laughed.

Pagarelli didn't see the humor in the situation. His eyes practically bore through me. "Honey?" he asked, his tone dripping with anything but.

"Uh, Mike's girlfriend in Punxy," I confirmed.

He wrote in his notebook again. "How did you find out about Honey?"

Answering the question was a bit tricky as it involved the second encounter with Ribar, something I hadn't informed the detective of. I paused too long, leaving it to Jess to answer. "Ribar told her."

Pagarelli slowly lifted his head and stared at me. His eyes darkened. He drew in what seemed a bottomless breath, holding it a couple of seconds before releasing it and boring those intense gray eyes into mine. "You talked to Ribar?"

Chapter Nine

Jess shivered. "He's one scary guy. The size of a grizzly bear. Mean as one, too."

I tossed Jess a dark look. *You're not helping matters.*

Pagarelli ignored her, still fixated on me, as if we were the only two in the room. "Ribar is dangerous. You should have called me when he approached you."

There was a softness to his tone I hadn't noticed before. Or maybe hadn't expected, given the circumstances. My emotions swirled.

Leaning against the back of the sofa, Pagarelli crossed his brawny arms and twisted his body fully toward me. "Enlighten me about Ribar's visit to your house, *Ms. Tuft.*" The emphasis he placed on my name left no margin for error. He expected me, not Jess, to provide the details. He was intimidating when he was in interrogation mode.

My mouth went dry. I took a drink of my tea. He waited.

"Ribar terrified me, of course, showing up without

139

warning," I began. "As he did at the cabin, he demanded to be allowed to claim his belongings."

"What exactly does he want?"

"He wouldn't give specifics."

Pagarelli uncrossed his arms and flipped to a new page in his notebook with a snap. "Tell me everything."

I related the particulars of the visit. When finished, I explained that I'd intended to call him this afternoon.

"The better intention would have been to call me immediately. I meant it when I said to call anytime." He took a breath. "Did he threaten you?"

My dry mouth caused my *yes* to come out as a weak croak.

He leaned forward and rested his forearms on his knees, only inches from me. "I don't care how many times a day you contact me. Being bullied by a criminal who is roughly twice your size is a reportable offense."

His stare penetrated my brain, suspending me in time for a few moments. All I could think about was his gorgeous eyes.

"What else?"

I blinked, coming back to the present. "Ribar wanted a key to the cabin."

Pagarelli rubbed his chin, slow and deliberate. "You didn't give him one, did you?"

"No."

"Good." He scribbled in his notebook.

Unfortunately, I couldn't stop myself from asking, "Do you think Ribar knows about the money we found? Maybe he robbed a bank with Mike or something?"

"Ms. Tuft." The furrows in his forehead returned. "Please allow me to conduct the investigation. Conjecture leads to any number of invented scenarios. Let's stick to the facts."

He flipped to a blank page. "Thus far, we have Ribar, who wants something he left at the cabin. We have Samantha, who wants the cabin, you believe, out of entitlement and a bit of jealousy. It's possible neither was aware Hansen buried cash on the property."

"Samantha isn't destitute. The attorney told me Mike left her the house they shared." To myself, I muttered, "I can't believe Mike owned enough valuables to draw up a will. I don't even have one."

Jess perked up at my disclosure. "You should. Everything of yours would go to the state since you have no husband or family." She smiled at Pagarelli.

Her matchmaking brain was whirring, and I wanted to choke her.

"Ladies, we're veering off subject," he said. "When Ms. Banks discovered Hansen owned a remote cabin, perhaps she concluded you rendezvoused with him there."

"I've already told you I didn't."

He held up his hands. "I'm not alleging or judging. It's a plausible reason for Ms. Banks to fight you for ownership or harass you to forfeit your inheritance. By deceiving her, Hansen endangered you."

I blew out a breath. "She can argue all she wants, but Mike's attorney told me the will is legally binding. Hunter and I can handle her if she comes to my house again."

"You can file harassment charges or call me if she causes trouble."

"Between Ribar and Samantha, I could be calling you every day."

A slight smile softened his features. "I don't mind."

My heart soared. "I'll remember that."

Pagarelli coughed into his hand. "There's more to this case than what I originally thought." He twirled the pen in his fingers. "We need to cover all the bases."

Jess stroked her forehead. "This is a nightmare. I thought we were rid of the creep years ago."

"We?" he asked.

"Suzie, I mean, but I lived through the misery of those breakup days with her." She gestured toward me with her coffee cup. "We've been best friends since high school. Suzie was my maid of honor when I married Jake."

I willed Jess to stop talking. Embarrassment scorched my cheeks. "Jess, Detective Pagarelli doesn't need a rundown of my sordid history with Mike."

She looked wounded. "I'm only trying to help. Did you tell him Mike used cocaine after he hooked up with Samantha? It might be important."

Pagarelli nodded. "She did, and a cocaine habit could account for Hansen's money if he was also selling drugs to afford it."

I wanted to refute the idea that Mike sold drugs, but what did I know about him? Clearly, he'd shocked me in the waning days of our relationship.

"Mike didn't have a drug habit when I met him. I was furious when I caught him using, and I threatened to end our relationship. He swore it was the first and last time. He begged me to give him another chance." I folded my hands in my lap, staring at them. "A week later, I discovered his affair with Samantha, who also supplied him with drugs. No amount of his begging afterward changed my mind about ending the relationship."

I thought about average-looking Samantha and her quick temper. Her main appeal to Mike, I imagined, was introducing him to, and maintaining, a drug user's lifestyle.

When I caught them in the throes of passion in his bed, she didn't even have the decency to be ashamed. With a sinister smile, she'd said, "Oops," as if she had spilled a glass of wine instead of breaking up a serious relationship.

The encounter had devastated me. I'd bolted from Mike's apartment, knocking over a lamp I hadn't noticed through my tears. He called after me, shouting a string of apologies, while Samantha urged him to let me go. I slammed the door on our relationship, literally, and never looked back.

"Ms. Tuft," Pagarelli said, regaining my attention. "Are you okay?" He reached around me and plucked my tea from the end table, handing the cup to me.

I longed to close my eyes and forget Pagarelli sat beside me. Forget about Mike and Samantha and all the pain they inflicted.

"I'm going to get to the bottom of this," he vowed. "I'll call Ms. Banks in for questioning and see what part she plays regarding this case."

"What if she confronts me again?" What I really wanted to ask was, *Can I knock her senseless?*

"Seeing me here tonight, she may decide to leave you alone," Pagarelli continued. "But I can't guarantee it. I'm also concerned about Ribar." He paused. "My personal advice is for you to stay with your friend until I can figure things out."

Jess said, "I think so, too."

I didn't answer. I had the feeling he realized I wouldn't stay at Jess's.

The detective picked up his hat. "Call me if either one of them bothers you again. Don't answer your door if they show up. Keep Hunter close."

Without committing, I stood. "Thank you, Detective

Pagarelli. I appreciate your coming today. I'll walk you to the door."

Pagarelli followed me into the foyer, so close I could feel heat radiating from him. I opened the door, turned, and looked up at him. He smiled down at me before rearranging his face in a sober expression. "Promise me you will be careful. I would hate for something to happen to you."

A sensation I hadn't enjoyed in a very long time swept through me. "I'll be careful."

"Call me if you are the least bit endangered. I don't care what time. I'll be there for you."

I believed him. He walked down the front steps and slid into his cruiser. Jess bumped me from behind, causing me to jump. "You scared me."

She closed and locked the door. "He has a thing for you."

Taking in a deep breath, I let it out slowly. "Stop trying to put ideas in my head. He's doing his job," I admonished, though I hoped she was right.

"The police aren't that attentive. He comes personally to interview you every time you call to report anything upsetting."

"He's working a murder case. I found the victim. Of course, he's interested when I report possible suspects who come to my house."

"Didn't you notice the way he looked at you?"

"Like I'm a witness to a crime, you mean?"

She waved away my answer. "I'm telling you, he's attracted to you."

Strangely, I did sense a slight connection with Pagarelli during the visit. Because my dating life was nonexistent during the past year, I questioned if the attraction was simply loneliness on my part.

"You'll stay the night," Jess said.

"Stop." I raised my hand. "That woman is not driving me out of my own home. Hunter and a loaded .380 will scare her away."

* * *

I spent Thursday working on the latest proposal requested by my editor. I received an email from her, asking me to write a textbook on the subject of dealing with difficult people. She listed a few things she hoped I would include but left the bulk of the material to be covered to my discretion. The editor expressed her desire to present the proposal to the acquisitions committee at next month's meeting, and she asked if I could meet the deadline. As with all requests from my publisher, I replied *yes*. No matter the work or time involved, I would scramble to fulfill my promise.

The particular topic came at an opportune time, since Ribar and Samantha—two nasty, threatening people—were trying my patience and sanity. My research on the subject might help me manage, or at least survive, the two bullies.

I clicked on my computer file of the publisher's template. The company required all authors to complete the lengthy proposal form if they submitted an idea for a book. I filled in the general information on the introductory page. Then, I took out a new notebook to brainstorm ideas, such as chapter headings, scenarios, tips, and advice. I made note of HR personnel, small business owners, office staff, and other professionals who might be willing to discuss the topic with me.

I drew up a list of marketing ideas. Although the publisher's staff marketed the textbooks, they asked authors what they were willing to do to promote their own books, such as arranging speaking engagements. The template provided sections for the author to describe competing and complementary books on the same subject the author suggested, a requisite for nonfiction book proposals. The information allowed the publisher to determine if there was enough of a market for another book on the subject, or if comparable books were selling.

Contemplating material to cover, I brainstormed details for chapters along with their approximate page counts. I would adjust those figures once I dug into the research and wrote a sample chapter. Two hours later, I took a short break. Using my brain made me hungry for chocolate. I reached for the container of cashew meltaways on the corner of my desk.

My week continued to deteriorate with unwanted visitors. The doorbell interrupted my writing. Hunter followed me to the door, where I glanced out the window. Tom Hansen. I froze. My ex's barrel-sized brother contaminated my doorstep, the ballcap on his head as worn out as his faded jeans. The lackadaisical expression on his face didn't ease my fears. I went to the study, where I pocketed my pepper spray. Between that and Hunter, my courage was bolstered.

Tom and I never got along. Truthfully, I couldn't stand the drug-taking freeloader. Unlike Mike, Tom took drugs long before I met him. He also ran to Mike every time he lost a small fortune at the casino or got into a scrape playing pool or cards with the guys.

Tom couldn't hold a job for more than a few months. Once when Mike did Tom's income tax return, he produced eight W2 forms from various employers. Tom brushed off those turnovers, insisting he gained a lot of experience from the work. According to him, his bosses were all idiots. I formed my own opinion about who the real idiot was regarding his work situations.

In between paychecks, Tom opted to live off whatever handouts Mike's sporadic employment provided or from the money I gave Mike. Tom's parasitical, lying, unscrupulous lifestyle lent itself exponentially to my breakup with Mike. I resented paying his brother's bills when I was the only one with a work ethic. In addition, Tom drew Mike into get-rich-quick schemes that proved to be anything but lucrative.

I released a huge sigh, cracking open the main door. He grinned. "Hi. Bet you're surprised to see me."

Tom uttered the understatement of my challenging week. My four-legged guard stood beside me, ramrod straight, ready to pounce when given the command. Hunter growled, apparently sensing my distaste for the man on my porch.

Tom retreated two steps. "Still have the mutt, I see."

"What do you want?" My tone and emphasis on *you* would intimidate most people, but he merely grinned before spreading his arms wide. "Is that any way to greet your almost brother-in-law?"

"I wasn't engaged to Mike." His wheedling tone irritated me. "What are you doing at my house?"

"May I come in? Please."

Against my better judgment, I unlocked the storm door, allowing Tom inside the foyer, confident Hunter could manage him if the need arose.

Tom removed his stained hat, uncovering a flattened mop of hair. The greasy mess needed more than a good shampooing. "I'm sorry to say I bring sad news." Hypocrisy was scrawled all over his face. He paused, eyes downcast. I assumed he thought the expression would lend impact to his words. "It's Mike."

"You mean the fact that he died?" I enjoyed spoiling his performance.

He feigned surprise. "You heard?"

I suspected he already knew I had. He was a terrible actor. "Yes." My clipped answer matched my tone.

"Don't be heartless," he cajoled. "My brother loved you. He pined for you all these years."

"Pined for me? Are you reading romance novels now, Tom? What do you want?"

"Thought you might want to talk about the happy times you and I experienced with our dearly departed."

"Wrong." I swept a hand toward the door. "You delivered your message. I'm busy."

His forced smile tightened. "I wanted to have a friendly conversation. I drove all this way because I thought you'd want to know what happened to my brother."

"Now, you've told me."

"Aren't you curious about how he died?"

"Heart attack."

Tom grunted. "It's obvious you never cared for me, but I always thought you were perfect for Mike."

I folded my arms, propping myself against the still-open main door. "Perfect for supporting him, you mean. Along with you."

"I'm not the same person I was all those years ago. I'm clean now—almost a year. I work a steady job and rent an apartment." He showed his yellowed teeth. "A pretty woman keeps me company."

"Hooray for you." Sarcasm oozed from my words. "This little homecoming has been heartwarming, but you haven't explained why you're here. In my home."

"To inform you of Mike's death. As I said, he was still

crazy about you. He even knew what you were up to these past few years."

My chest tightened. "What do you mean?"

Tom smiled in the way people do when they think they're holding a secret over someone. "Mike obsessed over you. He took pictures of you." He chuckled. "Bet you're surprised. Mike was a sneaky one. He couldn't get you out of his mind, so he captured you in candid shots." He glanced down at Hunter. "Sometimes with the mutt."

The horror of knowing Mike violated my privacy returned, but now I had proof the pictures were the result of his sick, obsessed mind.

"Since my brother loved you so much, I wanted to offer my sympathy." He gave me a once-over. "Obviously, you aren't broken up about his death and don't need comforting."

I stared at his lying face. "I was over him years ago." I moved to open the storm door.

Tom averted his gaze. "I thought so, but I, er, heard Mike left you some property."

Finally, we were getting down to what the snake really wanted. Another handout from Mike, this time from the grave. "I don't care what you learned. My business doesn't concern you."

He straightened. "It does when Mike gave you what should be mine. I visited him in the hospital after his heart attack. My brother was in bad shape. I didn't think he'd last long." Tom clenched his battered hat with both hands. "I asked him about the cabin. Mike said his lawyer had his will, and I wasn't in it." His expression was a mingling of hurt tinged with anger. "Me," he railed, wringing the hat. "His own flesh and blood. Mike confided he left Samantha the house they lived in, along with an SUV."

Maybe Tom was a better actor than I gave him credit for. I decided to hear him out to learn what he talked to Mike about at the end. Did Mike confess a crime? Tell Tom he hid the money?

Tom glared at me. "The remainder of his estate, including the cabin, went to you. I got nothing." Hatred oozed from his last words.

I kept silent, hoping he'd continue.

"I pleaded my case as his sibling, the rightful heir. I questioned his loyalty." Tom's eyes glittered. "The bum laughed at me. Argued he left me out of his will for my own good." He took one fist from the ballcap to brush his forearm across his eyes.

As much as I wanted to throw Tom out the door, I listened with curiosity and a smidge of sympathy. Being excluded from Mike's will had genuinely hurt him.

"Did you ask Mike why he gave me the property?"

He scoffed. "Of course I did. Mike blubbered about loving you and making the biggest mistake of his life by letting you go." Tom ran a hand through his greasy hair. "I told you he was obsessed. I tried to reason with him, but you know how stubborn Mike could be."

I did. Both men were hardheaded. Did Tom's badgering worsen Mike's heart attack? Did he cut Mike's survival short with the added stress?

Tom raised his voice, flailing his arms. "Mike lived a lavish lifestyle while I scraped by."

Hunter growled.

Tom's eyes widened, his body jerking back at the sound.

I stroked Hunter's fur. "You'll want to keep your voice and arms down or Hunter will think you're attacking me."

Tom heeded the warning. With a defeatist attitude, he

said, "I was Mike's sole relative. Blood should have meant something to him."

"When your parents passed, did they leave you money?"

He opened his mouth but closed it again without answering.

"I'll take your silence as a yes. Mike turned his share into a small fortune. What happened to yours?"

Tom hung his head. "I owed a few debts. My investments didn't work out."

I suspected Tom had gambled it away. "If you two received the same amount of money, why do you insist Mike is responsible for you? You are a grown man. A brother, not a son."

He brushed me off with a wave of his hat. "You don't understand how brothers look out for each other."

His *poor me* attitude annoyed me. My old resentment toward him resurfaced. "What I can't comprehend is why you still won't accept responsibility for yourself and your actions."

"My brother was a stingy miser." Tom curled his free hand into a fist at his side, clenching the hat tighter in the other. "I needed cash. Mike had loads. He made me beg for a few bucks when his bank balance contained multiple commas. He lived it up while I scraped by."

"You said that already. Maybe he wanted you to stand on your own two feet for a change."

Tom stiffened. His jaw tightened. He spoke through gritted teeth. "We were family. He had an obligation to help me when he hit it big."

"What about your job? Your *woman*?"

"Mike was a lousy brother, period. By rights, I should

have inherited his fortune. You admitted you two weren't engaged."

I shrugged. "Who knows what ran through Mike's mind? When you visited him in the hospital, did he tell you he bought the cabin?"

He sneered. "You mean his hideaway from Samantha? Mike bragged to me the day he signed the loan papers. Even invited me there a few times." The smirk dropped from his face. "Hard to enjoy myself, though, while listening to him boast about the antiques and money he hid there from her."

Tom was a wealth of information and more than willing to share. "Why would Mike feel the need to conceal possessions from her when they lived together?" I asked.

"So the miserable woman couldn't get her mitts on the bulk of his money. She moved in with him after his investments made enough to afford a nice house, but she was clueless about his real worth. She hounded him to buy her jewelry and clothes. One weekend when he was at the cabin, she hired a company to put in an in-ground pool without his permission at the house they shared." Tom blew out a puff of air. "Mike came home after fishing to find the yard torn up. They cut down his favorite shade tree and threw away his hammock. He couldn't stand Samantha. Planned to leave her out in the cold."

"Did you know Mike was seeing a woman in Punxsutawney?"

Tom's self-satisfied grin answered my question. "She wasn't much better than Samantha with her spending habits. He didn't leave her a cent."

"How do you know?"

"I attended the reading of the will. Besides, Mike told me he only included you and Samantha." He snorted. "Mike dated two other women but decided you, his ex, deserved everything." He tossed me a sleazy look. "Why? You two playing around on the side all these years?"

"You're a jerk."

His eyes sparked anger. "Why else would he choose you over me?"

Because you are a whiny, needy child instead of an adult. "Mike made his decision. You'll have to live with it."

He pointed at me with the index finger of the hand that clutched his cap. "If you hadn't seen the stupid will, you wouldn't have known about the place. No one would have expected him to leave you anything. I would have assumed ownership of the cabin without any trouble from you."

"But there was a will."

"Which you wouldn't have found out existed if the second lawyer hadn't contacted you."

The hairs on the back of my neck stood on end. Second lawyer? Did Tom know Christopher Ryder was the first one who'd tried to deliver my inheritance? How else would he know a second estate lawyer contacted me? I tamped down my fears. "What about Samantha? She would have learned of the cabin during the reading of the will, too. Wouldn't she claim entitlement?"

"Samantha was oblivious to Mike's secret life. When the attorney read the will, she went nuts hearing about the cabin and everything that went with it."

You don't say.

"I figured if she sued for the property and won, I'd marry the old bag to get my hands on the cabin." He wiggled his eyebrows. "She has a soft spot for me."

His greed sickened me.

Tom scowled. "My whole future depended on you never learning of Mike's intentions."

"Sorry that didn't work out for you," I said with a heavy note of sarcasm.

He drew himself to his full height, glaring down at me. "Turn over the deed. The property is special to me. It means nothing to you. As I recall, you didn't enjoy the outdoors."

"Like you, I've changed. Hiking is my favorite pastime." *Not*.

Tom thumped his hands on his hips. "Here's the deal. I'll give you the contents. I'll take the house with the property."

"That's hilarious, considering I already own everything."

His face reddened. "I'll hire a lawyer. Tie up the estate in court for years. As Mike's brother, I'm entitled to a share."

What was it with everyone's claims of entitlement and threats of lawsuits? "I'll give you my attorney's name."

"How are you going to maintain the property when it's located hours from here?" Tom challenged. "The house will need upkeep over the years. You'd have to hire someone to do the work for you. The cabin is isolated. Perfect for thieves to break in when you aren't there. Believe me, it would be one giant headache."

The manipulating Tom I knew had finally resurfaced.

"How much will it take to buy you out?" he demanded. "Give me a figure."

As if he could afford it. "I'll inform you if I decide to sell. Have your lawyer contact me in a few weeks. You have my address." I reached out to open the storm door.

He grabbed my arm.

Hunter leaped up, latching onto Tom's wrist. With a

vicious scream, Tom forcefully shook his arm to dislodge him, but the dog held on. "Get him off me!"

"Hunter, release," I commanded. He obeyed, but he continued to prance around, baring his teeth and growling.

Tom staggered into the doorframe. "He bit me."

I stroked Hunter's head. "Good boy."

A scarlet-faced Tom rolled up his sleeve and shoved his arm toward me. "Look at these marks."

I gave his wrist a passing glance. "You're lucky. He would've broken the skin if it weren't for your sweatshirt."

Tom jabbed a finger in Hunter's direction. "Your dog is a danger."

"Only when violence is directed at me."

He yanked down his sleeve with an indignant huff.

I gestured toward the door. "Get out, Tom."

"This is not over." At Hunter's snarl, Tom stepped through the doorway.

"It is, as far as I'm concerned." I shut the door, locking it immediately. Tom pounded on it, yelling profanities. Barking, Hunter sprang toward the door. A few minutes later, I heard the sound of Tom's vehicle starting. The break in the curtains afforded me a view of his old green clunker of a car speeding out of my driveway.

Chapter Ten

Sufficiently shaken after the altercation with Tom, I lowered myself to the floor and threw my arms around Hunter's neck. "My brave dog." While clinging to him, I pondered what I'd learned.

Tom knew the contents of the will. How far would he go to guarantee I didn't find out about the cabin? Did he know of the hidden thousands of dollars? His vague answers left me questioning the possibility. In one way, I didn't think Mike would tell Tom he hid the money since he left him out of his will. On the other hand, Mike lingered near death when Tom last visited him. Mike might have mentioned the money while under the influence of medication.

Interestingly, Tom knew Honey. He could have told her Mike died, unless he didn't want Honey to attempt to collect a share of the estate.

My heart tripped into overtime. I had experienced Tom's bad temper multiple times while dating Mike. But could he really have killed Ryder to stop him from notifying me of the will?

I questioned whether I should call Pagarelli. Tom's threat of a lawsuit was hardly police business. However, he knew about the second attorney. That said, I had no proof he murdered anyone, nor did I truly think he was capable of it.

My deliberating continued with reliving Tom's temper tantrum. He threatened me and grabbed my arm, causing Hunter to attack him. I needed to get ahead of the situation in case Tom decided to sue me for a dog attack. *Yes, definitely call Pagarelli.*

I dialed his number, but a voice message said he was unavailable. I didn't want to discuss the incident in a voicemail. I gave my name and asked him to call at his convenience.

I decided not to chance being alone. I gathered my laptop and papers and headed to the coffee shop in town, where I could write while in the presence of others.

Sitting in my car in front of the café, I wondered how credible the threats to sue me were. I dialed Corey James. "My apologies for disturbing you again. I have a quick question I hope you can answer."

"It's no trouble. I'll do my best."

"Tom Hansen visited me. Do you remember him coming to your law office to speak with Christopher Ryder?"

"Yes. Christopher mentioned the visit to me. Tom Hansen came when Mike was in the hospital convalescing after his heart attack. He asked Ryder to declare his brother unfit. Mike told Tom he'd excluded him from his will and access to his estate. Tom wanted to vacate the will. Christopher informed him that Mike was still sane and had the right to name his heirs. He was entitled to eliminate his relatives."

"Tom would be angry about that." I pictured his livid face.

James sighed into the phone. "He went berserk, raging about hiring his own attorney to fight the will. The man had no regard for his brother lying in the hospital."

Anxiety grabbed me. "Tom threatened to sue me for the estate on the grounds that he is Mike's sole surviving relative. Can he? How likely is he to win?"

Corey James replied in a soothing voice, "You have nothing to worry about. The will is a binding document of Mike's wishes. Omitting his own brother from Mike's holdings was unfortunate for you, since it's causing you problems. However, Mike may distribute his estate as he wishes." He took a breath. "On the other hand, Tom might tangle your inheritance in the courts for years if he appeals after each court loss."

"I want to sell the property. Should I wait to see if Tom or Samantha files a lawsuit?"

"Go about your business preparing to sell. Hansen and Banks could be bluffing to see if you'll meet their demands. Why give them the satisfaction?"

"Won't a lawsuit cost me a fortune in legal fees?"

"I doubt they'll sue. They may try arbitration, hoping for a positive outcome. At any rate, I'll be happy to represent you and reach an agreement to satisfy all parties. In the meantime, stop fretting about a lawsuit they may never file."

Easy for him to say. Money would flow into his pocket, not disappear the way it would from mine if I had to defend myself in court. "I appreciate your advice. Thank you."

I disconnected the call with a nauseating headache. I hadn't heard from Pagarelli yet. I'd try him again later when my head cleared.

I entered the coffee shop and ordered an iced tea.

When my headache subsided, I worked on my project. Around five o'clock, I decided to wrap up my work early and stop at the grocery store. Jess had invited me to dinner, and I wanted to buy a few things to take with me.

* * *

I pushed my shopping cart through a colorful array of fruits and vegetables, my attention focused on finding the correct ripeness of bananas. A shrill, familiar voice shouted loud enough for half the store to hear. "You think you're smart, carrying on an affair with my fiancé behind my back."

Appalled at the shocking comment, I cringed as I spun around to face Samantha Banks. Her face, contorted in anger, gave the impression of an enraged bulldog. Her wild black hair stood on end from static, or maybe too much gel. She resembled a crazed lunatic from a horror movie. Since she didn't have a shopping cart, I figured she was stalking me again. Too stunned to speak, I gaped at her.

Samantha continued to blather on in a beastly tone. "Obviously, you were after his money, but you don't deserve it." She stabbed the space in front of me with a stiff finger. "He made his fortune after he dumped you. Every cent should go to me."

Having regained my composure, I ignored the gathering crowd and answered the accusation in a voice that was a notch above a controlled whisper. "First of all, I told you we never talked or spoke after *I left him*. Second, I was unaware of his economic status until his lawyer contacted me with details of an inheritance. Third, a legal wife may be entitled to his estate, which isn't necessarily the case for someone living with him for a couple of years without the benefit of marriage."

159

Scarlet coloring crept from her neck into her cheeks. I suspected Samantha itched to bash me over the head with a stalk of celery or pummel me with raw potatoes.

She sputtered and stammered before shouting, "Liar!"

Reasoning with her would be as futile as telling a two-year-old they couldn't have a lollipop. I dropped a bunch of bananas in my cart, whirled it around, and turned my back on her. She rammed me from behind with her solid, outstretched palms. My stomach smashed into the cart's metal bar, knocking the wind out of me. I lost my balance. Flinging my arms out to keep from falling, I latched onto the closest thing to stabilize myself. Unfortunately, my choice turned out to be a bin of apples. My hands flailed through the fruit as I flopped like a dying fish. Apples scattered across the floor, causing my feet to slide out from under me. I landed against a huge box of watermelons with a thump, denting the side of the carton and my pride, and bruising my rear, too.

A gangly teenager with a sparse chin beard was stocking vegetables nearby, and he ran toward me. "Are you okay?" He reached for my elbow and tried to help me up, but my feet skittered among the apples.

"That creepy lady pushed you," he said, his breathing labored. "What's her problem?"

I wanted to explain that Samantha was no lady, but I was too busy trying to get my feet under me. "Thank you," I mumbled, clutching his arm. After steadying myself with his help, I glanced around. "Where is she?"

"She ran off after you fell. Are you hurt?"

His concern was sweet. "No." My chest, back, and right leg ached, but there was no sense in alarming him further.

"We'll need to fill out an accident report," he said,

releasing my arm. He straightened his apron. His name badge read *Archie*.

"A report isn't necessary. I'm okay, Archie." Other than my pride, bruised just as badly as my body by the unwanted attention we'd garnered from other shoppers.

A man with a sober expression waded through the onlookers. Dressed in a white shirt, long sleeves rolled to the elbows, set off by a red tie, I guessed who he was before he confirmed it. "I'm Paul, the manager. Can I help you to the office?"

"I'm fine, really. Just embarrassed."

"You needn't be self-conscious. Witnesses said the woman verbally and physically attacked you for no reason. You'll need to accompany me to fill out a report for our records."

I opened my mouth to decline.

He quickly added, "It's our standard procedure in case any injuries appear at a later time." He swooshed his arm out in front of me. "This way, please."

"I'll take care of your cart," Archie said.

Head lowered, I followed the manager through the throng of customers still gawking at the scene.

After filling out the appropriate paperwork, I paid for my groceries and left the store, still shaken from the confrontation with Samantha. I planned to put away the groceries, except for the ones for Jess's dinner, and make my way to her place. I was grateful for friends to share time with after such a horrendous couple of days.

While helping Jess prepare dinner, I explained my horrid day to her, leading with my run-in with Samantha at the grocery store.

"The witch," Jess spat, pulling ice cubes from the freezer. "If I were with you, I'd have punched her in the mouth as soon as she uttered the first words." She set a glass of iced tea in front of me. "You should've told her off."

"I wanted to settle the score, but she left before I got to my feet. All I wanted to do then was leave the store and all the gawkers." I sipped the tea.

"Did you call Detective Pagarelli?"

I nodded. "Called him earlier, but his voicemail said he was unavailable."

"Where's your phone? Call him now."

I ran my finger up along the outside of my glass. "If he doesn't return my call in another hour, I'll call him again." I still needed to tell her—and Pagarelli, for that matter—about Tom's visit.

Jess picked up her phone from the counter. "Call now, or I'll do it myself. He said to tell him if she bothered you again." She frowned. "You are too polite to the woman. She should be arrested for assault."

"Filing charges would be more trouble than it's worth since Samantha only caused scrapes and bruises, no major injuries."

"The zany lady shoved you hard enough to fall. You could have been seriously hurt if you fell on a wooden crate instead of a cardboard box." She stuck a finger in the air. "I've got a better idea. Let's find out where she's staying. We'll wait for her to come outside, let her know she can't harass you. She needs to be set straight. She can't follow you or accost you in stores. If you let her slide with this, she'll become bolder."

"She is apt to do something crazier if I confront her, but I'll fight if she causes me physical harm. She'll have to go back home soon, then I won't have to see her. Besides, I'm not finished with my story." I took a steadying breath, launching into a rundown of my conversation with Tom.

"Are you serious? What does the slime think he will gain by coming here and bothering you?"

I placed silverware around the plates. "He is convinced he should own the cabin. He grabbed my wrist in front of Hunter."

Jess laughed. "I've got no doubt Hunter showed him who's boss."

"He sure did."

Jess stopped stirring the sauce she was hunched over. "You need to be careful, Suzie. Having Tom on your wrong side is dangerous." She lowered the flame under the pot. "Remember how he treated you those times you told Mike not to lend him money or his car? He went so far as to smash your SUV's headlights to teach you a lesson."

I cringed at the memory. Mike insisted I not press charges if Tom agreed to replace the lights. "He claims he's reformed. Got sober. Has a real job."

"I don't care what he claims, the guy is a notorious liar and troublemaker. You need to stay away from him."

I added water glasses to the table. "It isn't as if I went searching for him. He showed up at my house. Besides, he gave me lots of information. This could help us figure out what he, Samantha, and Ribar want."

"You need to tell Detective Pagarelli about Tom's terrible temper when he returns your call."

I groaned. "You're right. Tom is dangerous, and his mention of a second attorney may be important to the murder case."

"If Tom's after the property, he might know about the hidden money. If he cleaned up his act, Mike possibly confided in him."

"I thought about that, but then why wouldn't he sneak up there in the middle of the night to dig up the loot?"

"He may know Mike buried money on the property, but not where," Jess reasoned. "Tom could think Mike told you the money was there and you took it for yourself."

I rubbed my temples. "I can't worry about Tom right now. I need a clear head to finish an article for tomorrow morning."

"Jake's home," Jess said.

The second Jake stepped through the doorway, Jess bombarded him with details of Samantha's grocery store antics. While we ate dinner, she topped off the story with highlights of Tom's visit.

Jake had met Tom when I dated Mike. He disapproved of the guy from their first encounter when Tom tried to convince Jake to buy into one of his conniving schemes. Convinced Mike and Tom were into illegal activities, Jake refused.

"Can your week get any rougher?" Jake asked. "This inheritance brought all the creepy crawlers out of the woodwork."

"Please don't jinx me," I implored. "The week isn't over."

Jake gave me a sympathetic nod. "I assume you called Pagarelli."

"He was unavailable and hasn't called back," Jess said.

I rubbed my forehead. "I've called him a half dozen times this week. He's probably tired of me."

"No way. Pagarelli told you to call anytime. Besides, he needs updated on the trouble from Samantha and Tom.

He's working a murder case linked to your inheritance, Suzie, and these could be viable suspects. He asked you to call with related information."

"I know, but…"

With a wry smile, Jess said, "I think he enjoys hearing from you."

And I enjoyed the sound of his voice.

Jake planted his elbows on the table. "What if Mike gave Tom a key to the cabin and he used it to search for the map during Mike's hospitalization? Then, he visited you when his search was a bust."

My pulse jumped at Jake's suggestion. "Maybe."

"Tom poses a risk. He could return to coerce you into turning over the deed. You can't invite him into your home again."

I averted my eyes. "I agree. That was stupid. In my defense, I had Hunter and pepper spray."

Jess said, "We want you to be safe."

"We do," Jake agreed. "You're welcome to stay here as long as you want."

I thanked them both for the generous offer but declined. "Tom received the message that Hunter will guard me. And he's aware I own and can handle a gun."

My phone rang. "It's Detective Pagarelli."

"We'll give you some privacy," Jake said, steering an objecting Jess from the room.

Pagarelli apologized for the delay in returning my call. "We had some trouble in the eastern end of the county. How can I help you?"

He listened without interruption while I reiterated my interaction with Samantha.

"You have the right to press charges for assault and

harassment, though those cases tend to get sticky. At the very least, take pictures of the bruising or injuries."

I thought of the bruising on my backside and quickly dismissed his suggestion. "I don't want to press charges. I'm hoping she will go back where she came from and leave me alone."

"I have her on my list to bring in for questioning in the next day or two."

I closed my eyes, bracing myself for his impending reaction. "Samantha wasn't my only problem today. Mike's brother, Tom, paid me a visit. He wants the cabin."

"Did he pressure you?"

"No, but he gripped my arm, and Hunter chomped on his wrist."

I heard his sharp intake of breath. "He assaulted you? Are you hurt?"

"No, I'm fine."

"Hunter bit him?"

"Yes, but Tom was wearing a sweatshirt. Hunter's bite didn't break the skin. No blood. It might bruise, though."

"You were on your property when this happened?"

I cringed at the question. "We were in the entryway of my house."

There was a short pause before he stated, "I'm on patrol in ten minutes. I'll be over to take your statement."

"I'm getting ready to leave the Waters' house. I'll be home in fifteen minutes." I sort of enjoyed Pagarelli's personalized attention to my case, even if technically police work and his duty were his reasons. How pathetic was my social life?

* * *

166

Thirty minutes later, Pagarelli arrived at my house, greeted me, and patted Hunter's head. I led him into the kitchen. "Please, have a seat. I made coffee and iced tea."

He removed his hat, pulling out a chair. "Black coffee would be fine."

While I poured it, he opened his notebook, flipping through the pages with his thumb. "The brother's name is Tom Hansen?"

"Yes. Jake thought this information might be helpful to your investigation."

"Mr. Waters was right," he said, writing something down. "I need all the facts available. Money makes people desperate, which brings me to another concern of mine."

His pen stopped. He lifted his gaze to mine. "You shouldn't let anyone associated with this case into your home, especially if you are alone. For your safety. Desperate people are capable of anything."

He was right, but my instinct was to find answers for Ryder's family. Unfortunately, I realized those exact instincts put me in dangerous situations.

"Do you think Tom Hansen had knowledge his brother hid thousands of dollars on the property?" he asked.

I rested my arms on the table. "I have no idea. I haven't seen him since I broke up with Mike. Years ago, as I mentioned."

"Did Mr. Hansen say where he was staying while in town?"

"No."

Pagarelli tapped his pen on the tablet. "Did he state why he paid you a visit?"

"He wanted to inform me that Mike died and offer his condolences, although I'm certain that was a ruse. He's furious that Mike excluded him from his will. Tom thinks he's entitled to all of Mike's property because he's his sole living relative. I disagreed. He offered to buy the cabin. I said I was undecided about selling, which wasn't true, and he threatened to sue me. Then, he became angry. Tom has a dreadful temper."

"All the more reason to avoid him. Call me if he approaches you again. If I don't answer, call nine-one-one." Pagarelli stopped tapping. "Do you think Tom Hansen and Samantha Banks could be working together in order to steal your inheritance out from under you?"

"I guess it's possible. They both argued that they're entitled to the entire estate. They harbor an extreme resentment toward me. Tom bragged he would marry Samantha if she fought him for the cabin."

I reached for my glass of tea and took a long swallow. "They both referred to the estate attorneys. I told you Samantha mentioned Ryder. Tom claimed I would still be clueless about the property if the second attorney hadn't contacted me."

"Wait." He straightened. "Hansen's actual words were *the second attorney?*"

I nodded.

He rolled the pen between his fingers. "These two troublemakers and Ribar are connected to the murder victim through his law firm."

His choice of words caught my attention. "He was really murdered?" The idea of any of them killing Ryder troubled me.

"I'll tell you since it will be all over the news tomorrow morning. The coroner officially declared Christopher Ryder died of an apparent gunshot wound. He's conducting further tests that we hope will give us a lead on the killer."

My ears buzzed, drowning out the rest of his explanation. I wobbled on the edge of my chair.

"Ms. Tuft. Suzie."

He handed me my glass. I focused on his face as I sipped the tea. Setting the glass aside, I admitted, "Whiteford didn't actually confirm Ryder was shot, but I'd figured someone else was involved, or at least knew about it. Though, I'd hoped he died from a fall, not a killer. Believing he died from an accident didn't upset me as much."

"That's understandable since you found him."

I covered my eyes. "Don't remind me."

He laid a hand on my shoulder. "I'm sorry. I gave you a lot to process."

His touch did much more than comfort me. My arm tingled from shoulder to fingers. I lowered my hands as he dropped his from my shoulder and straightened in his chair. I didn't want this time with him to end.

Through fumbling thoughts, I asked, "Do you think Samantha or Tom would have killed for Mike's estate?"

He shook his head. "I can't say, but every lead is important at this point. Did Tom Hansen hint at returning?"

"I didn't give him the chance. I shooed him out and shut the door in his face."

He scribbled in his notepad, then glanced up at me. A slight grin relaxed his features. "You have a habit of slamming doors in your visitors' faces."

"The unwanted ones, yes."

Pagarelli held my gaze for a few moments, then returned to his notes. "Tell me exactly what took place after you shut him out."

"Tom pounded on the door. Yelled profanities. When Hunter barked, he drove off with the tires squealing." I donned a sheepish smile. "Guess his storming off suggests future trouble."

The lines on Pagarelli's forehead deepened. "It does. In the future, you shouldn't answer the door for Ribar, Hansen, or Banks. If they cause a problem on your property, call nine-one-one." He paused again, holding my gaze. "In the meantime, try not to antagonize Mr. Hansen. I'll run a background check, then call him in for questioning. I want an answer as to how he knew the second attorney visited you." He closed his notepad. "Are you staying here alone?"

"With Hunter."

His expression was hard to read as he glanced around.

"I always set my alarm," I said. "A warning shot from my gun should be enough to scare anyone off my property. I won't let anyone but friends inside."

My safety precautions didn't bring a smile to his face. He clipped his pen to the notebook before tucking it into his pocket. "I'll assign a patrol car to make passes on your road. Please be careful. Keep your cellphone and Hunter near."

He picked up his hat, pushed back his chair to stand. "Your home is nice, but it's isolated."

"One of my favorite reasons for living here."

He nodded. "I grew up near a wooded area. Nothing comes close to nature for showing you a good time."

"The peacefulness. The beauty."

He made eye contact. "Yes, the beauty."

The sincerity in his eyes made me wonder if his visits were more than a professional duty. Mentally, I shook myself, trying hard to remember that it was just Jess's constant badgering about Pagarelli's interest that caused me to see things that weren't really there.

"If you need to talk about anyone or anything related to this case, I'm a good listener," he said with a smile.

Before I could censor myself, I blurted, "What if I wanted to talk about something other than the case?"

He grinned. "Depends."

My heartbeat quickened. Hunter chose that moment to bump up against Pagarelli's leg. I loved my dog dearly, but I regretted his timing in this case.

The detective petted him. "Call me if you run into any more trouble, Suzie. Or if you just want to talk."

My heart tripped in double time as I accompanied him to the door. Hunter trailed behind us.

Pointing to the doorknob, Pagarelli gave me one last fleeting glance. "Lock this behind me." He disappeared without another word.

I closed the door, locked it, and rested my forehead against the door jamb.

Chapter Eleven

I awoke rested Friday morning despite my worries about Tom's visit. I turned Hunter loose to explore the house. He zoomed straight for the kitchen pantry, where I stored his doggie biscuits. Dancing in expectation of a snack, his nails tapped a rhythm on the ceramic tile floor.

I held up my index finger. "Okay, but only one."

Hunter vaulted two feet off the ground and caught the treat I threw in the air. One crunch and two bites later, he'd obliterated the biscuit. I raised my hands, palms up, in an *all gone* gesture, then let him outside, refreshed his water, and poured myself a glass of tea.

Before going to my desk to write, I brought Hunter inside, not wanting to be sidetracked with worry about someone coming to my door. I had a long to-do list to accomplish before Jess and I met at one o'clock for lunch. She'd arranged to take the afternoon off from her job.

Hunter kept me company in his corner bed while I finished a post for a client's blog. Next on my agenda was the book proposal my editor had requested. I created a list of ways employees tended to annoy their coworkers. A second list included ways employees irritated employers and vice versa. I strategized how to incorporate into chapters the various ways people aggravated and provoked each other. I could begin chapters with scenarios or anecdotes of each type of annoyance, followed by suggestions for tackling these problems.

The deeper I researched into workplace problems, the happier I was with my ability to work by myself from home. I appreciated interacting with people, but my circumstances lessened those day-to-day workplace irritations. I didn't worry about an officemate playing music too loud or gabbing about everyone in the workplace. No one blamed me for leaving the lunchroom a mess or eating all the doughnuts. I wasn't accused of hogging all the customers or taking credit for someone else's work. No boss hovered over me, micromanaging my work.

Three hours and a candy bar later, my brain shut down. I logged off my computer with enough time to exercise Hunter and take a shower before meeting Jess at the restaurant.

"How about a walk, big fella?"

Hunter sprang to his feet. For a split second, I considered taking my handgun, but I slipped the pepper spray into my pocket instead.

The cool morning air on my face and Hunter's brisk pace invigorated me. Spring, my favorite time of year, brimmed with its distinct fresh scents. Mingling smells of fragrant blossoms and grass drifted on the breeze. Once barren tree limbs sprouted leaf buds that would mature over the next few weeks. Wild berry bushes turned from bare, dead-looking sticks to branches with clusters of green leaves. Forsythias bloomed in riotous yellow along the hillside. Pink and white flowering trees dotted the landscape. After a long, hard winter, I was always surprised at how quickly nature renewed itself. I took it all in with a thankful spirit.

The hum of a car engine coming toward me from up ahead drew my attention back to the road. I nudged Hunter to the berm, shortening his chain.

A green vehicle cruised into view. My stomach flipped. Tom. I tramped a few feet farther into the woods alongside the road. The car skidded to a stop beside me.

Tom rolled down his window, revealing his glowering face. "I'm not done talking to you."

The venomous words he snarled twisted my nerves into knots. Hunter's growl assured me he would ward off an attack from Tom. I wrapped my fingers around the pepper spray can in my pocket. Ignoring him, I continued walking in the opposite direction he traveled.

He revved the engine, which I ignored. Then, he drove his car in reverse, keeping pace with my stride. Edging the car closer, Tom thrust his beefy arm out of the window. His steely fingers clenched my wrist in a vice-like grip.

In an instant, Hunter leaped, his nails raking Tom's hand. The man swore and released me.

I guess some people learn the hard way not to provoke a person's dog.

Tom rolled the pane halfway up, shrieking, "Keep your mangy dog away from me!"

"Keep your mangy mitts off me, and you won't have a problem."

With a grisly scowl, he shook his fist at me.

Hunter clawed the driver's side door, his nails screeching against the metal. His powerful jaws snapped as he lunged at Tom's face through the window. Tom sprang back, inching the glass up further until there was only an open slit at the top. He hollered, "I want the cabin. One way or the other, it'll be mine."

Hunter barked a reply. I tugged on his leash and walked us a few feet from the car. My lips curved in a sly smile. "Hunter doesn't like threats." I patted his head for effect.

Tom's face took on the characteristics of a gargoyle, mean and ugly. He stretched toward the glove box. Hand on the latch, he stopped as his gaze caught the view in his rearview mirror. He straightened.

I turned and began to breathe easier. A blue and white patrol car rolled toward us, its engine drowned out by Hunter's barking. The vehicle stopped, the door opened, and Detective Pagarelli stepped out in his crisp khakis and white shirt, handgun strapped at his side and hat drawn low on his forehead. He presented a formidable sight.

Pagarelli assessed the scene, appearing to sum up the situation in seconds. His jaw clenched, eyes hard and alert.

His brow furrowed as he scanned my face. "Are you alright?"

Although I nodded, I figured his police intuition deduced otherwise.

He cupped my elbow in his hand. "You're shaking. Was he harassing you?"

"Yes," I whispered.

"Did he hurt you?"

"No."

Pagarelli studied me another moment, then released me. "Wait here. I'll take care of this." Hand on the holster at his side, he walked toward the green car.

Tom lowered his window a few inches as Pagarelli approached him, and yelled, "She set her dog on me. Arrest her and destroy her vicious mutt."

Pagarelli shot Tom a look that instantly had the bully cringing in his seat. His voice stern and hostile, the detective replied, "From what I hear, you've been harassing Ms. Tuft."

"I didn't harass nobody," Tom insisted loudly.

Hunter growled.

Tom pointed. "That's what I mean. The animal is a menace."

Pagarelli bent, stroking Hunter's back. His reward was a tail wag and a tongue lick on his chin. When he stood, he placed a hand on the roof of Tom's car, leaning toward the window. "Seems to me he doesn't appreciate you bellowing at his owner."

Tom sputtered. "He attacked me."

"May I see where he bit you?"

Tom reddened. "He didn't bite me. He scratched me." Turning up his sleeve, Tom showed off the red stripes.

An amused Pagarelli seemed to enjoy toying with the man. "Ouch. Fortunately, you won't bleed to death with those wounds."

Tom yanked his sleeve down with a huff. "I could get rabies," he grumbled.

Ha. He'd give Hunter a disease rather than the other way around.

Pagarelli shot me a glance and asked, "Did Hunter have his rabies shot?"

"He did."

Furious, Tom slammed his hand on the steering wheel. "Look at what that scraggly mutt did to my car door!"

Pagarelli inspected the damage, taking his time. "I'd say you got off easy for antagonizing Ms. Tuft. A dog protecting its owner could rip a person to shreds."

Tom swore. "I didn't antagonize nobody."

"Mind your language, Mr. Hansen."

The use of his name clearly surprised Tom. His mouth hung open a moment, then he closed it with a snap. "If you aren't going to do anything about this, my lawyer will."

Pagarelli pulled a notebook and pen from his right front shirt pocket. "What's his name? I'll need to speak with him about these harassment charges."

Tom's face puffed up as if someone had used a bicycle pump on his cheeks. Red splotches spread. "Am I free to go?"

"Yes, sir." Pagarelli closed his notebook. "Mind your speed." He gestured toward the woods. "Never underestimate wild animals in the woods. They'll dart across the road and damage your vehicle."

Tom's ears turned red. He clenched his teeth as he put his car in gear and drove away at a slow crawl.

I nearly sank with relief as Tom's car disappeared around the bend.

Pagarelli placed a hand on my shoulder, turning those gray eyes on me. "Okay now?"

I managed a *yes*. He had a way of making me think he cared about me. "Thank you. I'm glad you happened along when you did." We held eye contact. My insides had a slow meltdown.

"I am, too." He slid the hand on my shoulder down to my elbow. "I would hate to see you hurt. Or worse."

I wilted under his touch. His eyes were mesmerizing. "I would hate that, too."

He dropped his hand from my arm, and it felt as if I'd been hit by a blast of cold air. I wanted his warm touch back.

"Now," he said, "tell me why you're walking this deserted road alone when people are out to hurt you?"

His question momentarily stunned me. "Hunter is with me." The dog bumped my hand as though confirming the fact. "He guards me. Tom was afraid to leave his car."

Pagarelli gestured toward my wrist. "He still managed to leave some nasty red marks."

Instinctively, I put my hand in my pocket.

Pagarelli stared down the road. "I doubt you've heard the last from Mr. Hansen."

I silently agreed, knowing Tom as well as I did.

"Do you want to file harassment charges?" he asked.

I shook my head. "It'll be his word against mine, and he'll complain about Hunter. I don't need the aggravation."

Pagarelli pursed his lips, his expression clouded. He reached down and scratched Hunter behind the ears. "Good job. Keep looking out for your mistress."

Funny he should use that particular word.

He straightened and tugged at the brim of his hat. "It'd be better if you stayed closer to home while Mr. Hansen is in town."

"I thought the same thing." I toyed with the leash wrapped around my palm, searching for something interesting to say.

"How about I give you and Hunter a ride home?"

My heart fluttered. I glanced at the cruiser. I wished to be in the car with him, but I hesitated, remembering the barred window in the back.

He interrupted my thoughts. "You can ride upfront with me. Hunter can go in the backseat. He's not claustrophobic, too, is he?"

His smirk almost did me in. "No, he isn't."

He coaxed the dog into the cruiser and opened the passenger door for me.

I slid onto the seat, my pulse quickening. *I'll be sitting a couple of feet from him. Oh, so close.*

Pagarelli handed me the seatbelt. I observed him walk around the front of the vehicle, then fold himself behind the steering wheel.

He started the engine. "First time riding in a patrol car?"

I was glad to be able to say *yes* to his question. I nodded. "Feels rather strange. Glad I'm sitting in the front."

"You would be surprised how many people I come across who are claustrophobic." He stared out the windshield.

His statement made me feel less self-conscious. "I'd go berserk if I was handcuffed or thrown into a jail cell. How do the claustrophobics you arrest deal with that?"

"We have ways to handle the problem."

The mere thought unnerved me. I didn't want to know the methods they used.

Pagarelli rolled along the road, windows wide open, his forearm relaxed on the door. He scanned the woods. "Do you hunt?"

"No. I couldn't kill an animal."

"I wondered when you said you own a gun."

"As I mentioned before, I practice at a local gun club with some friends."

"You a good shot?"

I smiled. "Good enough to make my friends jealous."

The remark earned me a grin. As if on cue, a flock of wild turkeys strutted across the road, their necks jerking in time with their steps.

He stopped to allow the turkeys to cross. "I might add this place to my list of hunting spots."

I might take up hunting if you're planning to be in my area.

Pagarelli swung into my driveway with ease. A pang of disappointment hit me. I appreciated his company.

He put the cruiser in park. "I don't suppose I can convince you and Hunter to walk over in the Waters' neighborhood where you are surrounded by houses and people."

Hunter lifted his head at the sound of his name.

Was Pagarelli tired of rescuing me? "I could, but I would miss the woods. This is the best time of year to experience nature." I breathed in deeply. "I love the scent of spring blossoms. All the different flowers are gorgeous for such a short time." I sensed his gaze on me, and I kept my eyes focused on the road ahead.

"My favorite time of year," he said.

It was as if he read my thoughts. If only his captivating smile hadn't left me tongue-tied. "Mine, too."

He exited the vehicle, let Hunter out of the back, and walked us to the front door.

My pulse raced as wildly as my heart. I reminded myself to settle down. This was not a date.

I unlocked the door and let Hunter inside.

Pagarelli moved closer, shifting from one foot to the other. "Tell you what. If you can't refrain from walking this road, call me. If I'm free, I'll tag along."

Time stopped. Did I hear him right? Was he proposing to accompany me on a personal basis? "I will."

"Okay. Deal." He gestured toward the house. "Keep your doors locked and the alarm on while you're here."

I reined in my crazy thoughts and saluted him. "Yes, Detective Pagarelli."

With a smirk, he turned and walked to the cruiser. I stood at the doorway until he pulled onto the road. Stumbling inside the door, I called out to Hunter. "I think he likes me."

Hunter barked his approval.

Hurrying, I rushed through my shower to be on time for lunch with Jess, eager to share the details of Tom's latest antics. I planned to keep the ride with Pagarelli to myself for now. No sense in fueling Jess's active imagination.

I laughed. Who was I kidding? I couldn't wait to tell her.

* * *

I backed out of my garage, keeping an eye out for Tom, and drove to the restaurant. My eyes wandered to the rearview mirror several times, but no one followed me.

The sunny day lightened my mood as I waited on the restaurant patio for Jess. Hanging baskets of bright petunias and pansies greeted guests. Long wooden boxes filled with additional colorful flowers and greenery lined the railings. I sank into one of the rockers with comfy oversized navy cushions.

Jess approached, dressed in a swirl print jumpsuit. She crossed the street in front of the restaurant. Together, we entered the lobby and were seated at a roomy table along the back wall by a hostess in a stylish white silk blouse and navy skirt. The sun spread its radiance through the bare windows.

Iris, our favorite waitress, was her usual upbeat and friendly self while obtaining our drink orders. "I'll be right back with your beverages while you gals look over the menu."

Jess snapped her red napkin open, placing the cloth on her lap. "Let's hear it."

I slid the silverware off my napkin and unfolded the cloth. "What?"

She clicked her tongue. "You have news. It's written all over your face."

I picked up my laminated menu. Jess reached over and lowered it onto the table.

"Out with the details."

I chuckled. "Oh, okay. I have news."

Iris returned with our drinks at that moment, making Jess bounce in her seat with anticipation. I imagined her mind telepathically screaming *hurry up!* at the waitress so she could hear what I had to say.

We placed our food order, Iris left, and I told Jess about the encounter with Tom. "You should've seen him squirm. He was furious that Pagarelli sent him on his way without arresting me and Hunter." I smiled. "Pagarelli appears whenever I need him."

"Talk about a personal white knight," Jess said, fanning herself.

"It's not like that. He was on patrol." I took a deep breath. "He gave me and Hunter a ride home."

"Suzie!" Jess shouted.

"Shh." I glanced around the room.

She lowered her voice to above a whisper. "Did you sit beside him? What did you two talk about? Did he ask you out? This is so exciting! Tell me everything." She rubbed her hands together.

I almost melted into the seat beside him. "Not much to tell during a one-mile drive. Spring is his favorite month."

She placed a hand over her heart. "Aww, and spring is yours."

I raised my eyes toward the ceiling. *Don't give her any more ideas.* "He dropped us off and left."

Jess flopped against her chair, her displeasure obvious. "He didn't ask you on a date?"

"No."

"You had your chance with him. Why didn't you invite him in?"

"He was on patrol. As in, working."

She reached for her drink. "Yeah, yeah. I only want you to find someone special to spend your life with."

The fact that I was single and not currently dating bothered Jess more than me. I cherished my alone time, although dinner and a movie with a nice gentleman appealed to me. I suspected as the years passed, I'd want a man's companionship, but I wasn't rushing into anything.

I folded my hands on the white tablecloth. "Let me tell you what I found online. Ribar had the lengthiest virtual footprint because of the arrests and convictions Pagarelli mentioned. He has lived in a half dozen places and is unemployed."

"Must be why he has time to hassle you," Jess groused.

I nodded. "Tom has a couple of petty judgments, nothing recent. His address is listed as his parents' home, even though he told me he has an apartment. He probably moved into his parents' place after they died."

"Figures," Jess said. "Anything not to pay rent."

"Samantha has an interesting past. I found articles about her marriage to a wealthy businessman. They divorced three years ago, and she received a hefty settlement. A couple of the news clips suggested a nasty split."

Jess gave her head a *la-di-da* shake. "Bet she cheated on him with more than Mike."

"You'll appreciate this tidbit about her. She was active online, posting daily until two days ago. She conceivably stopped because she's too busy shadowing me. She listed her status as married and her occupation as housewife, even though Mike never married her."

Jess pulled out her phone. "I've got to check Samantha's posts." Within seconds, she landed on Samantha's page and laughed. "Oh, man. This is priceless."

She tilted her screen toward me, exposing a photo of Samantha and Mike cuddling in happier times. The caption read, *My Lost Love*. Written underneath was, *I'll love you forever*.

Seeing Mike's face jarred me.

"He was leaving you, idiot," Jess snapped at the photo.

I fingered the edge of my napkin. "I've been considering motives."

"Uh huh." Jess scrolled through Samantha's social media pages, her attention diverted to the phone screen.

I ruminated aloud, hoping to spark something in my brain. "Everyone who approached me about the cabin seems to have a stake in my inheritance. They all wanted to keep Ryder from meeting with me."

Jess laid her phone on the table. "Your string of visitors this week is enough to make my head hurt. Ribar, Samantha, Tom. Honey might show up this week."

"I forgot about Honey. She's the person most entitled to the cabin."

Iris set our grilled chicken, strawberry, and pecan salads in front of us and placed a basket of warm rolls in the middle of the table. "Anything else I can get you?" she asked.

We shook our heads, and she left.

I picked up my silverware and speared a strawberry. "If Honey shows up on my doorstep threatening a lawsuit, I'm going to scream."

"Invite Honey in and call Samantha to come and meet

her," Jess chuckled. "Then, step back and watch the fireworks between them."

I sighed. "I feel sad for Honey."

Jess picked up her phone, swiping the screen. "I wonder if she has a social media account."

Really? "How can you find her with only her first name?"

"How many Honeys can be listed?" She frowned at her cell screen. "Oh. A lot." She turned off the phone and returned it to the table.

"I wonder why Mike excluded her from his will."

Jess blew out a puff of air. "You don't know what went on between them. Maybe he used her."

I lifted my iced tea glass. "It doesn't matter. If Honey put up with Mike, she deserves something."

Jess ripped apart a roll and slathered it in butter. "What about you? You invested enough time dealing with Mike's dreadful behavior. You deserve a reward. Apparently, he thought so, too."

She laid her knife across her bread plate. "Sell everything and be done with it. Put the proceeds in an account. Take a vacation. Marry the handsome Detective Pagarelli and produce a couple of beautiful kids."

I choked on the bite of chicken in my mouth.

Jess snickered.

"This is serious, Jess. I've been upset since learning the body I found is tied to my inheritance. Ryder died on my account."

"The guilt for his death belongs to the killer. You're an innocent party in all of this."

I paused, fork in hand. "Truthfully, the unwanted visitors this week have rattled my nerves."

"I can tell how upset you are. Let's switch to a happier

subject. You need a break from everything and everyone connected to Mike's property."

A break would be wonderful, but Ryder's death niggled at the back of my mind.

"Do you think you'll build up the nerve to ask Pagarelli out if he doesn't make the first move?" Jess asked.

I speared another ripe, juicy strawberry. "I have no intention of asking him out." I loaded lettuce on with the strawberry and topped it off with a pineapple chunk.

"Why don't you invite him to dinner for helping you? In this day and age, women ask men out all the time."

I put the forkful of salad in my mouth and chewed slowly, in silence.

Jess took the hint. "Okay, okay. Let's talk about vacation plans."

Throughout the rest of lunch, we discussed summer vacations. Jess and Jake secured reservations for an island resort. I planned to visit my cousin in Myrtle Beach. We decided to shop for vacation clothes together later in the week. A woman could always use a new pair of sandals.

By the time we were ready to pay the bill, I had relaxed. Iris collected our money and bid us a nice afternoon. Heading toward the all-glass door, still caught up in our chat about bathing suits, I glanced out and immediately gasped, backing away and pulling Jess with me.

"What?" she squawked, tripping over her feet.

I steadied her and whispered, "Ribar is outside." My heart pounded in overtime.

Jess paled. "Are you sure?"

"Positive. I'd recognize Paul Bunyan anywhere. He's even wearing the same flannel shirt and dirty hat he had on yesterday when he stopped at my house." I cringed. "He's waiting for us."

Jess edged around the hostess station. "I want to see." She peered out through the corner of the window, careful to keep herself hidden from view. Forehead creased, she suddenly flattened herself against the wall. "You're right. He's here." She rummaged in her purse for her cellphone. "Jake's home. I'm calling him to give us a ride."

The hostess approached us with a wary expression. We must have resembled two fugitives hiding from the law. "Is everything alright, ladies?"

I composed myself, offering what I hoped was a reassuring smile. "Yes. We're waiting for our ride. He's late."

The hostess thanked us for coming and walked away.

Jess blurted into her phone, in a too-loud, shaky voice, "Jake."

I put a finger to my lips as a caution.

"He's here," she whispered in a lower octave. "The man from the cabin." After a pause, she added, "Suzie spied him hanging around outside the restaurant. He's standing in the lot where she parked her car. We're inside." Another second ticked by. "No, he didn't see us. Hurry. Love you."

She disconnected the call but continued to clutch the phone in her hand. "Jake's on his way. He said to stay in here until he pulls up out front. He's also notifying Pagarelli that Ribar is loitering outside."

My limbs trembled. "Do you think he followed us here?" I knew the answer, but hoped I was wrong.

Jess's eyes were huge. "Yes, don't you?" Her lips quivered. "I'm scared. What if he confronts you when you are alone and forces you to give him the money?"

I shushed her again. "He may be unaware Mike buried the money."

"Then why is he so tight-lipped about what he has

stored at the cabin? You'd give back whatever he wanted if he said what *it* was, wouldn't you?"

She needed to ask? "Of course. Anything to get rid of him."

Jess fidgeted. "What if he flees when the police cruiser arrives?"

"Good riddance to him. Maybe he'll take a hint and leave town."

Pagarelli arrived before Jake. He didn't flash his lights or blare the siren. He parked the cruiser in the lot across from the restaurant and another detective in the car climbed out, strolling toward the parking meters. He appeared to check each car's meter status. Pagarelli remained in the cruiser. I couldn't catch sight of what he was doing.

Ribar continued his lackadaisical lean against his truck, smoking a cigarette, unfazed by the police presence.

Jake pulled up to the curb in front of the restaurant patio and turned on his four-ways. Jess and I pushed through the door ahead of two other women. We hurried down the steps as if escaping for our lives. My eyes were drawn toward Ribar, who flicked his cigarette onto the ground and opened his truck door.

We piled inside Jake's truck. "What about my car?" I asked.

"We'll come back for it later."

I peered out the back window as Ribar maneuvered his truck from the curb, traveling in the same direction. The detective checking the meters jumped into the patrol car. Pagarelli entered traffic two cars behind Ribar.

Jake turned off the main road. Thankfully, Ribar continued straight ahead with the cruiser following close behind.

"He's gone." I shifted around in the seat. "Pagarelli's following Ribar."

Jake's neck and shoulders were stiff. "I can't believe the outlaw followed you two."

"I'll speak to Pagarelli about his lurking around," I promised. My body shuddered from the cold dread seeping into my bones. Samantha, Tom, and Ribar were threats. "I'm sorry I dragged the two of you into this mess."

"It's not your fault," Jess said.

"I'm glad we can be here for you," Jake added.

I cherished my wonderful friends. "Can we swing back around for my car?"

Jess shifted in her seat to face me. "Why don't you stay with us for a few days, Suzie?"

"I'm confident Ribar got the message to leave me alone since Pagarelli followed him," I assured her. "I'll be extra careful."

Jess sighed. "I know, you won't let him run you out of your house."

"Right."

Jake dropped me off at my car. "Don't take unnecessary chances," he reminded me.

"Call me later," Jess shouted from her open car window.

Later after dinner, I received a call that frayed my nerves even further. After hanging up with the police, I called Jess. "The Punxsutawney police called me. The alarm went off at the cabin."

"Oh, no," Jess cried. "Ribar."

"He's in town. Maybe Tom or Samantha. Or Honey."

Jess put her phone on speaker so Jake could hear about the break-in. "What did the police say?"

"The security company monitoring the cabin called their station a few hours ago. Two detectives investigated and found someone had broken in and trashed the place. Whoever did the damage fled by the time the detectives arrived."

I sagged into a chair, resting my head against the back. "They overturned furniture, broke some things. They emptied cupboards and drawers, strew the contents everywhere. The police want me to come up, survey the damage, and determine if the intruders took anything. They doubt missing items will be recovered. Corey James gave me insurance information with the house papers. I'll call them, but how am I supposed to pinpoint what's missing when we didn't finish inventorying everything?"

"We're all off tomorrow," Jake said. "We'll take a drive up and check the damage before too much time passes."

Jess and Jake were coming through for me again. "I'm grateful for the offer."

"I'm curious about the boat and SUV," Jake said. "At least Mike had them insured."

"Forgot about those," I exclaimed. "I was thinking of all the antiques we didn't have room for in the truck to bring back here. The dining room furniture and the bedroom sets were fine quality."

"We'll leave around nine. Don't worry, we'll figure everything out."

"Maybe the three of us can determine if anything was stolen," I said. "I'll advise the local police we're coming."

I sighed. Another sleepless night.

Chapter Twelve

O n Saturday morning, we drove to the cabin as planned, unsure of what we'd find. My heart pounded faster with every mile, rising to a frenzy by the time we parked. I questioned why the break-in affected me so adversely. I had no attachment to the place, but I reasoned that it was a violation of my privacy and property just the same.

"The police will stop in to check on us," I said. "We can go inside by prying off the plywood they nailed over the door. The insurance adjuster will be here later this morning. We shouldn't move things until he sees the damage."

My stomach churned as I followed Jess and Jake to the front porch. Jake's boot hit the first porch step. He paused. "Let me look first. The key, Suzie?"

I held out the keyring. "Do you think the criminal came back?"

"I don't, but I'll determine what we're walking into." He mounted the steps, toolbox in hand, and ducked under the caution tape strung across the porch railing. "They broke in through here," he called to us, removing the caution tape and the board covering the door.

"Good thing they boarded up the place. This door won't close properly with the damage it sustained. The wooden frame is splintered, and the hardware is bent enough to prevent the lock from fastening." He crouched down to examine the latch. "The bolt is ruined. I'll pick one up in town after lunch, but we'll wait for the insurance adjuster's inspection before I make repairs." He ran his hand along the frame. "I'll need to replace this wood, too."

"Why didn't the security system stop him?" I bit my lower lip. Would my home system stop an intruder, or was I foolishly counting on it?

Jake shrugged. "I imagine he figured the police would take a while to get out here once the alarm sounded. If the criminal heard the sirens, he could run out the back and disappear into the woods. Chances of the police finding him would be slim." He pulled a gun from his side holster. "The burglar would be stupid to return to the scene of the crime. If he does, he's in for a rude awakening."

"Please be careful," Jess pleaded as Jake disappeared inside the cabin.

"What did Mike involve me in, Jess?" The wind rustled the leaves, fluttering my bangs. I stared at the cabin.

Slowly shaking her head, Jess sighed. "I wouldn't put anything past that lout."

A loud crack sounded from the surrounding woods. We both gasped, jumping in surprise.

"What was that?" Jess whispered. She ran for the porch.

I followed, less alarmed. I experienced such noises all the time in the woods near my home. "Maybe a deer or other large animal."

"A bear?" Jess put a hand to her throat.

Jake threw open the door.

"Ahh!" Jess cried out, arms flailing.

"What's wrong?" Jake asked, pulling her into his arms.

"You startled me," she replied, her chest heaving.

"We heard a noise," I explained, pointing to where the sound occurred. "Loud. Maybe a tree branch snapping."

Jake leaned over the porch railing. "If it's a deer or a bear, your screams will have scared it off." He gestured toward the door. "Prepare yourselves for a mess inside."

Jess and I stepped over the threshold, sucking in our breaths in unison. The place was an utter disaster. My stomach dropped. It would take an enormous amount of work before the cabin was ready to sell.

Jake wore a disgusted expression. "Every room was tossed. To wreck the place to this extent, the perpetrator spent a lot of time here. Either the police were slow to respond, or more than one person caused the damage."

Jess stood behind him, surveying the room with critical eyes. "Do you think they were searching for the money we found?"

"Or the map?" I asked.

"Could be either," Jake said. "We may never know, but I'm guessing they were after the map if they tossed the place like this. We'll go outside later and find out if they were digging around where we uncovered the cans of money."

"We didn't disguise the places where we dug. What if they found the holes and think I have the money?" I wanted to kick myself. "You can bet I'll keep Hunter close, now."

Jess patted my shoulder. "You'll be safe with us."

Jake said, "Notify the police. They can add extra patrols."

"What?" Jess glared at him, incredulous.

He swiped a hand over his face. "I don't think whoever destroyed the cabin will stop with this search, Jess."

Her eyes were watery, and I watched as she began to shiver. "Do you think they'll come after us? Are we in danger?"

Jake put his arm around her waist. "These culprits have all of our addresses and know we can identify them. That puts us in danger, but I think they'd be stupid to come after us in town when the police are actively interviewing suspects and working the case."

"They are stupid," Jess confirmed.

"We can't underestimate them," I said. "Ribar, Tom, and Samantha are trouble. Who knows who else is involved?" I looked to Jake. "What should we do?"

"We'll inform our local authorities. I'll have my buddies keep an eye out for strangers in town."

Jess looked on edge despite Jake's promise. He kissed her forehead. "Don't worry, baby. I'll protect you."

It was sweet how much he adored her. "Maybe Honey and her friends did this," I reasoned. "If she's angry enough."

Jake nodded. "If Honey has a key to the cabin and tried to enter, she knows I changed the locks. It's possible she retaliated." He placed a hand on each of our backs, giving a light push. "Check if her boxes are still in the closet. I'm going to investigate the shed and garage."

We had a difficult time passing through the wrecked great room without stopping to assess the damage or tidy the area, but we were on a mission. We skirted around upended sofa cushions and pillows scattered across the floor, taking care to step over broken knickknacks.

"What a mess," Jess said.

The disaster continued into the bedroom. We stood in

the doorway, stunned into silence. My spirits sank to the floor when I saw the rumpled bedspread and strewn pillows.

Dresser drawers we'd emptied on our previous visit had been pulled out and discarded on the floor. A lamp lay in their midst, its shade deformed from being stomped on.

I walked over to the bathroom. *Ugh.* The beautiful spa-style retreat was in complete disarray. The candles were smashed, as was the mirror on which they sat. The ceramic towel rack, stripped from the wall, had been cracked in half. The shower door hung ajar, revealing a roll of toilet tissue discarded in the whirlpool tub. I picked up the fancy gold soap dispenser from a puddle of spilled liquid on the floor.

Breathing a sigh, I was thankful for removing the personal products from the drawers already. At least they hadn't ended up scattered and smashed with the rest of the bathroom contents. I stared at the strewn items, trashed candles, and soap dispenser. I would make the needed repairs to the damaged wall, which held the towel rack, and replace the shower curtain.

"Whoever did this should be knocked silly," I called to Jess.

She walked around the dresser drawers, muttering to herself.

In the bedroom, I checked on Honey's boxes. I opened the door to the oversized closet, then sprang back with a scream. Something squeaked while scurrying out from one of the upturned boxes of Honey's clothing. The varmint ran out of the closet and raced across the top of my shoe. "Eek, eek!" I danced in circles, my mind unsure of which direction to run.

Jess whirled. "What happened? Eek!" Within seconds, she was busy doing her own hopping around. She lunged, landing on her knees on the bed. Scrambling to a sitting position, she flattened herself against the headboard. "How did that thing get in here? What is it?"

I took a few deep breaths and followed her gaze. A red-tailed squirrel sat upright on the dresser, still as a statue, peering at us with glassy eyes. What a relief to discover he wasn't a supersized rat.

"He's a squirrel," I said, breathless. "I opened the closet, and he shot out like a clown from a circus cannon. Scared me silly."

"I'm not crazy about sharing the room with a wild animal. Let's chase him out the patio door."

I nodded. "You go around that way and open the door. I'll walk this way to shoo him out." I held up a hand. "Slowly."

We each stepped forward. The little varmint vaulted from the dresser and landed, clinging, to the ceiling fan. Jess covered her head with her hands and leaped from the bed with a squeal. We both scooted toward the far wall.

"Do you think he has rabies?" she asked.

"I'm not giving him a chance to bite me to find out."

Jess kept her hands over her hair. "If he jumps on my head, I'm going to faint."

The squirrel flung himself from the ceiling fan to the bed, skittering around on the mattress before launching himself onto the nightstand, scattering flowers from an over-turned vase.

"I'll grab a box from the closet and attempt to catch him." I inched along, my back pressed firmly against the wall.

The squirrel dropped to the ground, where he scuttled across the floor. Outsmarting me, he didn't head for the patio. Instead, he scurried out the bedroom door and down the hall.

"He's headed for the great room," I shouted.

We collected ourselves, hurried down the hall, then skidded to a halt in front of the fireplace. I glanced around the room. "Where is he?"

Jess's head swiveled. "I don't see the little rascal."

I threw up my hands. "Wonderful. We'll never find him. He'll chew through this horrid sofa and build a nest inside." I lifted a cushion from the floor. Jess did the same.

"Grab an end," I instructed, grasping the arm of the sofa. "He might be underneath."

We tossed the pillows onto the sofa, moving every piece of furniture. He was nowhere to be found. I ran my forearm over my brow. "With this open floor plan, he could be anywhere. I'll check the dining room. Stay here, and call me if you spy him."

"Sure, leave me here with the monster," Jess whined.

I rolled my eyes. "Really?"

"Really. I'm coming with you."

We searched through the dining room chaos, but we didn't find the squirrel.

"He'll die in here and stink up the place like the one Jake found in the fireplace," Jess said.

We gave up, disgusted, and returned to the great room. I gestured around the area. "Let's work on figuring out if something is missing."

We walked around, trying to recall what was in each room, while trying not to disturb anything until the insurance adjuster assessed the situation. I snapped pictures of the mess and of two tall broken antique vases.

"I'm glad Jake suggested we take home some of the

antiques when we were here last time. At least those items survived. Destroying them would constitute a senseless loss, considering the values the estate firm placed on them," I said.

We searched in silence, my thoughts churning to remember what else of value was in the room. The couch cushions had been ripped apart. "Someone was thorough," I said, holding up a shredded pillow.

"After the map," Jess said.

"Unless they didn't want to leave anything useful," I suggested. "If Honey or Samantha did this in a fit of rage, their motive would be to ruin everything, whether it was valuable or not."

"Trashing that gaudy couch wasn't the worst idea," Jess reasoned.

"Why would someone destroy valuable antiques instead of stealing them?" I wondered aloud.

"Who knows." Jess held up a battered painting. I shook my head at the pathetic damage to a work of art and went about photographing it.

Jake reappeared in the doorway, followed by a gentleman in a gray suit. "This is Henry Hoagg, the insurance adjuster."

We exchanged pleasantries, and the man went to work with his camera and tablet. He finished his assessment within forty-five minutes.

"Ms. Tuft," he said, "I'll work up the figures and let you know where we stand."

"Is it okay to clean this mess?" I asked.

"Yes, I have all I need."

I thanked Mr. Hoagg and bid him a good day.

Jess checked her watch. "Jake wants to eat lunch around one. That gives us about two hours." She picked up a battered throw pillow from the floor and tossed it to me. "Shall we begin?"

"I'll get the rubber gloves from the laundry room."

Returning with cleaning supplies in hand, I sighed for what felt like the hundredth time. "Detergent pods are scattered across the floor." Frowning, I handed Jess gloves and a rag. "There's a puddle of mixed liquids on the floor. The fumes gagged me. I opened the window to air the room out before we work in there."

"Did you check the back bedrooms?"

"Destroyed."

Jess crinkled up her nose in disdain. "Couldn't the jerk leave one room intact?"

"Apparently not."

We started the disgusting job of picking up the litter left by the intruder. The room reminded me of a scene from a movie, with its upholstery ripped to shreds, lamps and vases smashed.

"Hey, remember the frame with Honey's photo?" I asked, straightening a lampshade that had survived the abuse.

Jess pointed at the end table beside the sofa. "I left the picture right there. Upside down to hide her face."

"I thought so." I glanced around. "I don't see it anywhere."

She blinked. "Do you think Honey was here and took it?"

I swept bits of glass into a pile. "Not if she didn't take her clothes."

"Samantha, then."

I extended a dustpan to Jess. "She'd take the picture for spite."

"Or to track down the woman Mike cheated on her with." Jess squatted in front of the heap of broken glass.

I swept the debris into the dustpan. "Or to throw her in the trash." We glanced at each other, thoughts whirling.

In the kitchen, the condition of the area bordered on revolting. We waded through cans, spilled dry goods, and smashed dishes to the refuse container in the corner. An empty garbage bag was the only thing inside.

"No surprise here," I said. "Why would a criminal use a trash can when they could throw everything on the floor?"

"The pig," Jess groused.

"Hog," I countered. "No photo here. Guess they took it." Jess dumped the contents of the dustpan into the receptacle.

We returned, disheartened, to the great room to finish cleaning and tidying. While Jess ran the vacuum cleaner, I gathered scattered logs and returned them to the basket near the hearth.

"Here's the photo!" I shouted over the whirr of the vacuum, pulling the frame from under the grate in the fireplace. The corner had been dented, the glass fractured. I dusted ashes from the glass with my gloved hand.

Jess switched off the vacuum. "Samantha must have tossed it in there out of jealousy."

"No. I found it positioned as if it was flung from the end table without a thought." I held the dented metal out for inspection. "The corner's caved in from hitting the side of the grate, and the glass has a roadmap of cracks. I don't believe the intruder had anything against Honey."

Jess flicked her wrist. "Throw it back. We'll start a fire and burn the thing when we're finished cleaning."

I shook my head. "I'll put it in one of Honey's boxes when I repack them."

Jess clicked her tongue. "She'll think you smashed the glass because you were jealous she was with Mike."

"Then, she'd be wrong."

I didn't catch the comment Jess made under her breath, and she refused to repeat it.

In the dining room, we discovered smashed crystal candleholders and broken glass from a picture that had fallen from the wall. I ran my hand over a gouge in the table, where a chunk of wood was torn away. I guessed that the wrought iron wall hanging had probably bounced off the surface on its way to the floor. Overturned chairs were piled in a haphazard fashion, one upholstered seat shredded.

Working without a break, we had the great room, dining area, and bedrooms tidied and cleaned in two hours. We piled the filled garbage bags by the door, turning our attention to the kitchen.

Jess texted Jake to tell him we needed another hour or so before taking a break for lunch. Still cleaning the boat, he agreed.

The mess in the area was enough to make me want to give up. I was beginning to think this kind of chaos and destruction was the work of a scorned woman, narrowing my list of suspects to Honey and Samantha. Could either one of them have killed Ryder in a similar fit of rage?

It seemed that by the time the intruder reached the kitchen, his or her anger hadn't subsided, resulting in the tearing of food boxes and dumping their contents out, along with all the sugar and spice containers.

The refrigerator door remained ajar. Since only bottled drinks were inside, nothing had spoiled. Unfortunately, the freezer yawned open, too, and its contents had been dumped on the floor, where they thawed. The food was ruined but not rotted, and I considered it a small win. We planned to discard the freezer contents, but I wanted to take the frozen foods home to dispose of in proper rubbish containers.

"What a jerk," Jess snapped. It had become her favorite word for the intruder.

I whirled around. She stood staring at the stove knobs, which lay crushed on the floor, apparently from a heavy foot.

"There is no reason to deface the stove," she fumed, picking up the knob fragments. "Why?" She held out the pieces to me.

I laughed at her serious, quizzical expression.

She pulled back the offered scraps. "What's so funny?" she asked, her tone admonishing.

"Ironic, not humorous. Why wouldn't the person break a few knobs after gouging the dining table, smashing objects, and ruining a ton of food?"

Jess smirked. "You're right. I lost my common sense for a moment." She laughed along with me.

"I think lunch is long overdue, don't you?" I suggested.

"Definitely. Let's get ourselves cleaned up and worry about the rest of this mess after we eat." She pulled her cellphone from her pocket. "I'll text Jake."

I picked up a soggy freezer bag. "Are you sure you don't want to fix lunch here?"

Still laughing, Jess replied, "Can't. Some *jerk* broke the stove."

I dropped the thawing package. "Thank goodness. I think this bag held a squirrel or rabbit."

"With our luck, it would be an opossum."

We were still laughing when Jake came into the cabin. "Glad you two are having a good time while I'm slaving away outside. They sacked the garage. Someone removed the boat seats and dumped a can of oil over the interior. He left the SUV doors open. The battery's dead. I'll jump it with the truck battery before we leave for home."

"We're having fun cleaning up the garbage in here," Jess said in a mocking tone. She spun around the room, arms spread wide. With an abrupt stop, she added, "Oh, and someone smashed all the stove knobs for an extra special touch."

Jake surveyed the kitchen's destruction. He shook his head. "Incredible. We should be able to order new knobs." He nodded toward his wife. "Do you think you can write down the model and serial number from the back if I pull it out a bit?"

"First things first. Lunch."

We returned to the great room. "What damage was done in here?" he asked.

"Smashed knickknacks, vases, and lampshades. That kind of stuff. The dining table has a huge gash and there's a frayed chair seat."

"Are Honey's clothes still here?"

I nodded. "Yes, they're in the closet, but someone dumped them out of the boxes I put them in. I'll have to repack them."

Jess flapped her arms as if to take flight. "Oh, oh, wait until you hear this." She detailed the squirrel incident, presenting a monologue worthy of an Academy Award. In her version of the story, the frightened creature was a vicious animal bent on mauling us to death. Her wild eyes and flurry of gestures amused Jake.

When she finished her tale, he remarked, "He may have come down the chimney. I'll close the flue. With any luck, the critter found his way outside. Squirrels and chipmunks chew through wiring and damage other things."

While Jake bent in front of the fireplace, I said, "I guess we can eliminate Honey as a suspect since her clothes are where we left them."

"I wouldn't rule out anyone just yet," he replied. "The police dusted for fingerprints. With luck, they'll find the looter."

Jake stood, rubbing his hands together. "You two pack Honey's boxes while I wash for lunch. I'll load them in the truck. If she's at the restaurant when we stop, we'll leave them with her."

I countered by saying, "Or, we can keep them here, find out if she's at the restaurant, and tell her we'll drop them off at her house. Then, we'll have her address."

Jess nodded. "Your investigator's mind always hunts for clues."

Jake arched an eyebrow. "We don't need her address because we aren't supposed to investigate this case. Remember?"

We discussed the break-in and our various stages of cleaning during the drive to town. I made a list of supplies we needed from the hardware store, including a new lock.

The restaurant was busy. While waiting to be seated, I searched for Honey, hoping her red hair would stand out among the staff. The hostess seated us just as I spied Honey's long crimson ponytail. Her back was to us, taking an order for the guests at another table.

"There she is," I whispered with a slight nod. Jake and Jess glanced over.

"I hate to admit it, but the photo doesn't do her justice," Jess said. "She's prettier in person."

I concurred, arranging my paper napkin on my lap. "When she comes, I'll ask her to speak with me."

"Wait until after she brings our food, will you?" Jess begged. "I don't want her to spit on my salad."

"Eww. Don't say such a thing." It was too late. Jess had put the thought in my head, making me want to wait until after we finished our meal.

Honey arrived at our table quickly, pen and paper poised in her hands. She wore a smile on her face. At least, she did until she zeroed in on me. Then, she did a double take. The blood drained from her face, and her smile dissolved. She looked as if she wanted to run. Seconds passed. Honey stiffened, pursed her lips, and stepped forward. With an edge to her voice, she spoke only one clipped word. "Drinks?"

We ordered beverages. Her reaction made me self-conscious. I decided not to delay the inevitable, even though it felt awkward. "Hello. I'm..."

"Suzie Tuft," she snapped, sneering.

Chapter Thirteen

T he venom in Honey's voice raised goosebumps on my arms. My instincts warned that she was about to tear into me. I wondered if she planned a verbal or physical attack.

Jess spoke up, foiling my strategy to bolt to the ladies' room. "I'm Jess Waters. This is my husband, Jake. We're Suzie's friends."

Honey glared at me, ignoring her. "I suppose you recognized me from my photos at Mike's house." She leaned closer. "Take a good look. I'm the woman you locked out of the home I shared with him. Hope you haven't come here to gloat."

So, she did try to enter the cabin. I opened my mouth, then quickly closed it. From the corner of my eye, I saw Jess squirm in her seat.

Honey's eyes flashed. "Think you're smart for stealing the place from me?"

I remained mute. Honey prepared for a fight. Nothing I could say would temper the hatred she launched at me. I let her talk, hoping she would say something to help me figure out why Mike left me the cabin in the first place, and what Honey was capable of.

"We shared a year's worth of happy weekends," she said in a soft voice. "We had extra days together during the week when he managed to escape his sour girlfriend." She studied her fingernails, though her mind seemed elsewhere. "We loved each other."

Saddened by the pain in her voice, I realized her vented anger distracted her from heartache. I'd used the same tactic myself when I discovered Mike's infidelity. "I'm sorry for your loss."

Honey's head snapped up. "Ha. I'll bet you are."

Her reaction caught me off guard, although I should have expected such loathing.

She lowered the notepad to her side, fisted her free hand around her pen. "You never treated Mike right. I can't understand what he saw in *you*."

Taken aback, I stared at her. "You don't know me."

Her face reddened, either from embarrassment or ire. Her voice rose. "You ran him into the ground. You broke his heart."

Mercifully, our table was tucked in a corner, not in the middle of the room crowded with diners. I worried the restaurant patrons would hear a skewed version of my failed relationship with Mike from his mournful girlfriend.

Honey shoved the notepad and both fists into the front pocket of her apron. She spat out in disgust, "He never recovered from your rejection. Your betrayal."

Heat crept up my neck with the arousal of my anger. Not wanting to alienate Honey before learning whatever she knew about my inheritance of the cabin, I tamped down my feelings.

Jess said, "Wait a minute..."

Speaking an octave higher, Honey overrode her objection. "Mike kept a box hidden in his closet filled with old pictures of you. He never noticed I went through them. I wanted to shred that trash into a million pieces, the way you shredded his heart. The poor man couldn't shake off the past, even after you cheated on him."

"He...he told you I betrayed *him?*" What an incredible liar Mike was.

"I loved him better than you ever could," Honey continued. "I was faithful to him. I dreamed of the day the two of us would burn your photos and cheer as the past turned to ashes."

"Well, aren't you Little Miss Hypocrite?" Jess noted sarcastically. "You were dating a man who was cheating on the woman he lived with."

Honey started toward Jess.

Jake held up a hand and cleared his throat. "Mike stalked Suzie."

Honey jerked her head toward him. "You lie."

Unflappable, he continued, his voice low and assertive. "I'm telling the truth. Many of those pictures you found were recent. He secretly photographed Suzie on her porch. Entering and leaving stores." Jake glared at the woman. "Mike even photographed her in my yard last month."

Honey whipped her hand out of her apron pocket, stabbing a finger in my direction. "She ran off with someone else. If Mike hounded her, he wanted revenge."

Her words hit me as hard as her venomous tone. "He was unfaithful to *me*," I countered.

She gritted her teeth, hissing barely above a whisper, "Liar."

"You're out of line, lady," Jake said. "We want another waitress."

But Honey wasn't finished with me. "What did you do to force Mike into signing our cabin over to you? It's mine. My sweat went into decorating the place."

"Explains a lot," Jess mumbled. Jake laid a hand over hers.

Honey sent Jess a withering glare.

My stomach tied itself in knots. "I hadn't seen or heard from Mike in years, Honey. And I sure didn't know he had a will."

Tears welled in Honey's eyes. "He planned to leave Samantha. We were to be married in a few months. We arranged to relocate to another country." Her mascara ran in rivulets. "He would have forgotten you if we'd escaped all the horrible memories." She swiped her cheek. "Mike saved money for us. A fortune. We would've enjoyed an even more wonderful life than the one we already shared." She used a corner of her apron to wipe her face. "Except you ruined everything."

Hearing Mike had planned to escape to another country convinced me he had obtained his money illegally, including the cans he buried.

I didn't see the restaurant manager approach until he stepped between Honey and our table. "Everything okay here, folks?"

"No," Jake replied, his voice calm. "Please assign us a different waitress."

The need to defend myself before Honey left plagued me. "You can't blame me for Mike's heart attack."

She sidestepped the manager, creeping closer to me. "He died from the dagger you left in his heart." Tears streamed down her cheeks. She swiped at them with her fingertips, but their furious flow continued.

"Take your break," the manager stated to Honey. She

fled, wailing. I sat open-mouthed as she scurried around the counter before disappearing through the swinging doors to the kitchen. The manager folded his hands in a prayer gesture, obviously beside himself with embarrassment. "I'm sorry for that display. Honey is one of our best waitresses. Please, enjoy your lunches on me today."

"It's okay," I assured him. "I understand she's upset over the recent loss of her fiancé." I twirled the end of my hair around a finger. "We knew him."

"I'm sorry for your loss, too," the manager said. "I'll have someone else serve you at once." He trotted off, beckoning another server.

"That was interesting," Jess said in the wake of his departure. "Honey is certainly delusional."

I shook my head. "No, she really loved him."

Jess smirked. "Another sucker."

I blinked. She was right. I was the first of many.

"Jess," Jake cautioned.

She slapped a hand over her mouth. "Sorry. I didn't mean to imply you were one."

"No offense taken." How could I be insulted when Jess spoke the truth? "Mike promised Honey he would leave Samantha and marry her. You saw how broken up she was. Honey loved Mike."

Jake said, "Her sorrow was the only reason I didn't jump to your defense when she began badgering you. I thought my interference would make matters worse."

The manager reappeared with a tray of mixed appetizers, sliding it in the middle of the table. He added a stack of small plates. "On the house. Enjoy."

When he was out of range, I said in a hushed voice, "I'm glad you spared Honey's feelings, Jake. I've experienced heartache like hers." I twisted my napkin. "Perhaps, I caused Mike more pain than I understood back then."

Jess shook her head. "If Mike hadn't tried cocaine, things might have worked out between the two of you."

"Would they?" My mind drifted back to the last painful days of my relationship with him. To the evening I arrived at his apartment to surprise him with a romantic dinner. I let myself in with the key he'd given me, pushed open the door with my shoulder, arms laden with groceries. I called his name, then the ground seemed to shift under my feet.

How many times had I relived the moment Mike streaked out of the bedroom wearing a horrified expression and a pair of unzipped jeans? No shirt. No socks. "Baby," he'd slurred. Samantha flitted out moments later, wearing Mike's robe, loosely belted, her black hair tousled. She wore the grin of a satisfied victor.

Adding to my anguish, Mike's glassy, ill-focused eyes rolled toward the coffee table in the middle of the room. There, I spied the drug paraphernalia, the traces of white powder. My mind scrambled to comprehend. Understanding had dawned on me, then. I'd unwittingly walked in on his drug-fueled tryst. My ears rang as hot blood rushed through my veins. How had I missed the signs?

I closed my eyes as the hurtful memory settled over me again. No matter how many years passed, the pain had the ability to return with an intensity that brought me to tears.

Jess rubbed my shoulder. "Are you okay?"

Nudged back to the present by her gesture, I empathized with Honey. People in love were often blind to the unpleasantness in a relationship.

"Do you want to skip lunch?" Jake asked. "Or order food to go?"

I waved a hand. "No. I'm having a sad moment. It will pass."

"Then, we're definitely having chocolate dessert," Jess insisted, scanning the list of choices.

I forced a smile. "See, you cheered me up."

Jess helped herself to a fried onion and a cheese stick. "At least you wised up and ditched the idiot."

"He wouldn't have changed," Jake assured me, spearing an appetizer onto one of the plates. "I've known plenty of Mike Hansen types. Most were unfaithful to the women they married, no matter how many times they tied the knot."

Jess drummed her fingers on the table. "If Honey somehow found out Mike left you the house up here, she might have tried to stop Ryder from telling you. I mean, what are the chances of you learning the place existed unless you were notified?"

I scooped marinara sauce on my plate from a small bowl. "I don't see her as the killer, but maybe someone who trashed the place to keep me from enjoying or selling it."

Jake said, "Honey is angry enough to explode. There's no telling what she'd do."

I plunked my elbows down on the table, covering my face. "Why didn't Mike give Honey the cabin if he planned to marry her?" I raised my head, focused on Jake. "Why?"

He shook his head. "Hard to say what goes through a person's mind."

"Honey created her own mess by taking up with Mike," Jess reminded me. "She admitted knowing he lived with Samantha while they dated. He was with them both the entire year."

Jake paused his fork over his plate. "Here's my take. If

Mike and Honey intended to marry, she had a key to the place. When she heard he died, she could've packed her things and taken them to her own place if she thought she'd be thrown out. But she left her personal items there. Honey must have believed Mike would leave her the property." He dipped a half strip of zucchini in the marinara sauce and ate it in two bites. "Imagine her surprise when I changed the locks."

"She'd be shocked," I said. "Furious. I wonder how she found out I was the one who inherited the cabin. Samantha, Ribar, or Tom, do you suppose?"

"Not Samantha," Jess said.

A tall, thin blonde woman with green eyes stopped at our table, her pen poised on a notepad. "Honey isn't feeling well. I'm Bella. I'll be your waitress."

Hoping to find out more about Honey, I said in a sympathetic tone, "I'm sorry to hear she's ill. Does she live far? Will someone drive her home since she's sick?"

"She's okay to drive." Bella tapped the notepad with her pen. "It's not too far."

"How fortunate she lives close to work." I wore my most compassionate face. "I heard she suffered a recent personal loss."

Bella creased her lips, tipping her head. "Yeah, her boyfriend died. Cute guy. She was crazy about him." Bella relaxed her arms. "They were to be married."

I maintained a supportive attitude, hoping to learn something new. "A wedding. The poor woman must be devastated."

"Yeah. A couple of us cover for her on days she can't drag herself out of bed. I was one of her bridesmaids. I mean, I would've been." Bella gestured around the diner. "She also asked two other waitresses to be in the wedding party. It's been rough on all of us seeing Honey a mess." She swiped at a tear.

I removed a notebook and pen from my purse. "What's Honey's last name? I can leave a sympathy note for her."

"It's Tannihan, but I can give the note to her, if you want."

I scribbled the name and put away the notepad. "Thank you. I'll tell you when I write my message."

We gave our order, and Bella left.

Jess clicked her tongue. "Well, aren't you Little Miss Detective?"

Jake approved. "Pretty slick work, but Bella might find herself in a lot of trouble for giving you so much information about Honey. Things like her last name and address should be kept confidential."

"I don't plan to tell anyone."

"We should be able to find Honey's address. You can mail her the stuff she left behind."

"Send it COD," Jess suggested.

We finished lunch and thanked the manager for the complimentary meals. After buying supplies for the damaged lock and door, we returned to make the needed repairs. Getting out of the truck, Jake scanned the property. "Before I fix the door, I want to hike to where we found the money. I've been wondering if whoever broke into the cabin also went to the place where we dug up the cash. If they did, I would be able to see signs of a person walking around the area."

I had one foot on the first porch step. Pivoting, I stepped down. "Me too. I'll grab my jeans and boots from the truck."

"It's up to you." Jake lifted his shoulders. "You can stay here if you'd rather work on straightening the house."

"I need to see the area for myself. Besides, I could always use the exercise."

Jake aimed his key fob at the truck, disengaging the lock with a snap.

Jess's head drooped. "I suppose I have to traipse after you two."

With a teasing voice, Jake replied, "You can always stay here to greet visitors. Human or otherwise."

I turned in time to see Jess stick her tongue out at him. "You're funny, dear. I can't believe you aren't a professional comedian."

Jake's laughter drifted on the breeze.

In the cabin, Jess and I changed from the shorts we'd worn on the drive into our jeans. We carried our boots to the porch steps to switch from our sandals.

"Ready?" Jake stood as we finished tying our bootlaces. He curled an arm around Jess's waist. "Is my baby prepared for some exercise?"

Jess's bottom lip protruded. "It's torture out there with the bugs and wild animals."

I snapped my fingers. "That reminds me, where's the insect repellent? We don't want to contract Lyme disease from the ticks."

Jess scowled. "You're not making me feel better about this."

I returned to the truck, plucking the repellent from our supply box.

"Grab water from the cooler while you're at it," Jake shouted.

* * *

We tramped through foot-high flora and plants. Even after applying the repellent, a flurry of teeny, irritating insects swarmed around our heads, buzzing at our ears. I couldn't distinguish if the teeny black dots I saw were the floaters in my eyes or insect bodies. I swatted, anyway.

"I can't see what's in these weeds," Jess complained, trouncing ferns with her boots. "What if I step on a snake? What if it bites me? Venom would go straight to my heart."

I hated to see my friend miserable on my account. It was another reminder that Mike had left me with a gigantic headache.

"Walk single-file behind me," Jake cautioned, moving to the front of the line. "The underbrush has grown higher and thicker since the last time we trekked through here. I'll flatten and cut as much as I can with the sickle." Jake, astute enough to bring the tool from the shed, wielded it from side to side, blazing a narrow trail.

I held a tree limb pruner, useless except for parting briar bushes in our way. I was not a trailblazer, by any means. I preferred walking on a worn path rather than carving out my own. America was lucky I missed the era when people were expected to travel westward to settle the West. Left up to me, the West would still be unsettled.

The difference a week made in the woods' regeneration amazed us. Instead of shuffling through dead, dry leaves on the ground, we trudged over dense moss through knee-high vegetation. Hidden roots snagged our boots every few feet, tripping us, slowing our progress. The trees, too, came to life with new greenery, forming a canopy overhead that would only thicken with the warm weather.

Every so often, a branch snapped, followed by the sounds of scurrying animals. Each sound grabbed our attention, causing our heads to swivel every which way.

"You should have brought the riding mower," Jess told Jake. "Suzie and I could've ridden behind in the cart."

"A mower is useless with all the downed branches and fallen trees. I would need to zigzag around all the roots, and I'd be slapped in the face every few feet by low-lying branches or briars."

"A whack might teach you to stay out of the woods," Jess grumbled.

"We're coming to the clearing soon," I said, offering words of encouragement that I hoped would ease Jess's distress.

"The field will be knee-high by now," Jake said, dousing my optimism.

Jess and I issued twin groans. Perspiring profusely in the humid air, my sticky skin chafed under my damp clothes.

As Jake predicted, the field we needed to cross to reach the trees where we found the hidden treasure was fully overgrown. He hacked a decent path for us with the scythe. Unfortunately, bugs and weeds flew in his wake, further souring both Jess's and my mood. We swatted to no avail. I wished for a plastic bubble to crawl into, or at least a huge can of flying pest spray. We would have had to bathe in insect repellent to ward off this many pests.

Jess gagged, trying to clear her throat. "A bug flew in my mouth!" she cried. She doubled over, gasping and spitting. Jake offered her a bottle of water. She straightened, fixing Jake with an evil glare. "Give me that," she demanded, swiping the bottle from his hands like a greedy child. After rinsing out her mouth, she drank her fill, then shoved the bottle at him.

Jake cooed, "I'm sorry, baby. You okay?"

"Not even a little bit," she groused. "Go on." With a

snap of her wrist, she motioned for him to continue slicing a trail.

I'm sure she wishes I'd never inherited the cabin.

We hiked in silence, wiping our brows and shooing away pests. Several yards short of the treeline where we'd found the money, Jake announced, "I don't see signs that anyone came this way." He did a three-hundred-sixty-degree turn.

"How can you be sure?" I asked.

"The area is overgrown with undisturbed wild vegetation." He hooked a thumb over his shoulder. "Look at the trampled path we left behind."

I surveyed the area. "Couldn't the weeds have straightened up if they were trampled, not cut? New growth could cover the flattened weeds."

Jake smiled. "Nature does regenerate, but not enough overnight to disguise a man-made path through here."

"What if they took a different route to where the money was buried?" Jess suggested.

"Trespassers still would have left their mark," Jake explained, frowning. "I wish I'd filled in the holes we left last week. They'd be overgrown by now. I should have anticipated someone else would be looking for the loot."

I pruned a dead branch about a half-inch in diameter, hanging low before my eyes, for the simple reason I'd brought the stupid trimmer and had yet to trim anything. "If they didn't know the cans were buried, why ransack the cabin?"

"Good question. I think the intruder guessed Mike hid a great deal of money but didn't know where. I'd bet they searched the cabin for clues, thinking Mike left the map."

"Too bad for him," Jess said.

"Or her," I amended.

"Or her," she agreed.

Jake led us onward, slicing through the high weeds. "Additional hidden cans of cash could have been left off the map."

"Mike invested in antiques," I said. "Maybe he has other investments. Stocks? Bonds?"

Jake nodded. "It's possible."

We reached the first spot where we found the buried cash on our last trip. Jake looked around. "The weeds in this area are undisturbed. No one came through here unless they flew."

Jess's whole body sagged. "We suffered through this ordeal for nothing," she groused.

I silently agreed. Hot, sweaty, and bug-bitten for nothing. I shooed away a droning honeybee. "I've had about enough of flying, buzzing things."

"Can we go back to the cabin now?" Jess whined. "I'm all stinky and sick of these bugs."

"I want to check one of the other places first," Jake replied.

Jess frowned. "Of course, you do."

"Do you want to wait here for me?" He raised his eyebrows.

Jess glanced at me with pleading eyes. I loathed slogging my clammy self to the other sites only to learn no one had visited them. "I'll start back with Jess. We'll stay on the path we made and go straight to the cabin."

The relief on her face was almost amusing. Jess was not the outdoorsy type. I wasn't thrilled plodding through overgrown woods, either, but I coped better than she did since I often hiked ready-made trails.

Jake hesitated. Finally, he handed me the scythe. "Take this in case you run into trouble. Don't cut yourself."

"What about you?" I asked.

"I'll take the pruner." He took the tool, making a face that showed he doubted its ability to be of much use.

Jess and I slogged back the way we came. What seemed ages later, we arrived at the cabin, too exhausted and dripping with sweat to continue cleaning. We each took one of the bathrooms we'd cleaned, showered, and dressed in the extra clothes we'd had the foresight to bring. We'd assumed we'd be filthy from tackling the cabin mess, though, not an impromptu hike.

Jess came into the great room, where I was examining a broken lamp. She was in the midst of towel-drying her hair. "I'm a new woman. No more woods for me."

"I'm sorry to drag you through the buggy weeds. I owe you big time, Jess."

She smirked. "I'll collect someday."

Jake returned. He confirmed that no one had visited the other treasure spot and went about repairing the door lock. "We'll come in the morning to finish cleaning," he said, packing up his tools.

I groaned inwardly. I couldn't bear the thought of returning in a few hours, even though the work had to be done. I could only imagine how disheartened Jess was.

"You're taking us out for dinner tonight after dragging us through the woods," Jess advised him.

Jake laughed. "Anything for my pampered baby and her best friend."

Jess fixed him with *the look.*

Chapter Fourteen

On Sunday, Jess convinced Jake we needed a break from all things related to Punxsutawney, then she called me. "Grab your purse. We're going shopping. I need a distraction to take my mind off your troubles. You do, too."

Who could argue? "I'll be over."

I pulled into Jess's driveway an hour later, and she hopped in the car. We drove to the outlets, chatting about everything but the cabin. The warm sun and cool breeze created perfect weather for us to duck in and out of the shops. We strolled from store to store, trying on summer clothes and sandals. As usual of late, our conversations wound around to my unexpected inheritance.

"Why not keep the boat?" Jess suggested. "It will be fun to take it to the Pittsburgh River festivals."

My back was to her, and I held up a pale blue T-shirt. "And be reminded of Mike every time we're on the water? No, thank you."

"He won't be on your mind if you ask Detective Pagarelli to come along."

I turned around, offering her a frown. Truthfully, I wouldn't mind sailing away with Pagarelli if I was convinced he was as interested in me as I was in him, but I wasn't going to tell Jess that. She wiggled her eyebrows. With a sigh, I threw the blue shirt over my forearm.

Jess picked up a raspberry-pink blouse with yellow lemons. "He's been single a long time."

I eyed her suspiciously. "How do you know?"

Squinting at the price tag, Jess replied, "He's Georgianna's neighbor."

"She mentioned that at book club. So?"

Jess held the uniquely patterned blouse in front of her. "What do you think of this?"

Bright. Bold. Flashy. "It's you."

"It is." She folded it lengthwise. "I bumped into Georgianna at the pharmacy, and she asked how you were doing."

"Jess." I doubted Pagarelli's name happened to come up in casual conversation. Knowing my friends, they were scheming.

Her expression turned sheepish. "What?"

"You haven't explained how you found out he's been girlfriendless for a while."

She shrugged. "I mentioned to Georgianna he was handsome. She said he was a great guy and couldn't understand why he was still single. Apparently, he dated a woman who moved out of state to take a job. Their long-distance relationship fell apart."

Jess glanced at the shirt I'd draped over my arm. "You ready to check out?"

"Yes. How long ago?"

"The breakup? I don't know, I didn't ask." She pulled out her phone. "Want me to text Georgianna?"

I placed my palm over her phone. "No."

We took our place in line at the registers. "He sounds like a great catch, Suzie."

Each time we met, a pleasant reaction coursed through me, right down to my toes. Did I have a similar effect on Detective Pagarelli? His few personal comments encouraged me. "He hasn't asked me out."

"Maybe he needs a little push in the right direction," Jess said.

I closed my eyes, preparing to ward off Jess and her matchmaking. "Whatever you're planning, forget it."

Much to my discomfort, Jess continued the conversation as I laid my purchase on the counter. The sales clerk seemed torn between listening to her and ringing up my items.

"You need someone like Jake to share your life," Jess said.

The clerk punched keys on the register, but she'd turned an ear toward our conversation. Who wouldn't enjoy a juicy fixing-up-a-friend story?

Jess wiggled her fingers. "Sometimes you have to nudge fate."

"If his breakup was recent, I don't want to tempt fate if he's not over his former girlfriend."

"Nonsense. She's gone." Jess placed a hand on her hip. "What do you two talk about when you're alone?"

I accepted my shopping bag from the sales clerk with a polite *thank you*. I turned, whispering to Jess, "The murder case."

The clerk's eyes widened.

Jess handed over her blouse and slipped her credit card into the machine when directed. "He's collected all your confidential information. Why don't you ask him personal questions?"

The sales clerk glanced up while refolding the shirt, unabashedly interested in my response.

I wrapped my fingers around the corded handle of my shopping bag, holding it in front of my legs. "I found out he enjoys spring."

The clerk's cheeks pinkened. I gestured to Jess. "She's trying to catch your attention."

Jess finished her transaction, and we walked out of the boutique. "Why don't you ask Pagarelli where he lives? Specifically."

"I'll wait for him to offer."

We arrived in front of the shoe store. Jess held the door open for me. "I bet he's gauging how interested you are in him." She eyed me. "You *are* interested, right?"

Of course, I am. "At the moment, I'm fascinated by these cute beach sandals." To prove my point, I lifted a pair from the shelf and inspected them.

An hour later, we stowed our purchases in the trunk of Jess's SUV. Leaving the outlet parking lot, she said, "I need to stop by the bakery to pick up cupcakes I ordered for a coworker's birthday. Okay with you?"

"Absolutely. I could use a sugar pick-me-up, too. Did you taste the new praline scone Bre makes? It's delish. Plus, it's always nice to see Bre."

We drove into town, parking in the lot across from Bre's Bakery. I got out of the vehicle and slid the strap of my purse over my shoulder. Bre rushed to meet us when we approached the bakeshop door. "Suzie. Jess. I'm happy to see you two. Come in and have a fresh macaroon, on the house."

We exchanged hugs. Bre asked me if the police had

apprehended the killer of the victim I'd found. She frowned at my negative reply.

"It's a shame someone can kill a man, dump his body in the woods, and escape arrest. The murder is all my customers are talking about. They're worried for their children's safety."

"Totally understandable," I said. "The police are doing all they can."

Jess's preordered cupcakes, each topped with a summer flower surrounded by leaves sitting prettily on top of lush frosting, were gathered on a tray at the back of the counter.

Bre placed the cheerful cupcakes into one of her signature pink boxes. "I wish they'd hurry to solve this one."

"I feel it's only a matter of time before a suspect is caught." I eyed delectable treats in the glass display case in front of me.

"That's right," Jess agreed. "The police have some shady suspects to choose from."

Bre paused while boxing up the cupcakes. "Someone from around here?"

I threw Jess a look. "We don't know."

She held up her fingers, ticking off viable suspects. "Samantha Banks. Tom Hansen. Ribar."

"Maybe," I said, though unconvincingly. "The police need evidence in order to make an arrest."

Bre discarded the thin pastry paper she used to grasp the cupcakes. Folding the edges of the box lid, she closed and sealed it with her personalized sticker. With a glance out the window, she asked, "Speaking of Samantha, isn't that her?"

"Where?" My heart clenched. Her presence couldn't be a coincidence.

Jess and I spun around. Samantha loitered on the sidewalk outside the shop, her wispy hair fluttering in the wind. She seemed to be waiting. For me, I assumed.

"Can't she leave me alone for one day?" I lamented.

Jess turned to Bre. "Give me a can of whipped cream."

I gaped at her. "You wouldn't dare."

Bre hesitated, two fingers touching her lips.

"Come on," Jess coaxed. "I'm only going to scare her into scramming."

Brows knitted, Bre passed Jess the container. "Don't do anything to get me into trouble."

Jess shoved the box of cupcakes at me. "Hold these." She stomped toward the door. Bre and I followed at a safe distance. Whipping open the door, Jess said in a cheery voice, "Hello, Samantha."

"Tell Suzie I'm not leaving without the key to Mike's cabin," Samantha shouted.

Her finger on the trigger, Jess fired a torrent of whipped cream. The frothy stream jettisoned from the spray can, hitting Samantha squarely in the face.

The woman sprang backward with a scream. Undeterred, Jess filled Samantha's gaping mouth with the emulsion. Samantha wrapped a hand around her throat as she choked and spat. Blinded by the thick, sugary fluff smeared on her sunglasses, she crashed into a nearby urn, filled to the brim with flowers.

Bre grabbed my arm. We both gaped in horror as Jess shook the canister again. The next blast of spray coated the hair around Samantha's face and covered her ears. Whipped cream dripped from her chin onto her blouse. Bre cracked the door open a smidge in order for us to hear Samantha's retort. She let loose a string of profanities, condemning Jess and threatening to sue Bre's Bakery. A man darted across the street. Passersby gawked at the sight.

Laughing, Jess directed Samantha to vacate the premises unless she wanted another blast. Bre and I shuffled backward as our friend returned to the shop without waiting for a response, slamming the door behind her.

Samantha spat once more before clomping down the sidewalk, spewing bitter warnings loud enough for the entire town to hear. Within minutes, she disappeared from the parking lot.

Eyes wide, Bre looked horrified. I stood half stunned, half amused by Jess's antics. Jess returned Bre's nearly empty canister with a satisfied grin.

"I can't believe you squirted her in the face," Bre exclaimed. "What if she sues me over this?" Worry etched her face. "I could lose my shop." She held the messy can with the tips of her fingers. "I wouldn't have given you ammunition if I had known your intention."

Jess took a napkin from the counter, wiping at the whipped cream that had dripped on her shirt. "Forget about Samantha. What's she gonna say? I mugged her with a can of whipped cream? The only thing she suffered was embarrassment. Suzie can counter-sue for damages from the grocery store fiasco when Samantha pushed her, bruising her leg." She reached for the box of cupcakes I still clutched in my hands. "I'll take full responsibility if she tries to blame you. I'll say I grabbed the can without your knowledge."

"Jess, I hate causing you trouble," I said.

"You didn't. This little stunt was for my own personal satisfaction. That boyfriend-stealing, self-centered witch has irritated me for years. It's about time someone put her in her place, even if she did do you a favor by removing Mike from your life." She rolled her neck. "Darn, that felt wonderful."

"I need sweets," I muttered. "I'll take three praline

scones, please." I pointed at the shelf above them. "And one of those huge brownies with the nuts on top."

After washing her hands, Bre boxed the scones and brownie, applied her signature pink sticker to the box, and rang through our purchases.

"Contact me if Samantha bothers you," I shouted from the doorway.

"No, call me instead," Jess interjected, pointing to herself. "I'll run her out of town."

Bre picked up a fresh canister of whipped cream. Thumb poised above the nozzle, she held it high. "I can protect myself."

Although we laughed, my senses were on high alert as we made our way to Jess's car. I wondered if we would run into Samantha, lurking in the parking lot. Thankfully, the coast was clear. I breathed a sigh of relief, but I speculated as to what payback Samantha would inflict. She wasn't the type of person to let a slight against her go unanswered. Strangers milling around the bakery had witnessed her humiliation, which would only fuel her hunger for revenge.

I fastened my seatbelt and broke into my goody box. I couldn't wait another minute to satisfy my craving. "Want half?" I raised the brownie toward Jess.

"Not half. Break me off a corner. It looks yummy."

It was. One mouthful was enough to change Jess's mind about only wanting a fragment. Together, we devoured the thick, fudgy brownie before arriving at her house. When we pulled into her driveway, Jake was putting away the mower.

Jess said to him, "I told Suzie to keep the boat so we could use it this summer."

Jake slipped the lock onto the shed door. "It's a beauty."

"The boat is yours," I said.

Jake straightened, turned, and gaped at me. "What? No

way." He waved a hand through the air. "We can't accept a gift that expensive. You're our best friend. We're happy to help you. No need to lavish us with a costly gift."

"How costly are we talking?" Jess asked.

"A boat like that? Upwards of a hundred thousand dollars."

Jess's mouth fell open. "You're kidding me."

"I'm not."

I was dumbstruck. "For a boat? I figured the thing was worth a couple thousand."

Jake shook his head. "It's a brand new, fully furnished cabin cruiser. The girl's in excellent condition. I'm quoting the low end of resale. Check the insurance policy in the folder of papers from the attorney with the value listed."

At the current tally, my inheritance from Mike neared a million dollars.

Jess came out of her trance. "I didn't expect you to give it to us. I meant for you to keep it, and we could all go boating together."

"Forget the cost." I waved a hand. "You two helped me with the cabin and all the problems with it. Those hikes tortured you. Take the boat."

"Cabin cruiser," Jake corrected.

Jess shot him an annoyed look. "Jake is right. We can't accept it as a gift."

"Okay," I countered. "Then, I'll keep it. You can borrow it for the summer since I don't know the first thing about operating a boat."

Jess turned to Jake, who looked as if he wanted to protest further, but a slight grin turned the corners of his lips upward. "Deal. I'll keep it fueled and in excellent shape for you."

After Jake left to attend an evening meeting, Jess and I

sat in her living room with two glasses of wine. His absence meant we could discuss what had transpired at the cabin, and the progress I'd made with my amateur investigation, without Jake reminding us that we were to stay out of police business.

"If Ribar isn't the vandal, that leaves Samantha, Tom, and Honey," Jess reasoned.

I ran my finger along the stem of my glass. "Maybe Samantha and Tom ransacked the cabin together. Jake thinks the damage was too extensive to be done by one person before the police arrived."

"True." Jess yanked the pillow from behind her back. "Speaking of tossing things." She threw the pillow to the other end of the couch.

"Tom and Samantha are brazen enough to think I'll give up the cabin if they aggravate me." I sipped my wine.

Jess looked more comfortable without the pillow. She lounged against the arm of the sofa, loosely holding her glass. "Makes sense. They're both vipers who would stop at nothing."

"Isn't that the truth."

Jess's forehead furrowed. "How can we trap them into admitting their guilt?"

I deliberated for a few moments while Jess finished her drink. "By catching them working together."

"How?" Jess poured more wine.

"They live several miles from here, but we run into them at every turn. What if they are staying at one of the hotels or motels near town to keep informed of the investigation? We'll figure out which ones, then tail them for a day."

Her free hand flopped forward dismissively. "We can't set up surveillance at every inn around here."

"I'll bet Pagarelli knows where they're staying," I suggested.

"Yeah. I'm sure he'll be happy to share the details with you after his warning not to investigate."

"Good point." A brilliant idea struck me. Or maybe it was the effects of the wine. "We can enlist the book club to help."

"I'm listening."

"I'll ask the ladies if they'd be willing to sit in front of various motels in the morning and report if Samantha or Tom leaves." My enthusiasm grew. "They're intrigued by the mystery surrounding Ryder's death. They'll agree."

I saluted Jess with my wine glass. "Time to call a special meeting."

She clinked my glass with hers. "Here's to our plan."

"Okay. We'll split up the ladies' names and call them."

Excitement danced in Jess's eyes. "A real stakeout. This is gonna be fun. When and where shall we meet?"

"My house, tomorrow evening. We'll explain my idea to whoever comes and assign each one a place to stalk. First, we'll need a list of area lodgings."

We compiled a list using GPS from our phones to include all nearby hotels and motels. Of course, Samantha and Tom could be registered farther from town, but I had a hunch they'd booked locally. They wanted me to know they were close, ready to pounce if I spent their precious money.

"Is it too late to call the ladies?" Jess asked.

"Not this bunch." I checked my watch. "It's only seven-thirty. They're settling in with bestselling authors right about now."

* * *

After arranging the meeting with my friends, I lay in bed languishing in murky thoughts, too keyed up to sleep. Dead Ryder, spiteful Samantha, nasty Ribar, and wacky Tom swam through my mind. Did one of them kill the attorney to keep me from learning Mike's will existed? Where did Mike get the money for the cabin? What about the source of the buried money?

I mulled over the visits from Tom and Samantha. Suppressing the fact that I was Mike's heir benefitted them both in a significant way. No one, not even I, expected his generosity toward me. Mr. James changed that.

Oh, to be a fly on the wall with its thousands of eye lenses to see Samantha's reaction when she learned Mike owned a secret retreat. I envisioned the top of her head popping off in an explosion of anger, a cloud of smoke curling around her wiry hair. I imagined her losing her mind upon hearing I'd inherited the cabin and property, jealousy consuming her from head to toe.

Would Samantha's hatred and rage tempt her to stop Ryder from delivering the will to me? How crazy and irate would Samantha have to be to shoot him? Did she even own a gun? Mike did.

Then, there was Tom.

Chapter Fifteen

The next morning at six, I dragged my groggy self to the kitchen for a strong cup of tea and shooed Hunter out into the backyard. I filled my mug with water and placed it in the microwave. Propping my elbows on the counter, I dropped my head in my palms and closed my tired eyes. Where would I find the energy to work on my textbooks? The microwave dinged, startling me. Hopefully, a couple of cups of tea would give me the boost I needed.

Hunter didn't want to come inside. I left him to run in the yard and went back to writing. A while later, his bark drew me to the kitchen. Opening the back door, I assumed he wanted in the house. He didn't come. Instead, he jumped at the fence along the left side of the yard.

Probably a deer or other animal in the woods.

I shouted to him, but he ignored me. I went out on the deck for a closer look, but the animal must have run off with Hunter's barking. This time when I called, he came.

"What did you see out there, boy, a deer? It would be nice if we had a buck with a big rack running around. I could invite Detective Pagarelli to hunt near here." *And maybe come in for coffee.*

I tossed Hunter a biscuit, which he caught in midair before following me to my office. I worked until one, then shut off the computer and got ready to drive to the fruit market and bakery.

At Bre's shop, she mentioned the meeting I'd called. "I can't wait to hear your plan for Samantha. I'm willing to do whatever it takes to get rid of the woman." She grabbed a can of whipped cream from behind the counter. "I've got ammo for protection." We shared a gleeful laugh.

She dug into a glass jar. "Here's a biscuit for Hunter. See you tonight."

Back at the house, I ran the vacuum, cleaned the bathrooms, and tidied up. I'd just put the finishing touches on a fruit platter as my first guest arrived—Jess.

Dressed in orange pants and an orange and navy blouse, she balanced a tray of cheese and crackers in one hand. "Jake thinks we're having a book club meeting. I'll have to dream up other excuses if our surveillance drags on a few days. He would be upset to hear I'm working on this case."

"You'll figure out plausible fibs." I never underestimated her ingenuity.

I slid the fruit tray down on the table to make room for Jess's platter. "You can set that in the middle."

Her bracelets pinged against the wood as she lowered the tray. "What did you buy at the bakery?"

"Come see." I led her into the kitchen, where a plate of blueberry and strawberry scones rested on the granite counter beside another tray stacked with brownies.

"Yum. Is that a piece of broken scone?" She pointed at a jagged quarter-sized fragment.

I laughed as she practically drooled. "Why, I think it is. Help yourself."

Between chews, Jess asked, "How'd you sleep last night?"

"Can't you tell by the dark circles?"

"Yeah, but I thought I'd be polite and ignore them."

"You're a peach." I dropped a grape into my mouth.

"Sweet as can be." She sported an ear-to-ear grin, then sobered. "Seriously, you have to take care of yourself."

I scooped ice into a container. "I can't quit thinking about Samantha, Tom, and Ribar. Who knows if any of them killed Ryder?"

Jess lightly slapped her cheek. "Don't ask. If one of them isn't the killer, we have another maniac running around."

"I half expect another person to crawl out of the woodwork and claim a share of Mike's estate." My brain protested the disturbing thought.

"Don't anticipate trouble. We have enough shady characters to choose from. But speaking of Tom, he's skilled with a gun from years of hunting."

I handed Jess the ice bucket and picked up the pitcher of tea. "I doubt Tom could shoot a man in cold blood. Maybe they struggled and the gun went off, fatally injuring him." She followed me to the dining room. "I wouldn't put it past Samantha to kill someone, though," I added. "The woman is totally wacko."

Jess set the ice bucket on the table. "Ribar's another nutcase. What about Honey?"

I shook my head. "She seemed genuinely brokenhearted by Mike's death."

Jess disagreed. "Only if she didn't know Mike gave you the cabin. A woman spurned is nothing to take lightly."

The doorbell rang. The ladies arrived in a huddled group, having carpooled. We exchanged greetings. I offered everyone a drink, and we settled in the living room.

"Are you enjoying this month's book, Jess?" Bre asked.

"It's okay, but I prefer romances."

"What's wrong with murder mysteries?" Georgianna, the whodunit author, asked. Her silver hair was perfectly styled, as usual.

I stood at the head of the table and cleared my throat. Loudly. The ladies quieted. "Thank you all for coming. I asked you here to discuss the recent murder in town." I clasped my hands in front of me. "I have a huge favor to ask. First, I have to swear you to secrecy."

Georgianna rubbed her palms together. "Is this secret something I can use in my next novel?"

I tossed her a mischievous smile. "Maybe."

"Does it have to do with the loudmouthed woman Jess attacked with the whipped cream?" MaryLou asked.

Jess reached for a napkin and scone, grinning. "Heard about my little stunt, huh?"

The ladies started talking over each other, laughing about the incident.

I raised my voice to bring them to order. "It sort of has something to do with her."

MaryLou ignored me. "You've stirred a hornets' nest, Jess. Aren't you afraid Samantha's out for revenge?" She turned to Bre. "And what if she sues you or your bakeshop?"

Bre paled.

Jess snickered, unfazed. "I threatened to turn Samantha in for stalking and terrorizing Suzie at the supermarket. Told her she has connections at the PD."

It was my turn to grow pale. "Jess, you didn't tell me that."

"Don't freak out." She chomped on another bite of the scone. "I didn't give a name."

"Is your connection Nathaniel Pagarelli?" Georgianna asked. "My neighbor said he's a wonderful, thoughtful guy. And he's handsome and single."

"Oh, Suzie!" Bre gushed. "You're dating again? I'm happy for you."

My cheeks burned. "I have no connections with the police. You guys, I called you over here to help me with a problem."

"Ladies." Georgianna clapped her hands. "Let's give Suzie our attention."

They quieted enough for me to continue. "I need help determining if Samantha and Tom are working together to intimidate me into giving up the Punxsutawney property. They may have plotted to kill Ryder to stop me from learning about the place."

They gasped and muttered.

I paced in front of the table. "It seems they both will try anything to get their hands on my portion of the estate," I told them about the destruction at the cabin.

"That's terrible," Bre said.

"What can we do to help?" Georgianna had a gleam in her eyes.

As I predicted, the book club ladies were thrilled to help with the investigation. I passed out the photos of Samantha and Tom I'd copied earlier from the Internet. "These are the two you are looking to find. Jess and I made a list of hotels and motels in the area. We can split up and run surveillance on them." I laid out the rest of my plan.

We decided to sit in our cars early the next morning at various locations. We agreed to stake out the lodgings from seven until ten in the morning. We figured it would take two days to cover all the accommodations near town. If we didn't see either of our suspects during those morning hours, we'd expand the time for another session the following two days. After that, we'd give up the surveillance.

"Please don't let anyone else know of our plans. As I said, Detective Pagarelli warned me not to investigate on my own. The trouble is, I can't stop thinking about Ryder and his family. I want to do something to help find his killer."

MaryLou spoke. "We all want to see his murderer caught and punished. This crime has been a blight on our town. The Council met in a special session to determine how to prevent this horror from discouraging tourists in our area."

"MaryLou," Bre scolded, "This isn't about saving face for the town. It's about making our community safe."

We all had different reasons for wanting to find the killer. Bre was adamant about safety. I wanted justice for Ryder's family and peace of mind for myself. MaryLou worried about the town's reputation. Georgianna, being Georgianna, hoped for a new murder plot.

Jess said, "Yeah, and we want to protect Suzie. Banks and Hansen are evil. They've badgered and threatened her multiple times. They should both rot in jail. Maybe one or both are killers."

Heads around the room bobbed in agreement. The ladies expressed their concern for me and vowed we would stick together. The meeting ended on a high note, with every one of us eager to carry out our clandestine plan.

* * *

Tuesday morning, I sat in my car, drinking tea outside the hotel I'd chosen for my surveillance. An avid reader, I wanted to pick up the book I'd tossed onto the passenger seat, but I resisted the urge. I needed to keep my eyes glued to the front door.

I'd brought along my digital tape recorder to narrate notes for the textbook I'd committed to writing. After an hour of sitting and staring, I'd logged exactly zero words. With a sigh, I unwrapped a dark chocolate bar and bit the end. When all else failed, one couldn't go wrong with chocolate.

Finally, ten o'clock struck. Quitting time. Being stuck in my car watching for Samantha and Tom for hours had left me wound tight. I was antsy and needed a restroom. Tomorrow, I would skip the tea. I drove to Bre's Bakery to use the restroom. She pulled into the parking lot ahead of me, waving.

Inside, we compared notes. She hadn't seen either Samantha or Tom. I called the other ladies while eating macadamia nut cookies. No one had good news to report.

With a bid goodbye to Bre, I drove into the main part of town with the intention of stopping at the office supply store before heading home. I parked, checking my watch. Hunter would need to go outside soon.

I purchased paper and ink, then slipped on my sunglasses before strolling out the door. The sun shone brightly in the cloudless sky, a beautiful day to be outdoors instead of at my home workstation. I glanced at the time again while waiting at the crosswalk for the light to change. Out of nowhere, a man materialized behind me and grabbed my arm, nearly scaring me to death. I sucked in a breath.

His familiar voice snarled in my ear, "Come with me."

Ribar. I writhed to free myself, dropping my package. "Get away from me, or I'll scream."

Clutching my arm tighter, he held out his jacket pocket, his hand tucked inside. "You do, and it'll be the last sound out of your mouth."

I froze, recognizing the outline of a gun through the thin material.

He snorted. "We need to talk."

Really? From my perspective, I had nothing to say to him.

He waved the hidden weapon. "Pick up your bag."

My hand shook as I did as he commanded. Ribar nudged me away from the curb, toward a sidewalk bench. Temporary relief flooded me. He hadn't forced me into my car or his truck. Sitting in plain view of the public almost comforted me. Well, if I could find comfort in a criminal dragging me away at gunpoint.

"Sit down," Ribar ordered.

I lowered myself, stiff as a mannequin, onto the iron bench, clasping my package to my chest. Maybe the bulk would offer some protection if Ribar decided to shoot me.

"Here's the thing," he began, his voice low and menacing. "If you think you can swindle me out of my share of the money Mike and I made in our business dealings, you're wrong." He tapped his stomach with the hand buried in his pocket. "I worked for my third, and I intend to collect it. Where is the cash?"

"I don't know what you are talking about."

"Don't lie to me." He gritted his teeth, increasing the vice-like pressure on my arm. "Mike left you the house in Punxsutawney and all his toys. He gave you the money, too. He wouldn't have given it to the leech he lived with."

"I can show you a copy of the will," I said, panic rising. "He didn't mention money."

Ribar raised his free hand as if to slap me. He lowered it when a woman walked past. "How dumb do you think I am?" he hissed. "Hansen wouldn't leave a written trail."

Actually, I think you are very dumb.

He tipped back his dirty ball cap, scratching his head. "Mike had a heart attack before we could divide the money. I went to see him in the hospital. He assured me he'd stashed the money in a safe place, and I'd get my share when he was released. Only that didn't happen, because he died there." Ribar's eyes flashed. His jaw tightened. "I tried to convince him to tell me where he hid the money. Mike claimed he was the only one who had access."

"Then, you have your answer."

Ribar shook my arm. "Don't get cute with me."

My curiosity once again exceeded my common sense. "Why was Mike the one who kept the money?"

Ribar sneered. "He had the cleanest record. He also made a bundle of legitimate money in the stock market."

So, it was true that Mike's stocks had done well. Could Tom be part of the business dealings? "What about Tom? Maybe he has details."

"You think I'm stupid?"

Why, yes, I do.

"Tom's looking for the money, too. I need to find it before he rips me off the same as his brother did," Ribar replied.

I continued to push my luck, hoping that if I kept Ribar talking, Pagarelli would rescue me as he had done in the past. After all, he seemed to mysteriously appear when I found myself in trouble. "Why would you go into business with Tom? His track record for making money isn't exactly stellar."

To my surprise, Ribar laughed. "Him being a loser made the plan even better. If we were caught, Tom and I could claim we'd lost our money gambling on the horses and at the casino. We'd be arrested for the scam, but we'd be out in a few years. The money would be waiting for us when we were released."

"Why didn't you have a failsafe plan in case something happened to Mike?"

He scratched his chin with the point of the pocket holding the gun. "I admit, we were stupid not to have a backup."

You think?

"Didn't expect him to have a heart attack at thirty-six." He lowered his arm, relaxing it against the back of the bench. "We planned to divide up the score in two weeks when our fake passports were ready. Except Mike went and died on us."

"How inconsiderate of him," I mumbled.

"Tom and I think Mike stashed the money in a bank out of the country." Ribar's eyebrows knitted together, forming a single bushy brow across his lined forehead. "It's not like he could bury all those bills in his backyard."

My face heated, and I willed myself to remain calm before Ribar suspected I'd discovered that Mike had done exactly that.

Ribar continued. "There's got to be a record of the bank name or account number. My guess is Hansen would've hidden the information at his secret hideaway. Which he gave to you." He glared at me. "I want my money."

"How would I know how to reclaim your money if it's in a bank?"

He leveled a vicious scowl at me. "You'd better hope Mike left directions or information for you."

I lifted my chin. "I haven't had anything to do with Mike for years."

"So you've said." He bounced the hidden gun against his thigh. "For my troubles, I deserve his share of the loot, along with my own. Don't you agree?" He didn't give me time to answer. "Now, I'm gonna ask you once more. Where is the cash?"

"What makes you think I have your money?"

"He left you the house and property. And his boat, which is kind of funny, since he named it after Honey. The Honey Bee." He laughed.

"I can't explain why he left me his estate."

Ribar sneered. "Of course you can't." He brandished the pocketed gun. "Quit stalling. Believe me, it will only get worse for you. Do you have his bank account numbers or a key to a bank box?"

"The only keys I have are to the house, boat, and SUV. Ask Samantha Banks about Mike's bank accounts. She lived with him." All true, except I didn't admit to finding the thousands buried on the property and banking it.

"Samantha. Hansen planned to dump the ugly tramp for Honey." He raised a hand. "Before you say Honey has the money, she doesn't. I've already talked to her. Mike cut her out of his will completely. She loved him, and he burned her."

Ribar hunched closer to me. "That leaves you. Obviously, you and Mike had an affair going on if he gave you what should have been Honey's share. Hansen must have left a note pointing you to his hidden cash."

Was it incomprehensible for people to understand Mike and I were not having a fling? I agreed with the bizarreness of his choice to leave me a small fortune when he had other women in his life, but maybe his unpredictable, sketchy past might have accounted for his odd decision.

"I don't have a note. Tom visited Mike at the hospital. Maybe he forced Mike to reveal where he hid your money."

Ribar's forehead wrinkled, considering the possibility.

I gathered the courage to ask what I'd been wondering all along. "Did you break into the cabin?"

He drew back, his eyes widening. I'd caught him off guard, but he rebounded instantly. "I'm the one asking questions. All you need to know is you'd better find my cash."

Since we sat out in the open with people wandering the sidewalks, I harbored a moment of bravery. "What if I don't? Are you going to kill me like you did Christopher Ryder?"

Another stunned expression caused his jaw to drop. "I didn't kill nobody."

Although Ribar seemed taken aback, I'd read that most murderers claimed they were innocent and had one excuse after another for their crimes.

"What I'm going to do is watch your every move. You won't be able to use a cent without me knowing. If you squander one dollar of my cash, you'll see my face." He gestured with the hidden gun. "And this."

What a scary threat—Ribar loitering in the shadows. How could I make him understand he was wrong? But was he? We'd found a hundred and twenty thousand dollars. Was the money Ribar referred to his half of what they stole from unsuspecting investors?

With false bravado, I lifted my chin. "Spend all your waking hours tailing me. It will be a waste of time. I have no idea where Mike stashed his money."

His voice rose. Ribar poked his chest. *"My* money. I never should have trusted Hansen with seven hundred fifty thousand dollars."

My mouth dropped open at the staggering amount.

Ribar surely read the surprise written on my face. He released my arm, stood, and tipped his hat. "I'll be seeing you around." He strolled away as if we'd been discussing the weather.

Shaken to my core, my whole body stiffened at the thought of him stalking me. After several deep breaths, I headed to my car, my head swiveling in every direction. Once inside, I locked the doors, closed my eyes, and worked on calming myself before calling Detective Pagarelli.

Knock, knock. Knuckles rapped on my window. My eyes flew open and I screamed.

Chapter Sixteen

My racing heart failed to slow after I recognized the face staring at me with concern. I opened the window. "Georgianna," I exclaimed breathlessly.

"Suzie, are you alright? Are you ill?" She rested the back of her hand on my forehead. "You're pale as parchment paper."

Not wanting to drag her into my drama, I shuffled my hand in a dismissive wave. "I have a headache and closed my eyes for a minute. You scared me when you knocked."

"I'm sorry. I was afraid you were sick." She drew back, nodding toward a nearby restaurant. "Do you want a cup of tea to help your headache subside before you drive home?"

I didn't. "Sounds nice."

We walked across the street to the corner café and ordered drinks and chocolate croissants.

"My headache could be from not eating," I lied. "This chocolate should do the trick." I took a bite. The flaky pastry and dark chocolate melted in my mouth. Headache or not, it was delicious.

"I'm sorry we didn't learn where Tom or Samantha are staying during this morning's surveillance," Georgianna said. "Maybe tomorrow we will."

"I hope so."

Georgianna added sweetener to her herbal tea. "Have the police made any progress on the murder of the poor man you found? He's been on my mind."

I longed to shove everyone associated with the case out of my brain for a few hours. "They're investigating several possibilities but haven't found anything solid yet."

"What about you?"

"Me?"

"Did you research the victim's background after MaryLou made the suggestion?" She lifted her blue flowered cup from its matching saucer and blew on the tea to cool it. "You're an ace at Internet stuff."

I shook my head. "No time for extra research. My editor assigned a new business book. I'm busy working on the proposal."

"What's the subject?"

"How to deal with difficult people."

Georgianna laughed. "Save me a copy. I could use help dealing with quirky readers who challenge me during book signings."

Remembering Jess's predicament at work with a cranky coworker, I said, "Seems lots of people need help dealing with others."

By the time Georgianna and I finished our drinks and said goodbye, I felt better. Not great, but improved. On the drive home, I wavered about calling Detective Pagarelli since I bothered him so much. On the other hand, Pagarelli's job was to protect people, and Ribar had terrorized me at gunpoint. My anger kicked in, boiling my blood. I vowed to call Pagarelli the minute I got home.

* * *

I arrived home around one, and Hunter greeted me at the door. "Hello, boy. I'm happy to see you." After letting him out into the fenced-in backyard to run, I dialed Pagarelli and recounted my confrontation with Ribar.

His voice churned with anger. "He held a gun on you? Are you okay? Where are you?"

"As I explained, I didn't see the weapon, but the outline in his pocket resembled the shape of a gun. He scared me, but I'm fine now. I'm home."

"Why didn't you come to the station and report him?"

"I was a wreck. Georgianna saw me sitting in my car and surmised something was wrong. I didn't tell her about Ribar, but I did have a cup of tea with her to calm my nerves. I figured I'd call you from home, where we could talk in private."

"Is Hunter with you? Did you set your alarm?"

His dire tone sent a chill through me. "Hunter is outside. I'll set the alarm when he comes into the house."

"Bring Hunter inside now and set your alarm." He paused. "You'll need to come down to the station and fill out a report."

I rubbed my forehead. "Can I do it tomorrow? I'm exhausted from the whole ordeal."

"I'll come to you. I'll be there in fifteen minutes." He disconnected the call.

A tingle raced up my spine at the thought of seeing him. I was happy he was on his way, even if it was for police business. I reapplied my makeup and brushed my hair.

Hunter sprinted at the sound of the doorbell. I peeked out the window, then opened the main door. Hunter pranced with excitement upon seeing Pagarelli. I let the detective in, and he gave Hunter's ears a rub. Then, he tipped his hat at me, turned around, and locked the door.

In the kitchen, I poured Pagarelli a cup of coffee before we sat at the table. With his prompting, I repeated the encounter with Ribar while he took notes.

"Did Ribar hurt you?"

I pushed up my sleeve, revealing the start of a bruise from Ribar's fingers and thumb. "He gripped my arm hard enough to leave this."

Pagarelli's expression morphed from professionally neutral to a visibly tight jaw and creased forehead in an instant. "We'll file a complaint for assault."

I yanked my sleeve down. "Ribar told me Mike owed him a share of seven hundred fifty thousand dollars."

Pagarelli looked up from his notebook. "That's a lot of cash."

I nodded. "He admitted to pulling off a scam with Mike and Tom."

Pagarelli wrote down the information. "I'll work on this angle."

I resisted the urge to chew on my nails. "Do you think the hundred twenty thousand we found is part of the scammed money?"

"Possibly. May I have your permission for detectives to search the Punxsutawney property?"

"Yes." I pictured men with shovels leaving huge holes in their paths. "Are you planning to dig up the entire area? There are several acres."

"They'll use metal detectors."

"Oh." I felt silly.

I filled out the paperwork Pagarelli had brought with him while he finished his coffee. I hated for him to leave. I asked, "Um, any further clues about who murdered Ryder?"

He closed his notebook. "We're closer to bringing in a couple of suspects."

"Let me guess. Ribar tops the list."

"His actions toward you have moved him to my number one spot." He eyed me suspiciously. "I don't want you to have contact with him for any reason."

"I don't plan to." I wiped the condensation from my glass with my index finger. "I think he ransacked the cabin, but I don't believe he killed Ryder."

Silence stretched for several moments. When I dared to glance at Pagarelli, I squirmed under his glare.

"What makes you say that?" His voice held a heavy mix of irritation and scolding.

I cringed. *Too much information. When will I learn to keep my mouth shut?* "I, uh, asked him."

He rested a forearm on the table, placing the other on his thigh. "You asked him?" He paused after each word, his voice flat.

I swallowed. "He wore a guilty expression when I asked about the ransacking. It disappeared when I accused him of killing Ryder. His face showed genuine surprise."

"You accused him of breaking and entering *and* murder?" His cheeks grew redder. "Ms. Tuft..."

Unable to take the reprimanding a second longer, I leaped from my seat. With averted eyes, I scooped my glass from the table. "Could we discuss this later? I'm having dinner at Jess and Jake's." I reached for his mug. He placed a hand over the top, stopping me. I glanced up and met his eyes, now softened.

"I don't want to see anything happen to you," he whispered, moving his hand over mine.

My heart thumped.

He cleared his throat. "Call me the minute Ribar approaches you again."

"I will." He kept his hand over mine. The warmth of his touch spread up my arm.

"Or if Hansen or Banks bothers you."

"Okay."

He pulled away, tucking his notebook into his pocket. "I'll wait here until you're ready to leave, then follow you to the highway."

I recomposed myself. "I'll be ready in a couple of minutes." I placed the cups in the dishwasher, missing his touch. How stupid was I to confront Ribar and then, afterward, admit it to Pagarelli? I was losing my mind.

Pagarelli followed me from my house to the end of the road. My limbs quaked the entire time. Having a cop follow me was nerve-wracking enough. The fact that I was falling for him only added another level of angst. I released a huge sigh as he turned the opposite way once we reached the highway.

I arrived at Jess's at five-thirty. She met me at the door, took one look at my face, and asked, "What happened?"

"Where's Jake?"

"Where do you think? Out in the garage. Want me to call him in?"

I took off my jacket, nodding. "I don't want to say this twice."

Jake and Jess sat captivated while I told them of Ribar's threat with the gun and Pagarelli's visit to fill out the incident report. Their facial expressions ranged from surprise to horror to sympathy.

"Thank heavens you're alright," Jess said. "What did Pagarelli say? Is he going to arrest Ribar?"

"I guess, since I filled out the paperwork he brought." I collapsed against the back of the chair. "Too much money and too many suspects are involved. I don't know where to go from here."

"The good news is that you are not responsible for solving the murder," Jake reminded me in a firm voice. "Pagarelli and the police force are on the case."

"I know, but there's something about encountering a dead body I can't shake."

Jess and I both remained mum about the hotel surveillance we were undertaking.

Wednesday morning, I sat in front of a different motel, hoping to see Samantha or Tom emerge. Minutes crawled by. My mind had plenty of time to wander and wonder. Once again, I brought the tape recorder with the intent of dictating a chapter for my textbook. It remained untouched. I tuned the car radio to music for company.

I glanced down at my phone as it began to ring. *Jess.* Excitedly, she advised that, from where she sat in front of a motel, she'd just spied Tom and Samantha leaving within minutes of each other. It was nine-fifteen.

"They walked from the hotel to the parking lot without acknowledging one another, and they left in separate cars," she explained. "If Tom and Samantha wanted to appear like they didn't know each other, they failed miserably. We caught them, Suzie."

My pulse thumped. "The question now is what are we going to do about it?"

"I know what I want to do." I heard her fist hit her palm.

"I'll call the ladies and tell them surveillance is finished. See you back at your house."

"Give me time to tail Samantha."

"Don't you dare. We know the two of them are working together. That's enough for now."

"Oh, alright." She sounded frustrated. "Remember, don't discuss this in front of Jake. He agreed with Pagarelli that we should stay out of police business."

We disconnected, and I proceeded to call my band of spies. They were disappointed that their involvement had ended. I assured each of them I'd be in touch if I needed additional help.

Arriving at Jess's house around ten from my hotel surveillance, my knees were stiff from sitting for two hours in a cramped car. Since Jess had taken the morning off work, we had time to discuss what we learned and how it could help solve the murder.

"If Tom and Samantha figured teaming up increased their chances to intimidate me, they're sadly mistaken."

"Yeah. You don't scare easily." Jess set cottage cheese and fruit on the kitchen island.

"Now that I'm positive those clowns are working together, how do I wreck their scheme?" I plucked a grape and pulled out the tiny bit of remaining stem.

Jess's forehead crinkled. "I'm not sure."

"At least we're aware of what I'm up against." I popped the purple fruit into my mouth.

"Yeah, double idiocy." She jabbed a fork into a piece of watermelon.

"Agreed. They're devious. We can't underestimate them."

"What's the plan, then?" she asked.

"It's under construction. I wonder if either of them hid items from the cabin in their motel rooms. They could be the vandals who turned the place upside down, instead of Ribar."

Jess poured tea over ice cubes in our glasses. "We'll wait until they leave the motel tomorrow morning to carry on their next attack against you, then sneak into their rooms."

I paused, my mouth hanging open as I held another grape in midair. "Have you lost your mind? We're not picking the motel locks." I shook my head. "This isn't a television show where we sneak into someone's hotel room without getting caught."

"What if I wear my cute little maid costume from last year's Halloween party?" Jess suggested with a dramatic curtsy. The costume she referred to had a ruffled white apron over a black strapless, mid-thigh length dress. Jess had worn black hose with red stilettos and a frilly headband to complete the outfit for the party.

I wagged a finger. "We are not posing as maids. We can't trespass on private property. Besides, that outfit is too sexy to pass for a regular maid's uniform."

She crossed her arms over her chest. "How else can we find out if they stole anything of yours?"

I stared at her. "Not by breaking and entering, that's for certain."

"Then ask Pagarelli to investigate."

"Rest assured, he's on it." I set plates and forks on each placemat.

We managed to fill our plates without further talk of breaking and entering. Near the end of brunch, my cellphone rang. "Pagarelli," I mouthed to Jess, my pulse quickening.

She snapped to attention like an eager recruit.

I tried to squash my delight. "Hello." My sultry tone sounded as if it belonged on one of those late-night commercials for chat-line *friends*.

"Ms. Tuft."

The smooth way he said my name intoxicated me. I cleared my throat and responded *yes* as normally as I could muster.

"I wondered if I could come by and talk to you. We've arrested Ribar."

My heart rate galloped at the thought of seeing him again. I also breathed a huge sigh of relief at learning of Ribar's arrest. "I'm leaving Jess and Jake's now. I'll be home in fifteen minutes."

"I'll stop by in a half-hour, if it's convenient."

"It is." I disconnected the call.

Jess asked, "What's going on?"

"Pagarelli wants to see me. He arrested Ribar."

Jess pouted. "Why couldn't you meet with him here? I want the scoop, too."

I gathered my purse and jacket. "I'll call you," I promised, rushing out the door.

* * *

Detective Pagarelli arrived ten minutes after I got home. I let him in and directed him toward the living room, where he removed his hat and sat. "As I informed you on the phone, we've arrested Ribar. We're holding him for accosting you with a weapon. However, charging him for the offense will be tricky." He pursed his lips a moment before continuing. "Ribar denies holding you at gunpoint or threatening you in any way."

"I didn't see a gun, but Ribar swore he had one in his

pocket. When he pointed it at me, the outline was unmistakable." I imitated the way Ribar waved it at me. "He certainly did threaten me. Several times, in fact."

Pagarelli referred to the notes in his ever-present notebook. "According to the statement Ribar gave, you two were having a friendly chat on a bench within view of several passersby."

My blood pressure ratcheted. "He's lying. We were on a bench in the town square, but we were not having a social visit by any definition. He *forced* me to sit with him."

Pagarelli flipped his notebook closed. "I believe you."

His sincere eyes and calm voice convinced me.

"The problem is a case of your word against his. If we proceed with prosecuting him, a conviction will be difficult." He paused. "These incidents are often trying experiences for the victim."

"Are you saying the vile man will walk away after intimidating me with a gun?" My voice rose. "He's free to come after me again?" I shoved up my sleeve to reveal the dark purple bruises remaining from Ribar's grip. "He squeezed my arm hard enough to leave marks, Detective."

"I don't want him to get off. I'm working on a solution."

I yanked down my sleeve. "Do that. I want him to leave me alone."

"We're holding him on stalking charges, at the very least." Pagarelli redirected his attention to his notes once more. "Video surveillance cameras at the office supply store and the restaurant show him following you. We'll continue leaning on him for the threats." He glanced at me. "I wanted you to be aware of the situation as it stands."

Silence stretched between us. I had the impression Pagarelli had something else on his mind. He flipped a couple of notebook pages. "Investigating Ribar's and Mike

Hansen's pasts, I uncovered a connection between the two of them and several lawsuits filed in Minnesota."

"Minnesota?"

With a nod, he glanced at his notepad. "They operated an investment scheme. From what we surmise, they bilked people out of close to a million dollars. A majority were vulnerable senior citizens."

A tiny gasp escaped me. "Was that the seven hundred fifty thousand Ribar claimed Mike was supposed to split?"

"I'll work that angle with him while he's in custody for your assault. A confession should be enough to put him away for a long time with his record. We think he and the Hansen brothers intended to skip the country before the lawsuits landed in court and the authorities came for them."

"They did. Ribar said they were waiting for fake passports."

He tapped his notebook. "I wrote Tom Hansen's information down and plan to chat with him about his involvement."

I released a sigh. "I hope Ribar is jailed for years and stays far away from me."

To my surprise, Pagarelli smiled. "I'll do my best."

He rose, and I accompanied him to the door. We said goodnight. Pagarelli stepped onto the porch, turned, and said, "It was nice seeing you again."

I returned his smile. "You, as well."

After gazing at me for a few long seconds, he turned and descended the steps.

With a smile on my face, I danced my way back into the kitchen.

* * *

I was perched at the desk in my office, with Hunter lounging at my feet, when my cellphone rang.

After a brisk hello, Georgianna launched into her opinion of our earlier hotel surveillance. "Since Hansen and Banks stayed at the same motel, do you think they schemed to murder the poor attorney?"

"I thought about that, but something seemed off. I know they don't want me to have the cabin, but I have a hard time believing they're killers. It's possible they joined forces after the murder," I reasoned. "Or one of them could be guilty without the other's participation."

"Bre said Samantha is a nasty loudmouth," Georgianna replied. "Mean women turn vicious when crossed. I once wrote a novel where a spurned woman killed her boyfriend who'd courted his ex on the side."

I sighed. "Mike and I weren't seeing each other."

"No, but by giving you such valuable property, Mike made it seem like the two of you were still an item. If I were Samantha, I'd think you and Mike had rekindled the flame."

"Maybe Mike wanted it to appear that way out of spite," I muttered.

Georgianna laughed. "I can come up with a lot of ways to be spiteful. None of them are as pleasant as receiving a fortune."

"Mike would have to presume Samantha would go nuts when she learned he owned the cabin, and he'd expect Tom to fight for ownership of the place."

"You're making it easier to peg them as killers," Georgianna stated.

"Except Ribar is a possible suspect."

"Oh, now you're talking. From the way you and Jess described him, he's a scary one. I'll bet he murdered the attorney."

A minute ago, Georgianna had pegged Samantha or Tom as the killer. "Conjecture won't convict any of them. We need proof."

"Is Ribar staying in town?" Georgianna asked.

"Probably. He lives in Punxsutawney but pops up everywhere I go."

"Do you want us to search for his hotel? We'll need his photo."

My mood sank. Why hadn't I given Ribar's picture to the book club ladies when I organized the surveillance, instead of only fixating on Tom and Samantha? I deserved a swift kick for missing the opportunity. "Thanks for the offer, but we need to lay off investigating for now."

"Are the police close to arresting the murderer?"

"They aren't sharing information with me at this point," I confessed, avoiding mention of Ribar's incarceration. After all, his stint behind bars could be short-lived.

"You found the victim." Georgianna huffed before continuing in an overconfident tone. "You should be included in updates of their investigation."

"Yeah, that's not how it works. Believe me, I want to be kept in the loop, but they won't disclose any details. The police only involve me if I'm helpful to them in some way because of my inheritance."

"That earns you the privilege of receiving regular reports."

Too bad Georgianna wasn't handling the investigation. "For all my curiosity, I didn't find enough evidence to help convict anyone."

"Meet me for lunch tomorrow. We'll put our heads together to figure it out. I've read and written enough mysteries to give you some hints."

"Thanks, Georgianna."

We decided to meet at the restaurant in town at noon. I welcomed her offer to help sort out the clues we'd found so far and to brainstorm others. She was adept at penetrating the minds of the murderers in her mystery novels. Maybe the process would help in real life.

To refocus on my work, I needed fresh air to clear my mind of Ribar, Tom, Samantha, murder, and everything to do with the cabin.

"Want to go outside?" I asked my furry companion.

Hunter sprang to his feet, charging downstairs. I shooed him out the back door into the yard, then settled at the deck table with my notebook and laptop. The smell of fresh-cut lawn and blooming lilacs made for a soothing balm. Closing my eyes, I breathed deeply for several minutes before getting down to business at my makeshift workspace on the outdoor furniture.

I wrote diligently for two hours, then stopped for lunch. I phoned Jess and told her Georgianna had called.

"What did she say?"

I repeated the gist of our conversation. "We're meeting for lunch tomorrow."

"I'm coming," Jess said. "I'm as invested in this as you are."

As my friend, I agreed she was invested to some extent, but it wasn't on the same level. "What about your job?"

"My hours are flexible. Where are you meeting, and what time?"

Chapter Seventeen

G eorgianna and I greeted each other in the restaurant parking lot. We scanned the vicinity, wary of Ribar's, Samantha's, or Tom's presence.

"The area looks free of your stalkers," Georgianna said as we hurried to the restaurant door.

Once inside, the hostess seated us near a window, where I kept an eye out for Jess. She breezed through the door five minutes later, easy to spot in a dark green shirt covered in fluorescent pink flamingos and pale pink slacks. I waved her to our table.

"I love that shade," Georgianna told Jess. "It brightens your skin tone."

We ordered salads and informed the server we were staying for a meeting after our meal.

Georgianna rested an elbow on the table. "I admit, conducting a real stakeout gave me a new appreciation for undercover work. I wanted to fill in the time with writing or proofreading my new manuscript." She flicked her wrist. "But I was afraid I would miss something if I didn't watch the door."

"I craved tea, but I was afraid drinking would require a restroom break," I confessed.

We chatted away while we ate. Once finished, the server cleared the table and refreshed our drinks. We got down to business.

Georgianna and I pulled out our notebooks, eager to begin the process of catching a killer. Jess leaned over my tablet. I explained my thoughts on how Honey, Ribar, Tom, and Samantha fit into the puzzle. Reviewing my notes aloud, I observed my friends' faces for any indication something was missing from my investigation. Nothing registered.

"Tom and Samantha complained about Mr. James contacting you," Georgianna repeated. "Did Ribar or Honey mention him?"

"Ribar did not. But Pagarelli said Ribar and Mike scammed some people. What if Ribar knew Mike had a will and killed Ryder so he would have time to search the cabin after Mike died?"

"If a lot of cash was involved, that would make sense," Georgianna said.

I kept the seven hundred fifty thousand dollars Ribar mentioned to myself. Frowning, I offered, "A couple of things bother me about Honey. Who told her Mike died, and when? Ribar mentioned her, but he didn't say he told her Mike died. I suppose Tom could have. He knows her."

Jess suggested, "Maybe Mike called Honey from the hospital after the doctors stabilized his heart. Do you suppose she was with him when he died?"

"I know who could answer that question—Bella, the waitress at the diner where Honey works. She was pretty talkative when she served us."

Jess rubbed her palms. "Another trip to the cabin is in

our future."

"This weekend." I placed a napkin under my sweating iced tea glass and moved it farther from my notebook.

"What about Samantha?" Georgianna asked. "Wouldn't Mike be afraid the two women would run into each other if Honey visited?"

Jess slapped a hand on her chest, laughing. "Wouldn't that be entertaining to see? Picture Samantha imitating a screaming banshee."

Georgianna raised her eyebrows. "I read stories of brawls between wives and their husbands' mistresses. Hair pulling, fingernail raking, shrieking, and throwing things. It's not a pretty picture." She tilted her head. "Would Mike care at that point if Honey and Samantha met?"

"Samantha didn't know about Honey or the house in Punxy before Mike died," I reminded them. "While he was lying in a hospital bed, Mike wouldn't want Samantha to find out he cheated. He'd be at her mercy."

Jess nodded. "True. And she shows no mercy. I wish we had a contact at the hospital to find out if they fought."

Georgianna scrunched her lips. "Hmm. I'll see what I can find out from one of the nurses."

"Ribar knew that Honey and Mike dated," I said. "He might have seen her as a way into the cabin to search for whatever he was after."

Georgianna looked pensive. "How did Ribar hear of Mike's heart attack and eventual death?"

"Through Tom," I guessed. "He met Ribar while visiting Mike at the cabin. The police think the three men were involved in a swindling scheme. I don't know if Samantha met Ribar, or if she was part of the scam."

"You said you don't know who told Honey you inherited the cabin?" Georgianna asked.

I shook my head.

Georgianna appeared to mull over this information. "Honey could've tried to keep Ryder from giving you the cabin. You said she was incensed to learn you ended up the owner. Does she have a gun? Can she fire one?"

I tapped my pen against the page before me. "Mike had a weapon collection in the cabin. He taught me to shoot my handgun before I took lessons at the range. I imagine he target-practiced with Honey."

"Are you saying Honey shot Ryder?" Georgianna's eyes narrowed.

"No, but I wouldn't put it past her to be working with Tom or Ribar to take the cabin." I tapped my tablet, adding, "We need to find answers."

"How?" Jess threw up her hands. "You can't ask Mike himself unless you hold a séance." Jess paused, leaning in. "Are you planning a séance, Suzie?"

Georgianna stifled a laugh.

"Don't be ridiculous." I rolled my eyes.

"Ridiculous is thinking you'll get answers from Honey, Ribar, Tom, or Samantha."

"Hmm." Georgianna drummed her fingernails on the table.

"What?" Jess turned to face her.

"I was thinking," Georgianna said. "If I were writing a mystery novel about this, I'd make Corey James the killer. Tell me about him."

"He's a nice man," I said. "He has no stake in the inheritance. What's his motive for killing his colleague?"

"Money, of course." Georgianna looked at me as if I were dense.

Jess and I exchanged glances. I hadn't told Georgianna we'd found the buried money.

Georgianna flipped her hand. "The property is worth hundreds of thousands. If James neglected to notify you of the inheritance, he could claim ownership. As an attorney, he has the means to record the deed in his own name without arousing suspicion." She tapped her finger to her chin. "He could rewrite the will to show himself as the rightful beneficiary. You would never know."

I breathed a sigh of relief as I listened to Georgianna explain her reasoning. "Ryder read the will to Samantha and Tom before his murder. They knew I'd inherited the property. If James tried to sell the cabin, those two would fight for a share from him, like they're doing with me," I countered. "The day after I found Ryder's body, James came to town with the intention of delivering the will to me. He handed me the deed, along with the keys to the house, boat, and car. He presented a list of valuable artifacts Mike stored at the house. Why do that if he wanted the place for himself? Besides, I spoke with him several times. He's always been professional and helpful."

"You make a valid point. He wouldn't have given you the deed if he wanted the property." Georgianna settled back in her chair. "If you don't think James is involved, let's consider each of the others."

We debated and outlined and reconfigured, but in the end, we chose no clear winner for the title of killer. Three heads did not appear to be better than one in this situation.

I tilted my glass toward Jess. "Here's to another trip to Punxsutawney to eat at the restaurant where Honey works. Hopefully her friend, Bella, is still in a chatty mood."

Jess raised her glass. "We'll have to tell Jake we want to finish cleaning. Can't have him suspecting we're working on the case."

Georgianna clinked her glass against ours. "I wish I

were able to take part in your covert op, but I don't want to scare away your snitch."

"You and your mystery writer's vocabulary," I said with a laugh.

Jess and I waved goodbye to Georgianna on the restaurant porch. Jess stayed behind to make a phone call, and I waited for her. Afterward, walking to the parking lot, she declared, "What a bust."

"Not necessarily. My pecan ball was yummy." I chuckled at the withering glare she gave me. "I never considered Corey James a suspect until Georgianna mentioned him. Now, I wonder if he knew Mike buried money on the property. If so, would he kill for it?"

Jess said, "The two attorneys were close friends. Ryder may have confided in James."

I unlocked my car door. "What about attorney-client privilege? Does it extend to partners at the same firm?"

"Even if it does, do you honestly believe they don't talk about their cases among themselves?"

I did, but Jess made me question my belief. I had some digging to do. Too bad discussing this new spin with Pagarelli was impossible. Input from his police brainwaves would have been helpful.

I opened my car door. "If James suspected the money was on the property, he might have searched unsuccessfully for it before giving me the deed."

"Does that mean he gave up?" Jess wondered. "Or does he expect you to find it for him?"

The question sent a shiver down my spine. Was James involved somehow? I cringed inwardly. Just what I needed. Another suspect.

* * *

I slept fitfully. The murder, the break-in at the cabin, and the list of subjects clashed in a nightmarish vision during the night and woke me. The clock on my nightstand displayed two. I tossed and turned. The clock struck three-thirty. I rose exhausted. Makeup didn't cover the dark circles under my eyes. I walked Hunter before dragging myself to the library to do research.

Crossing the street to enter the library, I noticed a police car approach. As I stepped onto the curb, someone called my name, and I turned to spot Detective Pagarelli waving from the driver's side of the vehicle. He pulled up to the curb, sending my heart skipping.

Pagarelli climbed out, leaning his forearms on the roof. "How are things going for you, Ms. Tuft?"

"Fine, thank you."

"No one has bothered you?"

"Not today, anyway." I couldn't stop smiling, wishing for a way to keep the conversation going.

"Glad to hear it. Don't hesitate to call me." He tipped his hat. "You have a nice day."

Pagarelli's greeting brightened my morning. I practically sailed through the library doors and over to the reference section. Once I'd recovered from the encounter, I sat at a table and took down several notes. Then, I selected two books to check out at the front counter.

I left the library, lingering around the front steps with the hope of catching sight of Pagarelli's patrol car again. When I didn't see him, I headed home.

An email from my editor awaited me, and I groaned as I read it. She asked when I would be able to submit chapters to her. I certainly couldn't explain that I'd made little progress with the project because of my muddled mind. The return message I composed explained the designated subject required more hours of work than I had anticipated. I promised to deliver chapters in a couple of days.

After hitting send, my shoulders tensed. I needed to free my mind of the murder and ramp up my research and writing. After meditating for several minutes, I spent the rest of the morning diligently working on the manuscript, stopping only for a light lunch. The hours flew by. I wrapped up the session quite pleased with my progress.

The doorbell rang, startling me. With a bark, Hunter raced for the front door. My heart pounded, fearful. On my cellphone, I pulled up the picture of the visitor from my security system. My body sagged with relief at seeing Jess's face through the camera. "Coming!" I jogged for the door and tugged it open. "What are you doing here?"

"Well, hello to you, too." She stepped into the foyer. Hunter danced around her with excitement. Jess gave him a pat on the head and a dog biscuit from her pocket.

She handed me a bottle of wine. "You've been in a blah mood with this murder case. I'm here to cheer you up."

"I'll get the glasses."

Jess followed me to the kitchen. "Jake has a meeting tonight. We're on our own for dinner." She leaned back against the counter. "Do any writing today?"

I placed the glasses on the counter and rummaged in a drawer for the bottle opener. "Yes. I'm finally back in the groove. I'll meet my deadline if I continue at this pace." The wine opener popped the cork with ease. I poured each of us a generous glass.

Jess accepted the vino from my outstretched hand. "I'll drink to that."

"You'll drink wine to anything."

She clinked my glass. "Right, you are."

Removing a package of various cheese chunks from the

refrigerator, I pointed to the other side of the room. "There's a box of crackers in the pantry."

We carried our drinks and snacks outside to the porch. Hunter followed. He bumped open the door, tore down the steps, and zipped across the yard.

"You do have a lovely view out here in the wilderness," Jess admitted.

"This is my favorite spot on nice days. I love it when the trees sprout spring leaves that turn deep green in the summer. Fall is also gorgeous with all its vibrant colors."

"Yeah. Except for the isolation, it's great."

"Solitude is perfect for a writer."

"Until you find a dead body and the riff-raff breaks down your door."

I lifted my wine glass. "There are those little inconveniences." My mood turned serious. "I've been turning over in my mind the theory about Ryder confiding to James that Mike hid the money."

Jess shrugged. "It doesn't matter. You can't come out and ask James."

"Not directly, but maybe through a subtle approach."

"Like?"

"I'm working on it."

* * *

Jake drove the now familiar route to the cabin. I was eager to finish clearing the mess from the break-in and do a thorough cleaning. I hoped to turn the property over to a real estate agent friend as soon as possible.

Jess and I tidied and vacuumed the guest bedrooms while Jake did his thing in the garage and sheds. At least we weren't facing the same total disaster as the last time. The great room, kitchen, master bedroom, and bathrooms had been scrubbed and put back in order on our last trip. They remained clean and orderly.

We still had plenty of work ahead of us, including disposing of the broken items. After three hours of back-breaking drudgery, Jess texted Jake and suggested lunch in town.

He reappeared inside. "Don't you want to stay and finish here, then stop for dinner?"

Slumping forward, her arms dangling in front of her, Jess groused, "I'm hungry now, and the snack bars we brought didn't satisfy me. Suzie and I want lunch."

"Uh huh." Jake raised an eyebrow. "To question Honey, I assume."

Jess grinned. "Can't sneak anything past you, sweetie."

His gaze was wary, but his grin matched hers. It was cute how he couldn't resist Jess's charm, no matter what she wanted. "I'll go wash," he said.

Jess gave me a thumbs-up behind his back.

When he finished in the bathroom, Jake hauled Honey's boxes from the master bedroom closet and loaded them in the truck. On the ride to town, we compared notes on our progress at the cabin.

SUVs and gigantic, mostly black, pickup trucks crowded the diner lot. Jake dropped us at the door and went in search of a parking space. While waiting for the hostess to seat us, I searched for Honey but didn't see her. Was she in the kitchen or on a break?

We were led to the last booth at the back of the room, which made me wonder if the hostess recalled the distur-bance we'd caused during our last visit. At least the sunshine peeked in below the partially rolled-up window blind.

Honey's friend, Bella, approached our table. I recognized her immediately. "Hi."

She glanced at me, pulling her notepad from her pocket. "You may not remember me. We were here last week."

"I remember," Bella replied, her face blank. "You upset Honey. You're her fiancé's old girlfriend."

Bella's unfriendly tone made it obvious Honey had filled her in about me. "We dated eons ago. It's not worth mentioning," I said. "We've had no contact since."

She slipped a hand into her pocket. "Honey said Mike gave you their home."

I tensed at her accusing tone, but if I didn't win her favor, she wouldn't give me answers. "Correct, but his gesture shocked me. I didn't know about Honey."

Jake arrived, sliding in beside Jess.

Bella stared at her notepad as she rattled off the day's luncheon special.

Hoping to make peace with the waitress, I said, "We brought the things Honey left at the cabin. They're out in the truck. Is she here?"

Bella seemed to thaw. "She's off today, but you're welcome to leave them with me."

My smile was genuine. "Thank you."

Jake excused himself. "I'll go get them. Don't want to forget after we eat." He stood. "Two large ones. Where do you want them?"

Bella pointed her index finger. "In that corner behind the counter. My boss can put them in my car."

Jake said, "Put me down for a black coffee, a glass of water with lemon, and the special." He turned and left.

"How is Honey feeling?" I asked.

"Awful."

I mustered a sympathetic tone. "I hate to ask, but do you

know if she visited Mike in the hospital after his heart attack? Like I said, I hadn't spoken to him in years. I'm just trying to figure out what happened."

Bella seemed hesitant to respond. Just when I thought she wouldn't, she nodded. "Honey trusted Mike's doctors. They were confident of a full recovery. His death devastated her."

"Was she with him at the end?" I asked.

"No. He convinced her to go home since he was scheduled to be released in a couple of days. His brother, Tom, was supposed to drive Mike here. Instead, Tom called Honey when Mike passed." Bella wiped a tear. "Honey hasn't forgiven herself for not being with him when he died. She only agreed to leave the hospital because wretched Samantha had a fit when Honey arrived. The staff demanded quiet." Bella shook her head. "Honey worried poor Mike would suffer another heart attack from Samantha's ranting and stomping around like an angry bull." She straightened, composing herself. "That woman is the reason Mike's gone."

"Samantha's a lunatic," Jess mumbled.

"You got that right," Bella agreed, acknowledging her. "She's the reason Honey and Mike kept their engagement a secret. Mike planned to leave Samantha and marry Honey."

Jake returned to the table after putting Honey's boxes in the corner. Bella flipped a page in her notepad. "Are you ladies going to order? I have other customers waiting."

"Yes, sorry." I closed my menu. "The special and an iced tea, please." I didn't remember what the special was, but my appetite was nil, anyway. Jess placed her order, and Bella left.

As soon as the waitress was out of hearing range, Jake asked, "Well, did she answer all your questions?"

"Pretty much," Jess said. "We found out Honey visited Mike at the hospital, and Tom told her he died."

"We can guess Tom is also the one who informed her of the will," I added.

Jake leaned against the back of the booth. "Maybe."

"Why maybe?" Jess flung out a hand. "How else would she find out?"

Jake patiently explained. "When Honey tried to use her key to the cabin after I changed the locks, she may have contacted Tom or Ribar to find out what was going on."

I unwrapped the paper napkin from around my silverware. "True. She would not have known the will had granted me ownership of the cabin."

"Right," Jess said.

I shook out my napkin. "I never suspected she had anything to do with his murder from the beginning."

"Unless Tom told her before Ryder came to see you and she was angry enough to stop the attorney," Jake suggested.

"Ugh," Jess exclaimed. "You're talking in riddles."

The same thought swirled through my head. "Every time we eliminate someone, there's a glitch."

Jake glanced at us both. "Perhaps, you should stop trying."

"Ha," Jess replied.

"Ha," I repeated.

We returned to the cabin. One constructive result of the break-in was the thorough cleaning we accomplished. The property stood ready to be put on the market. I paused a couple of times to admire the payoff from our hard work. I

273

owed Jess and Jake a lot more than a boat for their support and labor.

By five-thirty, Jess and I patted ourselves on the back for jobs well done.

"Let's see what Jake completed." I headed toward the doorway.

"He probably spent the afternoon napping," Jess teased.

We searched for him in the garage, but the place was empty. With further searching, we found him in one of the sheds, packing tools into boxes.

"How was your nap?" Jess asked.

Jake shot her an offended look. With a hand over his heart, he replied, "That hurts. I labored for hours." He outlined his strenuous activities within the sheds and garage. Lifting a small shovel from the boxed items, he gestured toward me. "Figured you can use these hand tools yourself. My suggestion is to let the larger items go with the property."

"Whatever you suggest is fine by me."

Jake accompanied us to the garage and explained what he thought should stay or go.

I glanced around. "Why didn't Mike hide the map in one of the sheds or in the garage? It'd be tough sorting through all this junk."

"If I were Ribar, those are the first places I'd assume Mike hid directions to the money. Mike was the outdoorsy type who'd spend a lot of time using his gardening tools and mower. He likely took the boat out and tinkered with the engine most weekends while here. I'm surprised he didn't hide the map on the boat, though." Jake wiped his hands on a rag. "Mike took a chance hiding it, period. Someone could have poked around in here or the cabin and never found directions to the fortune."

Chapter Eighteen

Monday morning while steeping my tea, the question of whether Ryder told James about the buried money gnawed at me. If so, what would James do to get his hands on it? How well did James really know Mike?

I dialed his number. He answered in his professional lawyer's voice, and I identified myself. "I'm preparing the cabin to sell and wanted assurance the purchase was legal."

"As I mentioned when I turned over the deed, Mr. Hansen's file contained notes of an inheritance from his parents and additional money made from investments. I believe he day-traded stocks." James paused for a moment. "What makes you think he obtained his money illegally?"

"I know Mike. He wasn't financially savvy when I dated him."

"According to our records, Hansen purchased the house and property with cash obtained from stocks." He cleared his throat. "The will also stated you could keep money found on the property."

He remained silent. I did, too.

Finally, he spoke again. "If you find a large amount of money, I cannot vouch for its legality."

I laughed. "Wouldn't that be a nice surprise?"

"Do you know when you'll put the house on the market?"

"Hopefully soon."

"Let me know if you have other concerns. I'll be happy to help."

I disconnected the call, rattled by the reference to finding a large sum of money. Did James know of the hundred twenty thousand we found?

With a sigh, I called Jess. "Do you have a few minutes to talk?"

"Sure. I'm headed to the break-room. What's up?"

I fiddled with my favorite Mont Blanc pen. "I'm suspicious of Corey James."

"Why? What happened?"

"I called him, using the excuse I wanted to sell the cabin. He assured me the purchase was legal. But then, he mentioned that if I found a large sum of money, he couldn't vouch for how Mike obtained the cash."

"That's suspicious." She sounded breathless. "You informing Pagarelli?"

"Yes."

I hung up with Jess and immediately phoned the detective. I told him my suspicions, highlighting our phone conversation.

"Still working the case you aren't supposed to be investigating, I see."

I thought of protesting his sarcasm, but I realized the futility.

He continued. "I get that you can't help yourself, but your curiosity has put you in danger more than once. I'll look into James's background. For your safety, please refrain from contacting him for now."

My heart tripped. Pagarelli agreed James could be dangerous.

"Ms. Tuft, you need to distance yourself from this case. Let me work on options from my end."

"Okay."

Nervous, I hung up, adding James to the list of people who might harm me.

Gathering my laptop, notes, and pen, I left the house and drove to the café in town, hoping to lose myself in my work. I sat at a table large enough to spread my papers beside my computer. Digging through my purse for my pen, I stumbled upon two Mont Blancs. I stared at them. I only owned one of the fine writing instruments. Suddenly, I remembered that James had handed me his Mont Blanc to sign the inheritance paperwork. I must have kept the pen by mistake. I'd apologize and mail it to him.

My manuscript about dealing with difficult people took shape as the hour passed. Several scenarios of workplace squabbles and gossip sessions ran through my mind, providing me with lots of anecdotal material. I was officially on a writing roll.

"Hi." A body slid clumsily onto the seat across from me.

Having recognized the harsh voice, I gritted my teeth and glanced up from my keyboard. "What are you doing here, Tom?"

He scrubbed a hand across his stubbly chin. "Have you had time to consider what Mike's wishes would be if he had lived long enough to set things right in his will?"

I lowered my head and continued to type. "My attorney assured me Mike's will was current. He wrote it to reflect how he wanted to dispose of his property."

Tom snorted. "I heard you had some trouble in Punxy."

My head snapped up. "Who told you that?"

His pure evil sneer reminded me of a deranged clown. "Wouldn't you like to know?"

I'd love to smack that grin from your face. I wouldn't put it past Tom to be the one who ransacked the cabin. "Did you break in?"

Mischievous pleasure spread across his face. "Been meaning to thank you for ridding me of Ribar. Pain in my neck." He rolled his head from side to side as if to emphasize the fact. "I heard he blabbed about the Minnesota investment plan." He laughed aloud. "Idiot."

Tom sure had heard a lot of details. "Scam, you mean."

He stiffened, making him suddenly appear taller. "Since you're familiar with our venture, you know Mike held the profits for us."

"Stolen money, you mean."

He ground out his question between gritted teeth. "Where'd he hide the cash?"

I hoped my innocent expression came across as sincere. "How would I know?"

"Mike wouldn't go to his grave without leaving instructions for finding the money. I begged him to tell me where he stashed it when he was in the hospital. He wouldn't." Tom fisted a hand. "The bum remained tightlipped even when I tried to squeeze it out of him."

I fought to hold my face expressionless, although anger boiled inside me. Did Tom cause Mike's fatal heart attack with his badgering? After all, the doctors had thought Mike would recover. "Your brother might still be alive to give you your money if you hadn't bullied him."

Unfazed, Tom squinted at me. "Did you and your friends happen to find those instructions?"

His indifference toward my accusation disgusted me. Tom cared more for the money than his only brother. "No."

His fist tightened. "I don't believe you."

"That's your prerogative." I returned to my typing.

"Mike kept a box full of your pictures and some trinkets. I figured he hid bank information in it." Tom slapped the table. "I didn't see the box when I—visited." Tom shoved my papers aside, nearly spilling my tea. He bent his head close to mine. "You found the box and took it home."

He couldn't know for certain, but I wanted to put an end to his questioning. "Jake destroyed the photos for me."

Tom's face reddened, twisting into an ugly monstrosity. "What do you mean?" His voice rose.

"Those photos were an invasion of my privacy. Mike stalked me after our breakup."

"Where are the box's other contents? Did you find bank information? Routing or account numbers?"

My insides turned to jelly, along with my slipping confidence. "Jake threw the entire box and the contents into a bonfire."

Tom's smoldering expression burst into rage. His fists repeatedly pounded the table. A customer at the counter and the sales clerk turned our way. Tom didn't notice.

I trembled inside, afraid for my safety, although Tom would be foolish to accost me in the café. "Do you want me to call Jake so you can confirm it?" I picked up my cellphone.

He raised a fist, shook it inches from my face. "You'd like that, wouldn't you? Tell him big, bad Tom is with you."

The customer at the counter, a tall man with broad shoulders and a rock concert T-shirt that exposed his beefy biceps, walked over to my table. "Everything okay here?"

"Mind your own business, buddy," Tom snarled.

The man set his coffee cup on a nearby table. I feared he and Tom would come to blows. "I asked him to leave," I said, hoping Tom would go uneventfully rather than argue with the stranger.

Tom hesitated before raising his hands. "Sorry. A family argument." He stood. "I'll get my coffee to go." He retreated to the order line.

With a final hard stare at Tom, the man picked up his coffee. I thanked him, and he disappeared out the door onto the sidewalk.

I tried to return to my work but remained aware of Tom's presence at the take-out counter. I took my cellphone out of my purse and placed it beside my computer. Within minutes, Tom strolled by my table and pushed the lid closed on my laptop. "I ain't goin' nowhere," he whispered. "Mike gave you all his belongings, which means you are the only way to recover my cash."

"You're wrong," I said.

"Don't play dumb with me. Mike left directions for finding the cash at his Punxy property." He leaned forward and hissed. "A lot of cash."

"Maybe Ribar found the money and didn't tell you."

Tom snickered. "If that was the case, he'd be living it up on an island somewhere, not rotting in a jail."

"I can't help you, Tom. Go bother someone else." I fluttered my fingers in a *go away* motion and moved to open my laptop.

He slammed a hand down, pushing the computer closed again. "Not without my loot."

My blood and body froze.

"Is there a problem here?"

The sound of Pagarelli's voice thawed me. I glanced up,

meeting his steel gray eyes with every ounce of gratitude I could muster.

Tom's head jerked in Pagarelli's direction. He withdrew his hand. "No problem, Detective. Having a friendly chat."

Pagarelli's eyes bore into Tom. "It didn't sound friendly to me. Maybe you should be on your way."

Tom glared at him. Adjusting his shoulders, he plastered on a fake smile and walked out of the café. Tension released from my neck and jaw. I propped an elbow on the table, lowering my head into my palm.

Pagarelli laid a gentle hand on my shoulder. "You okay?"

His touch sent a snap through me. I lifted my head. "Just a little shaken." I was certain he heard the fear in my voice.

"What did he want? Sounded intense."

"Tom insisted Mike left clues to the money he held for him from the scam. He thinks I found those clues and stole the money."

"Don't let him frighten you into admitting anything."

Pausing, I realized I had never run into Pagarelli at the coffee shop. "I can't believe you showed up to save me from harm again."

Pagarelli lowered his well-built body into the chair Tom had vacated. "I pulled Hansen in for questioning about the Minnesota investment scam. He denied knowledge of the swindle, but my gut said he lied. I don't have enough evidence to hold him, but I wanted him to know we're on to him. I put a tail on him. The detective who followed him called in this location. When he remained for a time, I had a hunch you were working here. Hansen doesn't seem the coffee shop type."

I smiled. "I'm grateful for your instincts, which were spot on."

He returned the smile, pushing himself to his feet. "I'll let you get back to work."

I slumped against the back of my seat, dropping my arms to my sides. "I'm going to sit here and chill with my tea for a while. Tom ruined my creative streak for the time being."

"In that case, do you mind if I join you for a drink?"

Oh, wow. "Please do."

While Pagarelli stood at the counter and ordered himself a cup of coffee, I admired his profile, hoping his interest in me wasn't purely police business. Coffee in hand, he made himself comfortable in the seat across from me.

I nodded toward his mug. "Never acquired a taste for coffee, although both my parents drank it by the potful."

"Do they live in town?"

The usual pang hit me at their memory. "My dad died in an auto accident when I was young. After I started dating Mike, Mom moved to Florida to live with her sister, who never married."

"Sorry to hear about your dad. Do you see your mom often?"

"She flies up once a year, and I go there once or twice a year. We do regular face talks over the computer. What about you? Family in the area?"

"Oh, yeah. Lots." He pushed his hat up with a laugh. "My mom and two sisters are still trying to run my life. I sic them on my brother as often as possible."

I laughed. "And your dad?"

"My brother and I hunt and fish with him whenever we're free. My brother's a full-time fireman in the city. His schedule is as busy as mine."

We continued the pleasant small talk. Fifteen minutes later, he said goodbye and headed back to the station. My creativity didn't return for my writing, but it flourished in my daydream about Detective Pagarelli.

* * *

I spent the next morning working in my office. Around noon, the doorbell rang. Hunter sprang to his feet with a bark. I checked the home security cellphone app and drew back, confused. Why was Corey James here? I slipped my ever-handy pepper spray into my jeans pocket.

Hunter followed me to the door, which I opened, keeping the glass storm door locked. "Mr. James. This is a surprise." An uneasiness roiled in my stomach.

A muffled growl rumbled in Hunter's throat, his reaction to a threat. My senses rose to high alert.

"May I come in and speak with you?" he asked.

Sure he wouldn't try anything with Hunter by my side, I replied, "Of course." I unlocked the storm door, and he stepped into the foyer. Hunter circled him until I patted his head. "He's leery of strangers."

I was leery of James, too, but concluded Hunter would tear him apart if he tried to hurt me. In the living room, I patted my back pocket, reassured by the feel of my cellphone. "Please have a seat. Would you care for something to drink?"

"No, thank you." He sat. "I had a muffin and coffee from the bakery in town."

"My friend's place. Bre's the best baker around for miles."

"I agree. The muffin was tasty."

I opted for the chair across from him. Hunter reclined at

my feet. I studied the well-spoken, affluently dressed professional sitting in my living room, unconvinced that he was a cold-blooded killer. "Are you in the area for business?"

"In a manner of speaking." He unbuttoned his suit jacket. "I came to see you."

"Oh?" Apprehension washed over me.

"Nothing worrisome." He threw his arm over the back of the chair, seemingly relaxed. "Did you make arrangements to sell the Punxsutawney property?"

I breathed easier. "As a matter of fact, I'm turning it over to a realtor friend of mine. Is there a problem?"

"Possibly a small matter."

I stiffened. Did he know of the buried money? How?

James must have noticed the change in my demeanor, as he waved a hand. "I'm not here to confiscate any of your estate. I'm here in an advisory capacity. Your call yesterday made me think about the clause in the will regarding money on the property you inherited." He leaned in with a slight bend of his head. "I wouldn't want you to be hit with a large fine because you were unaware of the tax laws."

"Oh, I see." *He could honestly be trying to help me. But then...*

"A few bucks wouldn't matter, but several thousand dollars would require you to inform the IRS. I'm here as a courtesy. Mike Hansen was a valued client." He smiled.

I gave my brow a theatrical swipe. "Whew. The only money we found was loose coins in the couch cushions."

Although his smile remained in place, it appeared to lose sincerity. "Well, then, you have nothing to fear from the tax man."

Hunter's presence made me brave enough to turn the interrogation around. "I wondered about the clause myself. What do you make of it?"

He shifted his weight. "Perhaps, Mr. Hansen hid money he didn't want Ms. Banks or his brother to know he possessed."

I frowned, unable to break through the attorney's facade. "I suppose we'll never know."

He peered at me. "Unless he left some kind of hint."

I scrunched my forehead in mock confusion. "Hint? You mean a note?"

He dropped his arm, resting his hands in his lap. "Or a map."

"Pointing the way to buried treasure?" I slapped my knees and laughed. "Sounds like a plot for a movie."

His face remained unreadable. "Did you find anything?"

I sobered. "I didn't, no." I wore my best surprised expression. "Are you serious, Mr. James? I was kidding."

When he curved his lips upward, it appeared his face would crack. "I'm joking, of course." He rose. "I won't take up any more of your time."

We walked to the front door, silent except for another growl from Hunter. James glanced in his direction, but he didn't speak until he stepped over the threshold. "Nice to see you again, Ms. Tuft."

As I closed the door behind him, I didn't believe he thought it was nice to see me at all.

* * *

My surprises for the day continued with a call from Pagarelli. He asked me to come to the station.

A bundle of nerves, I sat in a chair across from him. My uneasiness stemmed from an overwhelming mix of being summoned and anxiousness to tell him about James.

He spoke in his professional tone. "Ribar pleaded guilty to stalking and harassing you."

"What does that mean as far as jail time?"

"Since we can't confirm he had a gun, those other charges won't be enough to hold him for long."

My spirits sank.

Pagarelli continued. "The good news is we tied him to the crimes in Minnesota. In a plea deal, Ribar admitted he and the Hansen brothers preyed on unsuspecting senior citizens. The three agreed Mike would hide the money for them until they could all arrange travel to a country without extradition. He confessed he threatened you, but he says he didn't kill anyone."

"Will the fraud charge keep Ribar in jail?" *Dare I hope?*

"For years."

Relief coursed through me, spreading warmth from my head to my toes. I no longer needed to fear that the man would terrorize me. He couldn't carry through with his threats. I would have happy-danced if Pagarelli hadn't sat across from me.

"As a bonus," he added, "Ribar admitted he and Tom Hansen broke into and ransacked your cabin in Punxsutawney to hunt for clues to the whereabouts of the money."

I snapped my fingers. "I knew Ribar looked suspicious when I asked him if he wrecked the place."

One look at Pagarelli's pursed lips, and I realized my mistake. I wanted to shake myself for the comment. I rallied my confidence and asked, "Will Tom be charged with fraud, too?"

Pagarelli remained quiet for so long, I didn't think he was going to answer. Finally, he winced. "We're still building a case. With information from Ribar, we hope to arrest Hansen soon. For now, you would do well to avoid him."

Knowing Tom could still harass me tempered my joyfulness. "Believe me, I don't go hunting him down. Does this mean Mike's cabin and property were bought with illegal money?"

"We determined the cabin and antiques were not purchased with funds stolen from victims. The property is yours free and clear of legal implications."

I couldn't wait to sell the place and be done with the troubles it caused me. "That's a relief." I cleared my throat. "Um, I have information for you, too. Corey James paid me an unexpected visit."

Pagarelli stiffened, wearing an expression of disbelief. "Why didn't you call me immediately?"

I felt as though I'd committed a crime and needed a defense lawyer. "You called a few minutes after he left. I figured I'd wait and discuss his visit in person since you asked me to come to your office."

His forehead creased. "Then, why didn't you tell me as soon as you sat?"

"I hoped you had good news for me."

He spoke in an exasperated tone. "I wish you'd be more concerned about your safety." He pulled out his notepad. "Tell me the attorney's exact words."

I repeated the conversation as best as I could remember, facing an outwardly annoyed Pagarelli. Once finished, I said, "He asked if I had found a map. Isn't that strange? Maybe even incriminating?"

"What's stranger to me is the fact that you let him in your house after you advised me you were suspicious of him."

"I had Hunter to protect me. You know how fierce he is when I'm threatened. And I had my pepper spray."

"I'm guessing you couldn't resist a chance to see if your hunch about James was correct."

Pagarelli knew me. I was certain my face indicated he'd guessed correctly, but I bolstered my courage. "I had my cellphone in my pocket and Hunter at my feet the whole time."

"Neither of which can stop a bullet," he snapped. "I don't know how to convince you that investigating this case is dangerous for you." He hesitated, and when he spoke again, the edge was gone from his voice. "I'm trying to keep you safe."

His remark and the way he looked at me sent shivers down my spine. "I'm glad you've shown up many times when I was in danger. I owe you a dinner."

"I'm worried about the time I won't be there when you're in a grave situation."

To avoid being further chastised by his glare, I stared at my folded hands in my lap.

He sounded different when he added, "And I'll take you up on dinner when I solve the murder."

I could have floated out the door, but I controlled myself. Rising to my feet, I extended my hand.

His hand warmed mine as Pagarelli shook it. "I'll walk you out."

After multiple visits to the station, I could find my own way out, but I didn't want to miss a few more minutes with him. My heart pounded as I glided down the hall beside him. We said our goodbyes, and he promised to keep me informed. I left the station, my hand still tingling from his touch, and drove straight to Jess's house.

Did Pagarelli feel the same strange sensations from my

touch as I did from his? I couldn't wait until our dinner together.

Jess answered the door with a potato peeler in her hand. "Hi. You'll stay for dinner." She closed the door. "Come into the kitchen and tell me what's up. You look like you have encouraging news for a change. You're positively glowing."

I followed her to the kitchen and poured myself a glass of iced tea. "I think Pagarelli is interested in me."

Jess put a hand on her hip. "Haven't I been telling you that? It's about time, but what brought on this sudden revelation?"

"I mentioned I owed him dinner for always showing up when I needed him. He said he'd take me up on the offer after they found Ryder's killer."

Jess clasped her hands together. "Great. If we can help solve the murder, you two can start dating."

I could only imagine the gears grinding in her head as she plotted.

"We have to get the gang together again and start assembling the pieces."

"I've been trying. At least Ribar is out of the picture." I filled Jess in on the situation. "Pagarelli assured me that he would be in jail for years."

Jess cheered. "That's huge. Good riddance."

"In other positive news, the cabin and property were not purchased with stolen money. I can sell everything."

"The sooner, the better."

"Pagarelli also thinks they'll arrest Tom soon."

Jess checked the oven. "Now, if we could somehow rid ourselves of Samantha, things might settle down around here."

"We still have a murderer on the loose." I laid a hand

against my cheek. "Oh, I was so thrilled about Pagarelli, I forgot to tell you Corey James visited me today."

"What? Why didn't you call me?"

Hmm, where have I been asked that before? I gave her details of the attorney's visit.

"He's the murderer," Jess said, slapping a hand over her mouth. "You could've been his next victim." She hugged me.

"I'm fine. Hunter would never let him harm me."

Jess looked unconvinced. "Is Pagarelli going after James?"

"He's investigating. I imagine he'll keep tabs on him until he finds solid evidence about who committed the murder."

Jess shut the oven door, tapping her chin with her index finger. "You know, James would have had access to all of Mike's files. Maybe Mike was afraid the money would never be found if he died, so he told Ryder it was buried. Ryder could have later told James."

"*If* Ryder knew about the money. Pagarelli advised me not to let James in my house again. I'll also avoid calling him."

"Good."

"I'm still not ruling out Tom. In fact, I'm not ruling out anybody. Even Ribar could be lying to save himself with a plea deal."

Chapter Nineteen

T he next morning, I enlisted my friend, Megan, a successful real estate agent, to handle the sale of the cabin and property. After attending high school and college together, we had remained close friends. I called her to discuss the property, cabin, and furnishings with a promise to drop off photos and keys at her townhouse.

Megan's cherry lips broke into a huge smile when she spied me through the frosted glass of her front door. She swung the door wide. "Come in." She hugged me. "It's been too long. I made lemonade."

"Sounds refreshing."

I glanced around the tastefully decorated foyer. Italian marble flooring, a sparkling chandelier, and huge colorful pots of healthy plants presented a welcoming sight. We passed a curio filled with porcelain lighthouses and a richly furnished living room on our way to the dining room table.

I handed Megan the envelope with keys and directions to the cabin. "All the furnishings can be sold with the place, or you can arrange to have them auctioned or trashed. Whatever you decide is fine with me."

We browsed the original photos Mr. James had given me of the unfurnished cabin, as well as the recent ones I'd taken with the furniture in place.

Megan studied each image. "This place is amazing. When you said you had a cabin in Punxsutawney to list, I pictured something resembling an old hunting camp. I'm looking at a hidden gem."

"You think someone will buy it?"

Megan brightened. "Definitely. I serve clients who search for remote havens like this. It's a shame you want to sell."

"It was Mike's."

She laid a hand on my forearm. "Sorry about the circumstances. Although you two ended things a few years ago, this has to dredge up unpleasant memories."

"The hard part is fighting off the vultures who want all of his estate." I wiped condensation from my lemonade glass with a finger. "I can't blame them. I don't feel I'm entitled to any of his property."

"It doesn't matter what the others want. Mike made his choice." She continued scanning the photos. "You want all this furniture to stay with the house? The sofa is ghastly and will go, but the dining room table is fabulous. It's as if two different decorators and budgets furnished the house." She held two prints side by side. "The difference between this garish bathroom and the posh spa of the master bedroom is striking."

"The entire place is a crazy contrast. Wait until you see the rooms in person. Take the table. No charge."

She lifted her head, gaping at me. "Do you know what

that table is worth? I couldn't accept something that expensive."

"Yes, you can. The intruders gouged the top during the break-in. It will need repaired. Otherwise, it could end up with a family of ten children who don't appreciate your fine taste in furniture and go on to carve their initials in the tabletop."

She laughed.

We discussed the details of the listing, including a decorating makeover, then caught up on each other's lives before our conversation turned to the murder.

"Have you heard if the authorities have arrested a suspect in the death of the guy you found in the woods?" Megan sipped her lemonade.

"Only what the newscaster's reported." Heeding Pagarelli's earlier warning, I declined to share further details.

"Finding him had to be terrifying. I don't know how you stay out there in the wilderness by yourself."

"It's a wooded area, but I'm ten minutes from town, and I'm not alone. I have Hunter."

"Oh, yes. How is your playful beast?" She took another sip.

"He's a hero. He scared off Samantha Banks and Tom Hansen when they threatened me."

A hand went to her throat. She gasped, "They did?"

I waved away her concerns. "With lawsuits." No sense in worrying her about my physical safety. "Hunter protects me, and my security system at the house is excellent."

Megan released a breath. "Thank goodness Samantha and Tom didn't get physical. As I recall, Tom was always a bit of a troublemaker."

"The estate attorney told me the will is a binding agreement and not to worry about their blustering."

"Why don't you stay with Jess and Jake until this is over?"

"I'm working on a book deal. I need quiet in the convenience of my home office with my equipment and research materials. Besides, I'm not letting those greedy jerks drive me from my house."

"Speaking of protection," Megan said, "The rumor at the flower club is that you're seeing a certain handsome police detective." She wiggled her eyebrows.

Heat flooded my cheeks, probably turning them as red as Megan's lipstick. "Georgianna," I grumbled.

Megan nodded. "He's her neighbor's nephew. Is it true?"

"Only in Georgianna's imagination. Pagarelli is cute and friendly, but we've only just met through the investigation. He hasn't asked me out."

She smiled. "How could any man not be captivated by you?" She touched the ends of my hair. "You are beautiful, talented, and a sweetheart."

"You're too kind, my friend. And you exaggerate. You've seen me angry."

She laughed. "Are you referring to the time Rafe Parker picked on you during our senior year?"

I cringed at the memory of my hormonal seventeen-year-old self having been pushed to my limits by one of the school bullies. I roared out of my introverted shell with the fierceness of a lioness to verbally put him in his place. He retreated in a hurry, which earned me the nickname Rocky for the rest of the school year. I slapped a hand over my eyes. "Don't remind me. Some fearlessness. I tucked myself back into my shell until graduation." I shook my head. "Is it any wonder I left town for college?"

Megan smiled. "But you're back here where you belong, and we love having you home."

And I enjoyed living among my friends. I raised my glass. "To friends." Megan clinked hers against mine.

* * *

When I returned home a few hours later, I was surprised to get a call from Pagarelli. "Ms. Tuft."

I rolled my eyes. His formal use of my name grated on my nerves. *We should be on a first-name basis by now.* "Yes."

"We conducted a background check on James. The investigation is ongoing. I can't give you details other than he has substantial debt hanging over his head. This could be a motive for his questioning regarding money found on your inherited property."

A cold chill settled over me. "Do you think he knows Mike buried the money?" I swallowed hard. "Do you think he murdered Ryder?"

"We've found no motive or proof of his involvement at this time."

Tired of all the investigation rules and Pagarelli's refusal to give me a straight answer, I snapped at him. "Don't you think I deserve to know if the man is a killer? He's been in my house."

"Yes, but we don't have solid evidence. In the meantime, don't let him in your house. If he comes near you, I want you to call me immediately."

Oh, do you? "Why? You don't have anything on him."

"Ms. Tuft." He sounded tired.

"And don't *Ms. Tuft* me." I didn't give him time to

answer. I hung up, my blood simmering. He still refused to share information with me even though my life was in danger.

And his moods were maddening. He could be sweet and personable one minute, the next, he reverted to police mode, treating me like one of the many victims with which he dealt.

"Come on, Hunter." I snatched his leash from the wall hook. "I need to work off this anger before I explode."

Walking on the deserted road cooled my ire and gave me time to think. Pagarelli need not have warned me to avoid James. There was no way I would allow him into my house again.

I fumed all the way to the end of the road. On the return trip, my anger had slowly but surely dissipated. By the time I rounded the curve in the road near my home, I was calm.

Then, I noticed James's car in my driveway.

A bolt of panic speared through me. I shut off the music on my cellphone and dialed Pagarelli, holding my breath that he would answer. He did.

"Corey James is at my house," I whispered.

"Don't answer the door," he warned, his tone sharp. "Maybe he'll think you're out."

Hunter spied James, barking in earnest. I juggled my phone while tugging his leash to keep him by my side. James turned our way and waved.

"Too late. We're standing at the top of the driveway. Hunter's barking his head off. James sees us. He's walking our way."

"Keep Hunter between you and James. Stay outside if you can. I'm on my way. Keep your phone on so I know what's happening."

"Hurry."

Pretending to listen to my music, I bopped my way down the driveway. When we were a few yards from each other, I faked turning off my phone and removed my earbuds. "Mr. James. Another visit so soon?" Hunter made a ruckus. I let him, clinging to the leash as he tugged. "What's on your mind?"

"I'm sorry to bother you, but I wondered if I might speak to you about the estate." He motioned toward the house. "Could we go inside?" Without waiting for an answer, he turned and started toward my walkway.

Stuck for an excuse to remain outdoors, I followed him. I fumbled for my key at the door to stall, mindful to keep my phone on.

James took the key. "Allow me." He turned the lock and pushed open the door. Stepping inside, he held the door as if he was the owner and I was the guest. I entered, nerves snapping all over my body. I unleashed Hunter. He barked and circled James. I allowed him to carry on for a few moments before asking him to quiet, hoping James got the message not to mess with me. Hunter hushed, but he stayed by my side.

"Shall we go into the living room?" I asked, hand extended to show the way.

Corey followed me, taking care to keep a distance from the dog.

"Can I get you something to drink?"

"No thanks." He took a seat on the sofa. "I only need a few minutes of your time."

I sat in a chair, Hunter at my feet, and placed my phone on the side table, the line to Pagarelli open. "What can I do for you?"

"Have you listed the Punxsutawney property on the market yet?"

"As a matter of fact, I gave the keys to a real estate agent yesterday."

A dark cloud passed across his face so quickly I wondered if I'd imagined it. "Sorry to hear."

My chest tightened. "Why? Is there a problem with selling?"

"Could be." He fidgeted. "I didn't want to show my hand, but you've left me no choice."

Fear consumed me. Hunter whined, sensing my distress. His ears went up, and he fixed his gaze on James.

The dog's motions didn't go unnoticed. James scooted back farther into the sofa, but he dropped all pretense of politeness. "Hansen buried seven hundred fifty thousand dollars on the property."

I didn't have to fake my shocked expression. We'd only unearthed a fraction of the money buried near the cabin. "What?"

"Don't play dumb. It doesn't suit you." He linked his fingers. "I could use that tax-free, untraceable money."

"What are you talking about?"

He stared at me with hardened eyes. "I want the money."

Hunter stood and growled, his body rigid.

James glowered. If looks could kill, I'd be dead. Terror shot through me. He slipped a gun from a hidden holster at his waist. "Keep that dog in line."

I stroked Hunter's head. I could not let James hurt my dog. "It's okay. Lie down."

The dog glanced up at me.

"Lie down, Hunter. Now."

He did as commanded, but he remained on high alert.

"That's better." A sinister smile marred James's face. "Now, where were we? Oh, yeah. You aren't a very accomplished liar. Where did Hansen bury the cash?"

"What makes you think Mike buried money?"

"Not think. *Know*. Christopher Ryder confided in me. Hansen told Ryder he buried the money so it would be untraceable. He hid a map in his Punxsutawney house. The one you now own." James leered. "Ryder advised against burying the money. He said you'd never find the map. Hansen assured him you would." James chuckled. "Said you were a clean freak and would eventually come across the directions when you prepared to sell."

"What if I didn't sell? What if I never found the map?"

"Ryder asked those same questions. Hansen insisted you would sell and find the map beforehand."

I bristled with the knowledge that Mike understood me so well. "He took a risk. The money could have stayed buried forever."

James shrugged. "Guess he figured it didn't matter in the long run if he was dead and couldn't enjoy it himself."

"Why didn't Ryder steal the money? No one would've ever known it existed."

"True enough. He told me the story after Hansen died. I wanted us to locate it, then split it." James sneered, "Honest Ryder wanted to return the money to the victims."

"You killed him."

He lifted his shoulders. "Didn't mean to. I liked him and didn't intend to hurt him. I offered to ride with him to deliver the news of your inheritance. I made sure no one knew I went along. We argued most of the way." He shook his head. "You weren't home when we stopped at your house. I grabbed Christopher's arm and pleaded with him to go back to the firm and forget about you. We could've searched for the map and money before notifying you of the property. Things got out of hand. I lost my temper and pulled my gun on him. We struggled. The gun fired."

His explanation shook me. My stomach churning, I wondered where around my property Ryder had met his end before being crudely disposed of up the road. Then, it clicked into place.

The pen Hunter found under my azalea was lost in the struggle. Ryder probably died right there.

"How could you throw his body in the gully like a bag of garbage? You don't do that to a friend. He had a wife and baby. He deserved better."

James showed no remorse. "I had to distance myself from him and this place. I couldn't take a chance that the police would suspect me."

Disgusting coward. "Why didn't you go dig up the cash yourself?"

"Believe me, I tried. I drove his car to Punxsutawney and ditched it in a manmade lake near Hansen's property. I walked back to the cabin and hunted for the stupid map everywhere. I examined each drawer, cabinet, piece of furniture—all the usual places. I scoured the garage and shed. I gave up, figuring I'd let the cleaning freak—you—retrieve it for me. I called my wife for a ride and went home."

He frowned. "I assumed you would be confused when you located the map, and you'd consult me. The trouble is, you didn't."

"Were you planning to steal the map if I'd told you I found it?"

He tilted his head. "Not necessarily. I'd have asked to show it to my colleagues. Make a copy for myself. Tell you we thought it was something he drew up for hunting. Dig up the money, then return the map back to you."

"How did you know Mike wouldn't tell Samantha and Tom about it?"

"Ryder said no one knew where the money was hidden. If we weren't close buddies and Hansen hadn't died, Ryder wouldn't have confided in me."

Such close buddies that you murdered him. I couldn't wait to see this man behind bars for life.

"As far as that ridiculous Banks and goofy brother went," James continued, "all I had to do was sympathize with them about you cheating them out of the estate and their greed took over. That's the reason they threatened and harassed you." He puffed out his chest. "They made themselves suspects in the murder investigation. No one suspected me." He loosened the knot of his tie with his free hand.

"Until now."

"Until now," he echoed, tapping the gun against his thigh. "Which brings me to you. As nice as this chat has been, it's time you were out of the picture."

"You're going to shoot me? You think you'll get away with murder a second time?"

An ugly sneer creased his lips. "With Banks and Hansen threatening to do you harm? I think I can figure out a way to throw suspicion on them. In any event, no one would suspect an upstanding attorney."

"Except you aren't upstanding. You're a debt-ridden phony."

His face turned scarlet, his expression a mix of disbelief and anger. "How dare you. Give me the map, and I'll make this quick. If not, I'll put a bullet in your dog for every minute you delay." He raised the gun.

With a vicious snarl, Hunter leaped on James, his powerful jaws snapping at the man's face, his nails raking his cheeks and neck. The gun fired, then fell to the floor. Blood splashed. My heart stopped.

Pagarelli smashed through the front door and charged into the room, gun drawn. He raced toward the attorney, picking up the discharged firearm from the floor.

"Hunter, heel," I commanded. He ignored me until I yelled a second time.

Pagarelli patted the dog's head. "You got him, Hunter. I'll take over now." He leveled the gun on a sniveling James. "Stand up. You're under arrest."

"What for? I didn't do anything." He held out his arms, his sleeves shredded and bloody. "The dog attacked me for no reason." He swiped at the blood on his face. "I'm injured."

I smiled. "This is when I tell you my phone had an open line to Pagarelli from the minute I spied you at my front door."

"You are under arrest for the death of Christopher Ryder," Pagarelli announced. "You'll also be charged with the attempted murder of Suzie Tuft." He read James his rights.

Hearing my name and attempted murder in the same sentence made me lightheaded. The realization that Hunter and I came very close to death hit me. My legs turned rubbery, and I crumpled into the chair.

James's eyes widened in surprise. "I...I didn't...this is entrapment!"

"Good luck proving you were framed. Turn around." Pagarelli nudged him forward, snapping handcuffs on his wrists. He twisted his torso toward me. "You're pale. Are you okay?"

I rose from the chair, having checked Hunter over and concluded he was fine. "I am now," I whispered.

Police sirens sounded in the distance.

"My backup," Pagarelli explained, heading to the door. He returned a few minutes later after handing over James to another detective, urging me to call Jess.

He stayed with me until she arrived. His presence both calmed and delighted me. I hated to see him leave.

* * *

I spent the next morning hiking in the woods with Hunter. I needed a break from the stress of the past weeks. The confrontation with James was the final event to wreck my nerves.

We hiked toward the creek that ran along the property, following it to where rotted branches and moss created a dam in the water. The sound of rushing water over the flat creek rocks soothed me. I sat on a fallen stump, closed my eyes, and meditated, breathing deeply of the woodsy smell. Hunter barked at a rabbit that disappeared into a hole.

When I returned home, I showered and dressed in jeans and a pink cotton top. I had plans with Jess to meet in town for a celebratory lunch.

As usual, I arrived at the restaurant first. The hostess seated me at a table in the middle of the busy restaurant. Jess sashayed in ten minutes later, clad in black and white checkered leggings and a white top. She rushed toward me, arms widespread. "You scared me to death." She wrapped me in a tight hug. "Don't ever let another killer into your house."

A couple seated at a nearby table gasped at her comment.

"I'm fine."

Jess dropped into the chair across from me. "Thanks to Pagarelli, your superhero. I need a latte. Where's our waitress?"

Pagarelli was indeed a superhero. I wished he were mine.

After Jess ordered her latte and salad, I told her, "The police recovered more of the money from the defrauded victims. They dug up several cans, similar to the ones we discovered. A chunk is still missing, but what they recovered will be returned to the victims."

Jess slid her elbows from the table as the waiter set a salad in front of her. "All of it?" She sounded disappointed. "I thought we'd travel."

"The money from the sale of the cabin can go toward traveling." I pulled apart my warm roll, slathering it with butter. "I'm thinking of contacting Honey to see if she wants any of the furniture."

"Why give her anything?" She stuck an index finger in the air. "Wait. Give her that horrendous couch and those hideous drapes." She stabbed a forkful of greens. "What is your realtor going to think when she sees the ugly decorating scheme? I hope you warned her."

"I've shown Megan pictures. She went up yesterday and hired a local decorator to make some changes. She'll take the woman's fee out of the sale proceeds. I'm not making the trip to see the result, but she said she'll take photos to show me. Megan had some of the furniture moved to the garage. I told her to sell it all with the house or auction off separate items."

"Sell everything. Honey can pay you if she wants something."

"It's not her fault Mike was a rat."

"How about you? Ready to date again?" Jess moved her eyebrows up and down a couple of times. "Pagarelli?"

"He hasn't called. I guess he didn't feel the spark I did."

"Bummer."

Yeah.

* * *

Two days later, a knock on my door startled me. The sight of Pagarelli on my front step sent my heart into my throat.

"I wanted to update you on the estate case," he said by way of greeting.

"Come in." I tamped down my excitement at seeing him.

Hunter, on the other hand, couldn't contain himself. He jumped up and down until Pagarelli rubbed his head and ears, praising the dog's bravery.

I let them have a few bonding moments before I interrupted. "Would you like coffee?"

"Sure." He followed me into the kitchen and leaned against the counter. I reached for a mug, aware he was watching me as I set the mug in position and pushed the button on the coffeemaker. I turned, and our eyes met.

He cleared his throat. "Corey James has been officially charged in Christopher Ryder's death. He pleaded not guilty, but the DA is confident we have enough evidence against him."

"I hope he serves the maximum time for putting Christopher's poor wife and child through this ordeal." I reached for a container of cookies I'd bought at Bre's Bakery. "Cookie?"

He hesitated but couldn't resist. He withdrew a macadamia cherry one.

I handed him a napkin. "My favorite, as you can tell by the amount of them I bought." I pulled one for myself. "Let's sit in the dining room."

As we sat, the container of cookies between us, Pagarelli continued to brief me on the outcome of the case. "Tom Hansen took a plea deal. He'll serve a few years. I advised Samantha Banks to leave town before I slapped her with harassment charges."

"Good riddance to all of them. I can't wait to get back to my normal life."

He brushed a hand across the table, clearing away a rogue crumb. "It's been a rough few weeks for you."

Rough didn't adequately describe my torture. "I put the cabin on the market. My friend Megan is handling the sale."

"I hope you get the result you want."

An awkward silence hung for a few moments. "I'm happy those poor people Mike stole from will get their money returned."

"Thanks to you for allowing us to search the property."

"Don't pin a medal on me. I couldn't, in clear conscience, keep that money. Do you think they'll find the rest?"

"Maybe."

Lost for words, I averted my eyes.

"How about that dinner you promised me?"

My heart thumped. I raised my eyes to him. "When do you want to collect?"

A lazy smile spread across his lips. "Since you helped me solve the murder, I think I should take you to dinner. Are you free Saturday night?"

For you, I'm free any evening. How could I resist his playful grin? "I'd like that, Detective Pagarelli."

"Call me Nate."

Acknowledgments

I would like to acknowledge and thank my critique group, Sharon Wenger, Darla Greco, Audrey Snyder, and Anne Tiller, for their time, helpful remarks, and keen eyes. A special thanks to Sandra Hahn for her reader comments, encouragement, and support.

Thanks to my agent for this project, Carol Woien of Blue Ridge Literary Agency, for her part in making this novel a reality. Also, thanks to Dawn Dowdle for bringing me into the agency—she will be missed by many.

I'm grateful to Erica and Michelle at Harbor Lane Books, who made editing with them a pleasure.

A final thank you to Niki and Ryan for always cheering me on.

About the Author

Bethany Barker is the author of nine nonfiction books, a dozen creative nonfiction stories, and The Suzie Tuft Cozy Mysteries. She is a member of Pennwriters and Sisters in Crime.

She has been interviewed for Yahoo.com, AARP Online, and CBSMoneywatch.com. She was video interviewed for ABCNews.com; appeared on Cornerstone TV, HMC-TV Channel 20, and WIUP-TV.

Visit her website www.carolsilvis.com, blog www.carol silvis.blogspot.com, and Facebook page at www.facebook.com/carol.silvis.

About the Publisher

Harbor Lane Books, LLC is a US-based independent digital publisher of commercial fiction, non-fiction, and poetry.

Connect with Harbor Lane Books on their website www.harborlanebooks.com, TikTok, Instagram, Facebook, Twitter, and Pinterest @harborlanebooks.

Milton Keynes UK
Ingram Content Group UK Ltd.
UKHW012014280324
440101UK00004B/420